T0117287

THE CLEANER

Second book of the
"Miandi" series

A.P. Lynn

Order this book online at www.trafford.com
or email orders@trafford.com

Most Trafford titles are also available at major online book retailers.

Printed in the United States of America.

ISBN: 978-1-4669-4199-1 (sc)
ISBN: 978-1-4669-4198-4 (e)

Trafford rev. 10/26/2012

www.trafford.com

North America & international
toll-free: 1 888 232 4444 (USA & Canada)
phone: 250 383 6864 ♦ fax: 812 355 4082

To Aunt Pat, who gave me the story idea.
We need to talk more often.

And to Covert.

Prologue

Christie Augustine stared at the house where all the misery had started. She made her concentration on it complete, until she was unaware of the damp, sleet-filled wind blowing about her. When she was small, this place intimidated the hell out of her. Now she realized that perhaps it wasn't the house, but what happened inside. It surprised her how growing up could change one's perspective on things—or make them clear.

She closed her pale green eyes. She pictured the house as it was when she had lived there: the flaking blue and white paint chips littering the porch floor, and naked light bulbs hanging in all the rooms. She recalled her bedroom was more like a closet, adorned with a lumpy mattress, a four-drawer dresser with three broken drawers, and outdated paisley-print wallpaper. She opened her eyes. In the bitter February darkness, she saw that its black shutters and front door were now gone. The windows on the first floor were empty frames of mildewed wood. The ones on the second floor barely maintained their fragile grip on the glass within them. The frozen yard was a makeshift junkyard. A six-foot-high wire fence encircled the property. Where the cracked and broken sidewalk met the fence, there was a public notice saying that the house was condemned and scheduled for demolition within a few weeks. Christie gave the sign a grim smile. She was about to save the taxpayers some money. It would not be standing by dawn.

She pulled her wool hat down over her bald head until only her eyes peeked out. She shuddered in her thick coat, but not because she was cold. The feelings were coming back. They dogged her daily since she arrived in Mason City. The wounds were raw and burning, as if someone poured salt into them. They intensified the moment she saw the house again. She fought them back, and reached out for the canisters filled with kerosene. She touched the gate with gloved hands. It opened easily, but she knew it would. She checked her surroundings, not expecting to see anyone. On a night like this, the homes would be shut tight and the curtains drawn. Nevertheless, she reminded herself to check each room carefully. She did not want any unforeseen events marring her plans of revenge. Once inside the living room, she recalled the building's structure, and the path she should take for maximum destruction. When she first scoped this place, she wanted to use her special accelerant here. Then she decided otherwise. This fire would be the first in a long line of them. It was important that these first few fires look like they were started by some juveniles, or a perhaps a homeless person trying to stay warm. By the time she was done, the one who had betrayed her most would be dead, and her heart finally cleansed of the misery and agony he had brought her.

She started at the top of the home and went from room to room, pouring kerosene as she went. She made sure each room had an ample supply of it. She paused near a corner of the living room where her mother had routinely beaten her. There, she took out a squirt bottle and sprayed some of the kerosene in a deliberate pattern on the floor. She had left it at every place she torched. So far, no one knew what it meant. She knew, for she had read those final reports in the places where it was found.

She walked backward to the front door and gave the house one last vengeful glance. She pulled a matchbook out of her pocket, lit it, and dropped it into the kerosene. The flames raced from the doorway to the edges of the room and up the rickety staircase. By the time she was at the gate, the first floor had ignited. By the time she had reached her car, the building was engulfed. She watched as the flames reached for the clouded sky above. She closed her eyes again. Some of the pain had gone away. In her head, she heard her father's shrieks as he died, burning to death in his bed. She smiled at the memory. It had been one of the happiest moments of her life. That clean feeling she got whenever there was a successful fire spread through her body. She couldn't wait to savor this feeling again. Unlike the others she had killed these past few years, she would stay and observe the final one, watching the look on his overly smug face disappear as he realized that he was about to die—and who killed him.

I

Four months later

Mason City Police Detective Mark Daniels did not need to have his best friend call to know that he was back early from his vacation. He just caught the expression of a junior officer as she purchased her snack in the complex cafeteria. "Stay away. He's on a tear," she warned him.

Mark smiled and turned to head downstairs to the subbasement. As he approached the doorway to the main computer room, he heard a male voice muttering under his breath: "Send me away for a while, and see how screwed up the system becomes. Thanks a bunch, Chief. I appreciate it."

Mark cleared his throat. Startled, the man looked up. Mark saw a touch of relief come to his blue eyes. Then his gaze returned to the screen. He rolled his chair closer and pressed his nose up against the screen.

His mind shot daggers at the gibberish of characters scrolling on its surface. "This is why I never go on vacation, you realize that?"

"Hey, don't look at me. I don't get anywhere near them."

"Yes. That's how I know it wasn't you who tried to download the complete service revolver manual onto the server." The man frowned and deleted the file with one keystroke. "Next time Ed, see me, and I'll give you mine."

"Tyler, you know Detective Peabody's not in the building?"

Technical Sergeant Tyler Martin ignored him. He reached up to scratch a spot on his chin, scarcely aware of the stubble that had formed underneath it. He flung a strand of long, dirty blonde hair out of his face, and chewed non-stop on the end of a pencil. Mark's focus traveled down to the mess below Tyler's snakeskin cowboy boots. Coiled computer cables and black surge protectors competed for floor space with crushed paper cups, chewed-up pencils, gum wrappers, and eraser bits. "That explains the tantrum. So, how's the newest 'no coffee' resolution going?"

"It's not," Tyler responded, punching a key especially hard. The computer beeped at him. "Oh, shut up." Then he looked at Mark. "Not you, I mean."

"No offense taken. How was your vacation?"

"I heard you took bets as to how long I'd be gone. Who won?"

"Harry Carson. He guessed 48 minutes."

Tyler glanced at his watch. "Forty two minutes. Pretty close."

"Tyler, we've known each other how long?"

Tyler paused in his typing and thought on this. "Ever since the Mallory pedophilia case, which was like what, ten years ago?"

"And in that time, how many times have you voluntarily gone on vacation?"

"Twice."

Mark held up a finger. "Once. The last time you were off was when you broke your left big toe kicking a computer tower, during one of your other 'no coffee' stints. C'mon. You just spent two months in L.A. working on a major project. Even computer techies need a break."

"My eyes are fine. My ears are fine. I don't have a bad prostrate, and I'm not on drugs, so leave me alone."

"If only Jessie could see you now. What would she say?"

"I think she would say thank you for staying with him, and keeping him from going off the deep end."

At that, Mark paused. Tyler realized what he said. He looked at his best friend, his expression mournful. "I'm sorry, man. I didn't mean for it to come out that way."

"I know."

Tyler studied the man before him. Mark's dark brown eyes were clear and the drawn, defeated look that his face wore in the seven months following Jessie's death and Charlie's shooting had dissipated somewhat. He had also resumed his exercise regime. The fit of his faded blue jeans and black T-shirt were a testament to that. "So how does it feel to be back on the job?"

Mark straddled a wooden chair near Tyler's desk. "Just like second nature. I'm glad I decided not to quit."

Tyler began to chew on a new pencil. "Glad to hear it, and how's the new tenant?"

"Actually, that's why I'm here." Mark leaned forward and his cowlick fell into his face, its subtle way of reminding Mark that he needed a haircut. He ran a hand through his dark brown hair, forcing it back. "I was wondering if you could do a little research on her for me."

"Sure, although she's been living there for what, two months now?"

"Not really. She's never home."

"Hey, all the more quiet for you. It still begs the question: why research her now?"

Mark gave him a synopsis of everything that had happened to him since he met his new tenant, a young African-American woman named Julie Warren. Tyler listened with feigned interest as Mark reminded him about Julie and the little information he had gathered about her. "So Julie was waiting for you when you get back. She takes one glance Jessie's studio and says 'yes', right?" Tyler asked when Mark finished.

"Yeah."

"When you drove me to the airport, you told me that she told you that she'd been looking for a while. Maybe she was just tired of looking."

"Tyler, she drives one of the new Ford Escape hybrids. You know how much those things run."

Tyler stopped typing. A dreamy look came across his face. "Leather interior?"

"The works man, straight off the lot and she got picked up from my place one night in a limo. She must come from money, so why would she want my place?"

"From what you've told me, she sounds like a trust fund baby. Maybe Daddy still holds the passwords to the accounts. She was looking for somewhere cheap, so she can afford to get away from him, and prove to Daddy that she can do it without his money."

"Then why would she pay her rent up a full year in advance?"

Tyler's brow furrowed. He stopped typing again and pulled the now-destroyed pencil from his mouth. "She paid up a full year in advance? You didn't tell me that before." He tapped it against his desk with an unusual amount of force. Mark watched and waited for it to break in two. "That's unusual. Did she give a reason?"

"Only that she travels a lot, and that she wanted to make sure that it was taken care of."

"What, she's never heard of online bill pay and automatic payments?"

"She's computer literate, so I would say yes."

"True, unless she didn't have time to, or she doesn't believe in banks being that secure."

"Maybe, but the next night, when she stopped by to pick up the keys . . ."

Mark drifted off, as he thought back to what his neighbor Ruth Johnson told him about Julie and her behavior earlier that same day. The night Julie came to sign the lease, he caught her studying Jessie's painting in his office. He could not be sure, but he swore she had felt or sensed something real from that painting. Then there was the fact that his mortgage was paid just a few days prior. He barely mentioned it to her. Had she already known everything about him before she showed up on his porch steps? He thought back to the Madison Evans case and the mysterious piece of land that had become the focus of it. At first, Mark and his new partner, Detective Cassie Edwards had a hard time tracking down the owners. In the end, the owner was Julie's employer. Then Mark discovered she was the daughter of the CEO, and the intended victim. There was a lot more to that girl than met the eye. Since she was never home to ask, how was Mark going to find it? He thought back to the slip of paper he received from the bank and an idea returned to him. "Ty?"

"Yeah?"

"How hard would it to be to trace a wire?"

"Not hard. Any bank can do it."

Mark bit his bottom lip. "Could you?"

"Sure. Do you have the routing information?"

Mark pulled out his wallet and retrieved the bank report that the bank manager gave him. He handed it to Tyler, who scanned it quickly. "San Francisco? It shouldn't be too hard."

"Just do what you can." Mark stood up and glanced at his watch. "I have to go."

Tyler laid the piece of paper down next to his keyboard. "I'll get back to you on this, but if you want me to run the background check, I'll need more info.

You got anything else on her, like her social security number?"

"That's on her lease, which is back at my place. Oh, I got her business card with me."

Mark opened up his wallet again and handed it to him. Tyler turned the well-handled card in his hand a couple of times. "The Foundation? I've never heard of them." He read the front of the card and snickered. "Nice slogan, though. Well, it's a start. I'll run her name through some databases, make a few quiet inquires, and see what I can dig up. Okay?"

"Fine, but don't get caught. I don't want you to lose your job over it."

Tyler smiled. "I won't," he assured him, "not if I'm discreet enough."

*   *   *

At a third-floor office of the Internal Revenue Service, just outside of Washington, D.C., an agent sat at his terminal, paging through a file. His computer beeped and he looked at his monitor. Across his screen came an encoded message. The language was one that only he could read. He processed the information it flashed, then typed a fifteen-character response, deleted it, then straightened his tie, and went back to the file he had been auditing.

Tens of thousand of light years away, a computer more advanced than any on Earth received his message. It was one of several messages received in the past few minutes. From its vast database, it began to download a file especially created for the inquiry put forth. Simultaneously, it transmitted an undetectable message to the subject of the inquiry:

It has begun.

* * *

Two nights later, Mark was in his living room, still pondering the cashier's check Julie gave him two months prior. He sipped a glass of ice water, and ran his fingers over the raised imprint repeatedly. He had never deposited it. He still feared someone would call and inform him that his loan was still in force, until he received the original note stamped "Paid in Full." Now that it was official, he wondered what he should do with the money. Should he save it? Should he use it to make some needed repairs to the place? Adding central air was not a bad idea right now. He recalled the meteorologist predicting a week of 90-degree plus weather with high humidity. However, there were all of Jessie's outstanding medical bills and a slew of other debts to be paid. He sighed. "Yep, except this wouldn't even put a dent in them."

The doorbell rang and he glanced at his watch. It was well after 10:00 p.m. Who would be bothering him at this time of night? When it rang again, Mark abandoned his glass, slipped his T-shirt back on, slid the check into the coffee table drawer, and went to answer it. Tyler stood on his porch. Unlike Mark, he had made it to the barber, and he had shaved as well. He jerked his head in the direction of Mark's garage. "Is she home?"

Mark looked up at the dark room above it that once was his wife's studio. "No. She's still in China, I think."

"Good." He sniffed the air. "Got any coffee?"

"Gave up on your 'no caffeine' bit, huh?"

"Five minutes after I started your research. It's been tougher than I thought."

Tyler followed Mark back to the kitchen. He danced in place while Mark brewed a pot. When Mark handed him a cup, Tyler promptly picked up a jar of sugar from the stove and started pouring. Mark winced. It always surprised Mark that Tyler had not developed diabetes or some other ailment, despite the fact that there was not an ounce of fat on Tyler's lean frame. Tyler took one sip, grimaced, and started pouring again. "Plain old Columbian beans, Mark? I thought I taught you better."

"Hey, at least it's fresh." He leaned back against the kitchen counter, crossing his arms. "So, this isn't a casual visit, is it?"

Tyler headed toward the cookie jar stationed by the refrigerator, shaped like a white cat. He picked up the lid and stared into it, his heart broken for a split second. "Nope. I thought I ought to tell you what I found out about your new tenant in person."

"Already? What did you find?"

Tyler took another sip and smacked his lips. "She's well educated, and smart as a whip, too. She was born in New York and raised practically all over the place. Orphaned as a baby; parents died in some sort of accident. Her guardian's a British citizen, and a direct descendant of the original founders of that corporation they run. She's also an Oxford graduate; she got her MBA from Wharton Business School in Philly, and her law degree from Howard University, all before age 25."

"Julie's an attorney?"

"Yep. Her job doesn't require her to go to court or anything, but it probably comes in handy."

Tyler paused to take another sip. Mark saw some of the agitation leave his lean body. He must have been desperate for caffeine. "One thing's for certain: this woman doesn't believe in banks or credit cards. I couldn't find an account in her name anywhere. Ran her social everywhere I could." He rubbed his stomach and grimaced. "You got anything to eat?"

Mark sighed and walked over to the refrigerator, where he retrieved some leftover fried chicken that Jessie's mom brought him. He set the plate down on the table. Tyler's eyes lit up in delight. He plopped himself in the chair directly in front of it, abandoned his mug, and attacked it with gusto. Mark took a seat opposite of him. "That doesn't make sense," Mark told Tyler. "She treated me to lunch the first week she was here, and she paid with a credit card."

"That's because it was probably the corporate account. Why carry one of your own when you have a company that can foot the bill?"

"True. What about the wire that paid off my mortgage?"

Tyler bit into a leg, chewed carefully, and swallowed. "No can do on that. I managed to trace it back to a bank somewhere in the Cayman Islands. However, they're sticklers about protecting their client's privacy."

"What about the cashier's check?"

"It's drawn on a Bank of America account that her corporation owns." Tyler paused in his eating, waving a drumstick at Mark. "Now that place is interesting."

"How interesting?"

Tyler set down his mug and chicken leg and pulled out a folded piece of paper from his back pocket. "Well, it's still a British corporation. Their main offices were in London until just before World War II. Its records date back to around 1650, and there're signs it's even older than that." Tyler took another bite of chicken. "It keeps itself pretty quiet. On the public side, there hasn't been too much action, outside of some hefty investments and land purchases here or there. Most of its work is charitable, helping other countries as well as individuals; lots of money being doled out to others in the U.S. and around the world."

"So?"

"So, it just had a change in its leadership. Your tenant's now its CEO."

"You're kidding."

"Nope."

Mark frowned. His waiting for Tyler to return and do this research had been worth it. Tyler found one piece of evidence to contradict one of her statements. As the daughter of the CEO, Julie probably could authorize the wire transfer that paid off his mortgage, as well as all the other gifts the Foundation bestowed over the past few months. She had done a good job of hiding that fact from him. She had no contact with the board, she told him that night when he asked her. Right: now, she *ran* the board. "What else?"

"Well, I had an associate who does grant work run the Foundation through some of the bigger grant-tracking websites. She isn't being paid any salary, and it's not because that place can't afford it. According to their tax returns, that place has a lot of money, and I mean *a lot*."

"Like how much?"

Tyler looked down at this notes. "Last tax returns showed more than forty billion dollars in endowment funds, and one hundred billion in assets."

Mark gaped. "One hundred *billion dollars?*"

"Yep. You name it, and they own it or have owned it at one point. That piqued my interest, so I tried to track down the phone numbers of the board members, just to talk to them, get their opinion of her. They're all unlisted."

"That's not unusual. With the load of money they have, they probably don't want people to be bothering them, hounding them for money they don't need or deserve."

"I thought that too, and then I double-checked the addresses. All of them live outside the country, except one. He lives up near the Canadian border. His address happens to coincide with that parcel of land that was subject of your property scheme case."

"That's impossible. They said no one lives there."

"Obviously not. However, I can understand why it would attract schemers like the ones you had."

"Why's that?"

"That land? Granted, it's on the edge of the reservation, but it's highly prized lakefront property. I double-checked the county land records again." Tyler pulled out another piece of paper and handed it to Mark. "This is where it gets interesting. Apparently, the Amendu, the native tribe up there entered into an agreement with some individuals who were part of the Foundation more than four hundred years ago. Since then, private builders, public corporations, the county road commission, the state, and the feds have tried to get their hands on it. However, they can't break the agreement the two of them have, and it's not from a lack of trying."

Mark read the page carefully. Tyler had printed out a new, larger map of the area, and had circled the land that belonged to the Foundation. He remembered seeing this before. It was a large area, with what looked like a two-lane highway running through it, situated close to the U.S.-Canadian border. He also remembered District Attorney Natalie Bishop explaining the agreement between the Foundation and the Amendu tribe. The land the Foundation leased was also part of the Amendu's burial grounds. Mark scratched his chin. "I can understand the lakefront land, but the burial grounds? Why would anyone want it?"

"That's the same question I asked the clerks up there. The land the Foundation owns only encompasses part of the burial grounds, and you can't have the one without taking the other. If you wind up taking both, Amendu law prevents you from developing either one.

One hint of a development plan, one whiff of a project that takes away an ounce of soil, and it forfeits back to the tribe." A quizzical look came across Tyler's face, and he put the bone down. "It's a funny thing. When I asked the clerk about it, he seemed pretty spooked about the place."

"How so?"

"Apparently, the agreement still allows the Amendu to bury their dead there, as well as perform their traditional ceremonies. After all, it is holy ground. It's considered to be haunted, too. Local legend has it that people have seen spirits in the nighttime; white figures walking through the trees, ghost shapes, weird noises, the whole bit. Overall, it sounds interesting. We'll have to visit it sometime."

Mark turned his attention back at the map. After a few moments of quiet thought, he looked at Tyler. Tyler blanched. That look Tyler hated was on Mark's face. It only meant bad things to come. He raised a finger. "Mark, wait a minute . . . ," he argued.

"Well, you want to visit it, and I'm not doing anything important tomorrow. Feel like a road trip?"

II

Mark and Tyler left from Mark's place before sunrise the following morning. They took Mark's Explorer, heading northeast along the main routes toward the Canadian border. They had planned on a long drive, but by hour six, they were getting a little restless. Mark began to think this was some wild goose chase. According to all they knew, there was something up here, yet they had not seen any sign of anyone living anywhere; just miles of empty road and forestland that didn't seem to end.

"There it is."

Mark followed Tyler's finger. Tucked away on the left was a dirt road, about roughly where the map said it should be, but easily missed if no one was looking for it. Mark pulled his truck up to the gate. They disembarked. Mark immediately noticed that there wasn't a sound about, not even a bird chirping or the sound of the wind. There were also no telephone poles, a mailbox, or any other sign that anyone lived there. "This must be it,"

Tyler said, checking the map and then looking up at the pale blue sky. He returned his gaze to the trees and frowned. "Homey place."

Mark took note of the barren trees that lined the road. He tried to make out what type they were, but they were more like wooden sticks poking out of the land. It was as if they never lived. A breeze suddenly blew and he shivered. It must be well over 80 degrees out, and it was only going to get hotter. Why was he cold?

Mark took off his sunglasses and walked up to the gate. The haunting silence emphasized the gravel crunching underneath his boots. He focused his attention on them. They looked new. They stood about four feet high, and stretched from one tree to another, blocking off any access outside of climbing over it. He tapped on them. A hollow, metallic sound echoed back. A long link of brand-new iron chain joined the gates together, and it had been recently fitted with a new lock. He looked up the path, squinting in the afternoon sun. "I don't see any signs saying we can't enter," he commented.

"Yeah, but there's no way we're going to be able to drive up there, unless you plan to crash the gate. Even if you did, the road looks like it would wreck your suspension."

Mark headed back to the truck to grab his cell phone and his gun. He stowed his weapon behind his back. Then he checked his phone to see if he was within range of a tower. The indicator showed that he was in a roaming area. He hit the call button, but got nothing but static. "Try your phone," he called out to Tyler.

Tyler pulled his phone out of his pocket and held it to his ear. "No signal. Well, so much for calling for help if we needed it." He pocketed his phone and then pointed toward the gated path. "Are we going in?"

"Hey, you said you wanted come along."

"Only because of that look you get when you sink you teeth into a problem that's vexing you. I'm just making sure that obsessive nature of you doesn't get you killed."

Mark took a deep breath and then headed for the path. Tyler sighed, grabbed his good digital camera from the truck, and followed him. They vaulted over the gate and started up the rough road. An eerie silence surrounded them. To Mark, it was as if someone had come through with a machine and vacuumed the sound out of the air, save their footsteps and their labored breathing. The trees were so tall, they blocked out the sun. Large patches of shadow formed around them. The dead wood gave way to hardwoods in full flower and luscious evergreens that shaded the path before them, which added to the uneasy, foreboding feeling. The forest floor was carpeted with fallen leaves, needles, and pinecones. Twice, they encountered enormous trees that had recently fallen. Too scared to walk in the woods, they struggled to climb them. Occasionally, they paused so Tyler could take pictures. Each time, they glanced behind them, hoping that they would see some sign of life. Even a bird flying by or a squirrel scampering in front of them would be welcome.

After walking for about 20 minutes, Tyler spotted what looked like a rooftop ahead. He tapped Mark on the shoulder. Mark jumped. Tyler held up his hands, and then pointed ahead. Mark nodded, and they quickened their approach. A minute later, they entered the clearing, and found themselves staring at a huge red barn. It looked brand new. Mark estimated that it was about half the length of a football field, with one set of doors on its left. The sun glinted off its silver roof. A small dock granted access to the lake. Across the lake was an island laden with more lush groves of undisturbed forest reflecting in the sparkling blue water. Mark now understood why people would be clambering for this spot.

A two-story farmhouse stood to their right. Unlike the barn, in its bright fire-engine red, the house was a faded yellow with most of its paint gone. The porch, which was probably a brilliant bright white at one point in its life, stood in disrepair. The intricate wood lattice that made up its railings was mildewed and rain-stained, and in some spots had begun to separate from the house. A few green wooden shutters clung for dear life on their rusting hinges. There was no smoke coming from the crumbling chimneys that stood at either end. "Why would anyone want to live in such a bleak place?" Tyler whispered.

"I have no clue."

They looked down at the grass below their feet. It was a sickly straw color, with faint patches of watered-down green sprinkled throughout. The place looked deserted, and there were no signs of foot or vehicle traffic anywhere. Tyler snapped some pictures, and then looked back first at the barn, then at the house. "Which one do we check out first?"

Mark nodded toward the barn. They started walking toward it, glancing around to see if anyone was there. They were about 25 feet away from the large door on the barn's left side when they heard a rough voice call out: "Where d'ya think you're going?"

The men whirled about. Behind them stood an older black man, shorter than them, slightly stooped, dressed in filthy, faded blue overalls and a red, tobacco-stained shirt. His tan work boots and the bottom third of his overalls were soaking wet. His shaking right hand held a well-used wooden bucket and the water splashing over its edge only made his pants and shoes even soppier. His left hand held a cane-fishing pole. His salt-and-pepper hair had receded slowly from his forehead. He looked at the two men through squinty brown eyes. "Who are you?" he asked in a tobacco-rasped voice.

The men reached into their back pockets. "I'm Detective Mark Daniels," Mark explained. "This is Sergeant Tyler Martin. We're from the Mason City Police Department."

They handed the badges to the old man, who set his bucket down and took them. He glanced at the badges, then back at the two men. "Mason City? Ain't that a little bit south of here?"

"A little bit," Tyler said.

The man handed the badges back to them. They realized that he reeked of stale tobacco juice, sweat, and fish. Mark and Tyler took a step back, wrinkling their noses. "A little bit out of your jurisdiction, isn't we?" the man asked.

Mark looked at Tyler, who gave him a blank look in return. If this was this so-called Russell Webster, he was nothing like they had expected. Mark's brain raced to come up for a legitimate excuse for their presence. "We're here as part of an ongoing investigation. We were looking to speak with a Russell Webster?"

"Investigation? What for?"

Tyler stepped in front of Mark. Behind his back, Mark saw him cross his fingers. "We're investigating a property theft scam," he explained. "Someone in Mason City claims they own this land, and they been selling it repeatedly to unsuspecting people for the past year or so."

"Property scheme? Don't know nuttin' about it. Who sent you here? How did ya'll find the place?"

Tyler's mind went blank. Mark took over: "Actually, we contacted the county clerk, who gave us directions. We don't mean to intrude. It's just that our victim gave such an elaborate and picturesque description of this place, we wanted to see if it was real. Please, does Mr. Webster live here or around here?"

The man's eyes traveled from Mark to Tyler. They didn't have to be law officers to tell that this old man didn't believe a word they were saying. "There's no Mr. Webster that lives here, and this be private land. You need to be a gettin' out of here."

He picked up his bucket and turned away from them. "Wait! Sir!" Mark called out.

The man paused and turned around. "What's your name, sir?" Mark asked.

"They call me the Caretaker."

"The Caretaker? Nothing else?"

The Caretaker looked at them in silence. Mark decided not to press it. "Mr. Caretaker, do you know a woman named Julie Warren?"

Mark wasn't sure, but for a moment, he thought he saw a quiver of fear flash in the man's eyes. He set down his bucket and cane pole and approached Mark. "Miss Warren sent you?"

"In a manner of speaking. Do you know her?"

"Her family's company owns some of this land. They pay me to take care of the place. Nice people they is." The Caretaker reached into his overalls pocket, and pulled out a package of tobacco. He extracted a big wad out and tucked some in between his left cheek and gum. His eyes watered up and he spat at the ground. "She be sending you up here to check on me?"

"No, sir. However, her name did come up. We were just curious as to why so many people would want it, and why she and her company fight so hard to keep it."

The Caretaker straightened up as much as his old body would let him. They heard his joints crack and pop. There was a note of pride in his voice as he answered: "Her guardian's family made a promise to them natives, and she's bound by family honor to keep it. That's what she's doing, and I'm helping her to do it. Who are you to be questioning it?"

"I'm not questioning it, sir. I'm just . . ."

The Caretaker shook a crooked index finger at the both of them. "This here is private land," he told them again. "You best be leaving, before I call the sheriff."

Mark was about to ask the Caretaker how he was going to do that when there were no telephone or electrical wires around, when he realized that there were goose bumps on his arms. Suddenly, he got the feeling that he was being watched. Tyler must have felt the same thing, based on the way Tyler gripped his arm. "We better go," Tyler whispered in a panicked tone. "This place is really starting to give me the creeps."

Mark had to agree with Tyler. He took one more look at the red barn, and then retrieved a business card. "Please, if you happen to see Mr. Webster, would you have him call us? We'd really like his input on this property scheme case."

The Caretaker took the card and stuffed it unceremoniously in the same pocket he had retrieved his tobacco. "He never comes here. He has no reason to. However, I'll write him a letter and let him know."

"Thank you. It was nice to meet you, sir."

Mark offered his hand. Grumpily, the Caretaker took his hand. Mark realized it was covered in fish film after he had closed his grip. He felt it squishing between his fingers. He grimaced, as Tyler grabbed his shoulders and guided Mark back toward the path. They took one last look at the Caretaker, who had not moved from his spot. They tried not to run and said nothing until they were certain they were well out of earshot. Then Tyler let out a low whistle. "That was educational. Outside of the lake and the buildings, there's not much here. Defending family honor is great, but why would somebody want to keep this land that badly?"

"Good question. Maybe the people at the Foundation can tell us."

"Say what?"

Back at the barn, the Caretaker watched and waited until he received the signal that the two men had passed the first marker. Then he straightened up to his full height. There was no shakiness to his hand when he went to pick up his pole and bucket. He looked to his left. The small door on the side of the barn opened, and a tall, well-built woman stepped out. If Mark had seen her, he would have recognized her as Julie Warren, his new tenant. She was as dark in skin tone as the Caretaker. She walked up to the Caretaker, her black robes flowing around her. Her eyes twinkled with amusement. "Well done."

The Caretaker bowed. "Thank you, *miandi*," he replied, his voice deep and booming.

The couple looked in the direction of the path. In the distance, she listened to Mark and Tyler talking. Mark was trying to convince Tyler to make the drive down to San Francisco to visit the Foundation's corporate office. She sensed that Tyler was not keen on making the trip. "We did frighten him, but it also seems I've only deepened Mark's curiosity about me," she said aloud.

"We warned you that could be a possibility."

"I know." She crossed her arms. "Tell NIK to reprogram the memory card in that camera they had. She can also lift the dampening field on their phones once they're 20 miles out of the area, and notify all of our contacts to be ready for further searches by the computer expert. This isn't over."

"You are not worried about them coming back?"

Julie's expression turned grim. "No. Not yet."

III

"Luck is definitely my lady tonight. No doubt about it," Anthony mused. He hummed along to his favorite Frank Sinatra tune as it blared from the speakers of his BMW. He adjusted the collar to his Ralph Lauren polo, and pulled his black sedan into the alley behind the Pulse, a local dance house in the heart of downtown Mason City. He felt the bass line from the club throbbing through the car. He glanced up at the star-filled sky, and then checked the time. "It's nearly 11:00. Would she come? Would she be on time?"

His headlights hit the far corner of the building. He scanned the dark alley quickly. There she stood at the back entrance to the club, just as she promised him, those fabulous legs sticking out of a black leather skirt cut to there, and only made even more beautiful by the black stilettos on her feet. Her black beaded top showed more than an ample share of her firm breasts. He especially loved the long blonde hair flowing down her back. He couldn't wait to bury his hands in it. She had been to the tanning salon, he figured, based on the glow of her skin. Anthony grinned. Dad would have a fit if he knew that here was here instead of working on that stupid Matherson appeal he wanted on his desk by 9:00 a.m. tomorrow morning. He didn't care. He was only going to law school to keep his dad from kicking him to the curb. Anthony knew that he wouldn't have work for a living. All he had to do was mention his dad's name, and his ticket was punched for the rest of his life.

Anthony climbed out of the car. He wrinkled his nose to the odors coming from the alley. He wanted to go inside and get her a little tipsy before heading back to his place, and screwing her all night. The Pulse was his favorite dance club. He was here regularly. It wasn't unusual for him to find more than one woman who wanted to date him. However, she had been a hard case, sitting in her corner table, watching, but never allowing any of the men who stopped to make it to the plate, let alone to first base. Then he tried. The minute she heard his name, she latched onto him. "Is your dad really *the* Michelangelo Della Torre?" she had asked, batting her crystal blue eyes at him.

"Sure is," Anthony had replied, giving her his best Cheshire cat grin. "The one and only."

He had wanted to do it with her last week, but she had begged off. "It's that time for me," she informed him. "I'm not into sex when that's going on." He thought about her all week, but didn't see her at the club. Earlier that day, she phoned him asking him to meet her tonight. His heart thumped in anticipation of what could be the best night of sex in his life.

He shut his door and started walking toward her. She had been looking up at the sky, not really paying attention. At his footfalls, she turned. He saw her eyes light up with delight. "Hi, Christie," he said.

She ran up to him and threw her arms around his shoulders and neck. She gave him a deep French kiss with lots of tongue. Anthony almost choked, but recovered quickly. He slid his hands under her top. *No bra. Hot damn!* After about a minute, she pulled away from him, panting. Her blue eyes sparkled with anticipation. "Oh Anthony, I've been thinking about you all week," she admitted, as she played with his shirt collar. "How about you?"

"Yes. It's great to see you again." He gestured to the building, where the bass line had changed, but not the volume. "So, should we go in?"

"No. Let's just do it," she whispered in his ear, sliding her tongue along the outside lobe.

"All right. My place is on the other side of . . ."

"No, not at your place. I want to go someplace out of the way, someplace unique."

"Unique?"

She smiled. "I like it hot, and I like to do it in out-of-the-way places. That way, we can do it all night and no one can hear us. I have everything we need in my car, like blankets, lotions, and toys."

Anthony raised an eyebrow. Exactly what had he gotten himself into with this woman? He hoped she wasn't one of those who liked to tie men up and beat the crap out of them. Then again, maybe that wouldn't be such a bad thing. "Where then? In my car?"

"No. I've already done it in a BMW." She paused for a moment, as if pondering. "I know! A storage facility! I haven't done it in there!"

"Where?"

"Oh, c'mon, it'll be perfect. We'll have loads of room, and maybe if we're lucky, we'll get one that has a sofa in it, so we'll be comfy." She slid her hand down his pants and gripped him. "C'mon? You're not chicken are you?"

"A storage facility?" he stammered. Where in God's name would he know of a storage facility? Then it hit him. It was perfect, out of the way, and he still had the key on his key ring. "I know a place," he whispered, sliding his hands to cup her round bottom. "It belongs to my dad. He'll never know. He never goes there."

"Really?" she asked breathlessly. She pressed herself into him, twirling a lock of his black curly hair around her index finger. She rubbed her stomach against his growing hardness. "It sounds wonderful. How far away is it?"

Anthony swallowed. *Damn! This girl really wanted it! How lucky could a person get?* "Not far," he managed to say. "We can drive there together."

"No." She slipped her hand in his, running her long nails against his palm. "Give me the directions. I'll drive. After all, we can't leave the toys and blankets behind, now can we?"

They climbed into her Expedition, and he directed her toward the east side of town. After about fifteen minutes, they reached their destination: Levinson's Storage Unit and Truck Rental. He gave her the key code so she could open the gate. She saw the camera mounted on top of the larger facility, but paid it no mind. He pointed to the right, and she followed the maze of copycat yellow metal structures with white doors toward the back corner. After a bit, she stopped in front of the end one, toward the back of the complex. Anthony examined his surroundings. All he heard was her truck engine, and except for the headlights of her car, there was little light around. He started to feel a little anxious. "Are you sure about this?" he asked.

She climbed out, a seductive smile on her face. "Sure. Aren't you?"

He smiled. What did he have to be afraid of? "You have a flashlight?"

"In my glove compartment. I'll get it."

While Christie rummaged in her truck, Anthony walked over to the huge door, unlocked it, and rolled it upward. He didn't really need a light to know what was in there: a few pieces of unused furniture and lots and lots of boxes. He cleared the center area during his last visit to allow for maneuverability. He thought to bring a futon here and use this place as a getaway from Dad. "Maybe I might still do that," he said aloud, thinking about what else could happen here. He took a few steps inside. "It's a good thing we brought you truck. I don't remember seeing any blankets in here."

"I guess it is."

"Okay. So, where do you want to put them, on the boxes, the table, or on the floor?"

"We'll figure that out, but before we do it, tell me again, what's your dad's name again?"

He faced her. "Della Torre. Michelangelo Della Torre," Anthony said proudly.

"Thanks. That's all I wanted to hear."

Suddenly she swung her arms and struck him on the temple with her purse. Anthony crumpled to the ground. He writhed in pain for a few moments before blacking out. He wasn't sure how long he was unconscious. As he slowly opened his eyes, he realized that his head hurt like the dickens. His pants were down around his ankles. He felt cold cement under him. He had to conclude he was still inside the storage unit. It was pitch black inside. "Christie?" he whispered.

He rolled over to help him stand up. He felt something wet on his back. He sat up slowly. His head spun. It must be because of the odd scent in the air, and the knot on the side of his head. He made to push himself to his feet, yanking at his pants as he did so. His hand landed in some liquid. He brought it up to his face to smell it. It was slippery and smelled like lavender. He looked down at his pants and his shirt. Whatever it was, his clothes were now covered in it.

Out of the corner of his eye, he saw a spark of light. It turned into a flame that grew longer and brighter. Within seconds, the entire room was ablaze. In the bright firelight, Anthony could read the logo of his father's firm on the boxes that now were catching fire as well. He turned, looking for her, but she had vanished. He could hear the fire growing. The flame wall grew larger. "Christie!" he shouted.

There was no answer. Anthony began to panic. The smoke began to fill the interior. He covered his mouth with his shirt, but soon, he began to cough. Frantically, he looked for a way out. He made his way to the garage door. Maybe if he made a run for it, he could reach it. He rattled the sliding bolt, but it had been locked from the outside. The heat of the fire had reached the structure, heating the metal. As he struggled with the bolt, it began to burn his hand. He yanked off his shirt and wrapped it around it, trying to force it loose. When that didn't work, he pounded on the door. "Christie? Someone? Anyone! Help me!"

A spark from the flames leapt onto him. Instantly, his clothes began to burn. Then the flames reached his skin. He screamed in agony, trying vainly to put the fire out. Everywhere he touched himself, flames burst out. Within a few seconds, his whole body was consumed. He stumbled forward for a few more seconds, and then collapsed, as the fire began to burn his still form.

Outside of the storage shed, Christie watched and listened. Her imagination fed the malicious delight she felt, as it gave her images of his clothing, and then his body catching fire. She caught the scent of his burned flesh and her smile broadened. "Like father, like son," she cackled. "It just goes to show that you shouldn't try to screw every woman that you meet. You just might just get burned."

With a satisfactory nod, she climbed into her truck. She drove up to the gate and it opened silently for her. Once she was outside of it, she parked her car, tugged the blonde wig off of her head, and tossed it into the back seat. She reached for a tissue and wiped the lipstick off. Then she reached into her eyes and popped out the blue contacts that she had inserted. She gazed in the mirror at herself. *No one at the club would recognize her if they saw her now*, she thought smugly. She gave one last, longing glance at the orange light. He really wasn't the person she was after, but the effect of his death was the same. She felt so clean, as if she had just taken a long, luxurious bubble bath. Without a second thought to the man who had died inside the inferno, she moved the gearshift into place and drove away.

IV

Mark stood in front of a semi-open door. Behind him, he felt something hot, and he smelled wood burning. Fire . . . he was inside a fire. It was moving closer to him. He walked to the door. Something told him there was someone was inside. He pushed the door open. In front of him was a dark-haired woman dressed in white, lying on a bed surrounded by smoke and flames. In the background, he heard a little boy's voice screaming. He reached out to her. "Mommy? Mommy!"

"Mommy!"

Mark sat upright in bed, his sweaty form entangled in the sheets. Bright sunshine shone through the windows, but the breeze that accompanied it was hot. He fought to untangle himself from his coverings, rubbing his scalp. His eyes bleary, he wandered over to the open window and stared out. A thick haze of clouds blocked the horizon. He could barely make out the tower that marked the location of the county complex downtown. He walked back over to the nightstand and snapped on the alarm clock's radio. He had tuned in just in time for the weather report. He groaned as they gave him the bad news: overnight, a huge warm air mass moved in from the southwest. High humidity and temperatures in the nineties were in the forecast for today and the rest of the week.

He decided to forgo his early-morning jog. Instead, he stumbled into the shower, lingering in the cold water for as long as he dared. As he towel-dried his hair, he figured he should dress light, so he reached for a pair of khaki pants and a white polo shirt. He pulled on a pair of socks, and reached for his boots. If the meteorologist was right, he knew that he would probably regret doing it in a few hours. He wandered into the sun-filled kitchen. As he crossed the threshold, he suddenly had a major craving for homemade oatmeal raisin cookies, like his mom used to make. He had not had any since she died. After her death, even the smell of them made him vomit, so why the craving?

He reached up to yank the chain on the ceiling fan and it began to spin. He walked over to the coffee maker and poured himself a cup. As he busied himself making breakfast, he stole a glimpse at the wall calendar. He noted the date. It was June 6. Today marked another anniversary, but not the one that people learn about in school. It was a personal anniversary: the anniversary of his mother's death. He paused in his cooking. "That explains the dream," Mark mused, "and the cookie craving." Subconsciously, he had to have known. He wondered if his father would remember what day it was today. Then he shook his head. He doubted it. His father never talked about that day, or his mother for that matter. Except for Mark, that part of his life didn't exist. "Don't dwell on it, Mark," he scolded himself, as he dumped the onions, peppers, and ham he had been dicing into the skillet. "Don't make yourself angry over something that you have no control over."

He finished making his omelet and ate it while reading the morning paper. Around 8:00 a.m., he retrieved his gun from the safe. He shut the door and lingered in front of Jessie's painting for a moment. How he longed to be there now, admiring the colors of the blossoms and flowers, feeling the cool breeze of those trees, and the touch of Jessie's soft hand in his. He stroked the outside of the frame. The pain of her sudden illness and death was still there, but nowhere near as bad as it had been a few months ago. "Acceptance," he realized. "Doc said that was the last stage of grief. Have I finally reached it?"

He locked up his house and turned toward the garage. Julie still wasn't back. Her windows were closed, the apartment was dark, and her vehicle wasn't in the driveway. She called him last night from Beijing and asked if he had installed the ceiling fan that she requested. She sounded upset about something. She made no mention of him visiting the farm, but he knew the land's caretaker must've called her to let her know that he and Tyler had visited, and that was the real reason for her call. He asked her when she thought she would be home. "I don't know," she answered. "Things here aren't going as well as I hoped."

After climbing into the truck, he turned the air on full and worked his way toward downtown. He stopped at the range for some target practice, and then headed for work. He parked his truck in its usual spot just before 9:00 a.m. As Mark approached the main entrance, he noticed something taped to the glass. A neon pink sign warned everyone that the air conditioning was out throughout most of the building. Mark made his way through the crowded main hallway to the elevators and as he did so, he heard someone comment: "Yeah. I heard the morgue is the only place with cold spots. Unfortunately, you have to be dead to enjoy it."

Mark stepped off the elevator onto the seventh floor, where the Serious Crimes Unit was located. He thought the elevator had been bad, but then he reached the precinct. He entered the double doors and took a step back. The precinct's windows faced the south. The blinds were closed but the heat filtered through, and radiated off everything. Even the desks felt hot to the touch. All of the windows that could be opened were, and some of his fellow officers had raided the local hardware store. Oscillating fans of various sizes rotated back and forth, rustling the papers on everyone's desk. Men had their shirtsleeves rolled up. Those who bothered to wear ties had loosened them, but their backs and arms were soaked with sweat. The women seemed to be fairing better, but not by much.

"Hey, Mark."

Mark turned toward sound of the voice. Cassie Edwards, his new partner had walked in behind him. Her fair skin looked a little darker than when he had seen her a day ago, and her sandy blonde hair, usually done up in a makeshift ponytail, hung loosely around her face. It also looked lighter and about an inch shorter. She wore seersucker pants and a lime-green halter top, which showed off her athletic arms. Her gun hung in its holster on her right side and the pendant necklace that the Amendu tribe gave her glowed against her skin. He gave her a smile. "Cassie," he said in return, "did you have a good day off?"

"I can't complain. How was yours?"

Mark thought about his trip up to the farm with Tyler and his encounter with the Caretaker. "Very informative."

"Mark? Cassie?"

The officers turned. Lieutenant Allison Michaels stood in the doorway. She gestured to them to follow her into her office. They looked at each other, and then made their way toward it. They saw she had a file tucked under her left arm. She closed the door and asked them to take a seat. "I'm moving you two over to arson for a little bit," she informed them, as she leaned against her desk, and moved her long bangs out of her face.

Cassie sat up straighter and her blue-green eyes sparkled. Mark's face fell. "Arson?" he asked.

"Yes. A series of fires that have been set these last few months have the investigators a little baffled. They asked me if I could loan them a fresh set of eyes for a time."

"Lieutenant, there's got to be something else for us to do. From what I recall, the buildings burned were abandoned, and no one's died."

"Not any more." Lieutenant Michaels pulled the file out from under her arm and handed it to Mark. "There was another fire last night at a storage facility on the east side; only this time, someone did die."

"Who?" Cassie inquired, as Mark took the file from the lieutenant and began to read.

"Anthony Della Torre. He's the youngest child of Michelangelo Della Torre."

Mark looked up, his eyes wide. "Michelangelo Della Torre?"

Cassie, who had grown up in Seattle and had only moved to Mason City a few months ago, looked at the others. "Who's that?"

"He owns the biggest law firm in town," Lieutenant Michaels answered. "He handles only the big profile clients. You might've heard of him. He was the lead defense attorney on the huge oil spill case up in Puget Sound a few years back."

Cassie's lips formed a beautiful open-mouth pucker. "Oh. *That* Della Torre."

"Are we sure that it was his son?" Mark challenged.

"His wallet was found outside the facility and according to the owner, Della Torre's code was the last one entered into the system. Dr. Foster's trying to make the final verification. The Chief thinks that another set of eyes may be a good addition to this case. Hopefully, it'll break before someone else dies, and there's something else."

Lieutenant Michaels gave them her warning stare with her steel gray eyes. "Della Torre's already hounding the mayor's office. He's offering a $50,000 reward for any information leading to an arrest and conviction, and a sizable donation to the police benevolent fund. He's already called me. I told them that you were on your way, so you better get going."

Cassie jumped out of her seat. She grabbed the file out of Mark's hands. "Where to?"

"The address is inside. You need to meet up with a Lieutenant Rutherford. He's been heading the investigation so far, and take it easy on the enthusiasm there, Cassie. This is only temporary."

"Yes, ma'am." Cassie turned to Mark and punched him playfully in the shoulder. He hadn't moved. In fact, he seemed to be in shock. "C'mon, don't just sit there."

Mark glanced over at Lieutenant Michaels. Then he turned to his partner. "Cassie, I'll meet you downstairs, okay?"

Cassie looked over to the lieutenant, who raised an eyebrow, but nodded. She gave Mark a small frown and headed toward the door. Lieutenant Michaels watched as Mark rose to close the door behind Cassie. She noted that he was stiff and uncertain. "What is it, Mark?" she asked in a concerned tone.

Mark fought to look at his boss. He realized that his pulse had quickened and his breathing had become slightly shallow. His hands were incredibly sweaty. He stuffed them in his back pockets, hoping that Lieutenant Michaels didn't notice his sudden gesture. "I was just wondering if maybe Harry or Ed might be able to take this case instead."

Lieutenant Michaels saw that the tension in him had suddenly increased. Her eyes narrowed in suspicion. "Why?"

He nervously ran his fingers through his hair. "Well, Della Torre knows my dad. He'll want constant updates, and then he'll spend most of his time telling him how lousy of an investigator I am."

"Which we both know is far from the truth."

Mark pretended to study the floor pattern. He needed an excuse, any excuse to get out of this case, so long as it didn't involve revealing the truth. "I'm just not comfortable with this, Lieutenant. I . . . haven't investigated any arsons. I wouldn't know the first thing to look for."

"Yes, but you have handled murder investigations. Della Torre asked for the best detective on my squad. So did the mayor and the Chief. Like it or not, that's you." She approached him, her arms crossed. "You know, there's a simple way out of this," she added.

"What?"

"Just stop being so good at what you do."

She smiled, turned, and headed back toward her desk. Mark smiled at the compliment. Then it dawned on him: he lost the argument. He opened his mouth again, but Lieutenant Michaels had already picked up the receiver on her phone. She gave him a small wave and then reached down to dial a number. Mark sighed and headed out to join Cassie at the precinct doors, pausing long enough to grab some extra pens and notebooks for himself. "Stop being good at what I do," he grunted. "Stopping the sun from rising might be easier."

* * *

Cassie read Mark the initial findings as he drove them to the site. When they arrived, the property owner directed them to the crime scene. It really wasn't necessary. Even with the windows up and the air running full blast, they could smell what had occurred here. Cassie pinched her nose and her face wrinkled in disgust. "God, that smells awful," Cassie muttered. "Maybe this isn't going to be as much fun as I thought."

A patrol officer directed them to the parking area. As they climbed out of Mark's truck, a man walked over to them. He was between Cassie's and Mark's height, with stooped shoulders. He had carefully combed what little black hair he had over his shiny head. There were permanent circles under his hazel eyes. His navy blue uniform had black stains all over it and cigarette burns on the sleeves. It smelled faintly of cigarette smoke, and it looked like it hadn't been washed in weeks. The pudgy, ash-stained hand he held out for them to shake looked too big for his body. He forced a grin to his face. Mark understood the gesture. *You're here, but I don't have to like it*, it meant. *Trust me pal, I don't want to be here, either.*

"You the detectives from Serious Crimes?" he asked, his voice hoarse and scratchy.

"Detectives Cassie Edwards and Mark Daniels," Cassie replied, displaying her badge.

"Lieutenant Lawrence Rutherford, lead investigator."

They shook hands. Then Cassie motioned to the burned structure behind them. "Is this the place?"

"Sure is. We're lucky the whole complex didn't go up, considering the damage." The lieutenant led them toward what remained of the unit. As he did so, he pulled out a beaten-up pack of cigarettes from his uniform pocket and lit one. He noted the startled expressions on the detectives' faces. "Hey, everyone has habits," he told them, while he fumbled for a lighter.

"Are you sure that it's safe to light that here?" Mark asked.

"Yeah. We've already been through it." He lit the cigarette and took a puff. They thought they saw his tension lessen a little. "Our victim got here around 11:15 p.m. last night."

"How do you know that?"

"The gate keeps a log of who punches in and when. He entered the code around that time. The fire department got the call about half an hour later. It took them a good hour or two to get it under control and prevent it from setting fire to rest of the complex."

"But why would he have been here in the first place?" Cassie asked, as she stared at the building.

"Good question. I think that's what you guys are here to help us figure out," another female voice said in reply.

Mark and Cassie turned. A woman, slightly shorter than Lieutenant Rutherford, stood behind them. She carried a metal clipboard and wore the same uniform he did, except it looked brand new, and it fit much better. Her shoulder-length brown hair was pinned back at the sides with two side braids, and her green eyes gave Mark a seductive perusing from behind her gold-wired frames. "Detectives Daniels and Edwards, Melanie Keegan, junior arson investigator," Lieutenant Rutherford said. "She's on assignment to us from the Seattle Fire Department for training and continual education."

"It's a pleasure." Melanie held out her hand and the detectives shook it. She gripped Mark's hand a little bit longer than necessary, at least so Cassie thought. "So? Here to rumble with the fire-loving weirdoes?" she asked, her eyes sparking in anticipation.

"I'm game if you are," Cassie said. She looked at Mark. He forced a grin to his face and nodded in agreement.

"Well, let us take you through what we think happened. I think you'll be intrigued."

Melanie moved to step in line with the lieutenant. He gave her a small smile. It didn't take too much for Mark to figure out that the lieutenant was smitten with her, but it seemed to be more of a fatherly look. Cassie fell into place behind them, while reaching for a pony-tail holder from her pants pocket. Mark stayed behind Cassie. As they approached the structure, Mark's pace slowed. He felt his hands go clammy. He clenched them into fists. Inside his head, the little boy from his dream screamed.

"Mark?"

Mark jerked. Cassie and Melanie were staring at him. He felt their eyes studying his face. Both of them noticed that some of the color had drained out of it. "Are you all right?" Cassie asked, reaching out to touch his shoulder.

He took a deep breath. "Yeah. Go on."

The two women exchanged glances, then turned to follow Lieutenant Rutherford into the burned-out hull. It stood about eight feet high and looked to be about 25 feet deep. Mark touched the frame and felt the charred remains of the wood and metal frame crumble under his hands. With reservation, Mark took a tentative step into the building. He smelled the remains of burnt cardboard, melted plastic and wood. He also thought he caught the odor of burnt flesh and something else. He tried to step again, but he could not move. In the distance, he thought he heard Cassie ask a question: "There's an odd odor to the air. What is it?"

"We're not sure," Lieutenant Rutherford said. "We think it's the accelerant."

"Accelerant?"

"This place couldn't have burned as thoroughly as it did without it, Detective." Lieutenant Rutherford gestured to the cement floor, where the black burn patterns from the accelerant were embedded into the cement, forming a human outline on the floor. "Whoever did this wanted this place to burn to the ground, and our victim with it. We've taken samples back to the lab to test it, but we don't know if we'll be able to get anything."

Cassie took out her notebook and began to take notes. After she finished, she carefully looked around. In the far corner, there were a few boxes that had miraculously escaped the flames. However, they bore the scars of extensive smoke and water damage. Whatever was in them was now worthless to its owner. "So who rented out this unit?"

"Della Torre's law firm," Melanie said. "According to him, he hasn't been out here to use it in about ten years or so."

The three of them continued to walk the structure for some time. Then Cassie noticed that Mark wasn't with her. She turned back. Mark still stood in the doorway. She noticed that a thin film of sweat covered his face. Cassie watched him for a moment. Then she turned her attention back to Lieutenant Rutherford around. "How did our victim get out here?"

"We suspect that the arsonist brought him here," Lieutenant Rutherford answered. "We didn't find any cars anywhere around here."

"Was there anything unusual found?"

"No. We've been concentrating on the burn pattern."

"The burn pattern?"

"It's how we determine where and possibly how a fire started."

"So what about it?"

"It's highly unusual," Melanie replied. She pushed down on the clip to yank something out from underneath the paper. "It seemed to start in that corner over there." Melanie pointed to a corner of the structure opposite the remaining boxes, where a trail led out toward the center of the building. "It also looks like they wrote something with the accelerant. We took some pictures of it."

She handed some pictures to Cassie. The flames had burned some sort of symbol into the cement. It was the strangest thing Cassie had ever seen. "Mark, come take a look at this."

There wasn't an answer. Cassie looked up. Mark still hadn't moved from his spot. She glanced over at Melanie and the lieutenant, and then walked over to him. As she approached, she could hear him gasping for breath. She placed a gentle hand on his shoulder and stared into his eyes. "Mark? Are you all right?"

Mark snapped out of his trance. When he realized that it was Cassie, he took a deep breath. "Yeah . . . yeah I'm fine. Why?"

"Mark, it's all right if you're a little jittery. I am, too."

"No, Cass, it's not that. It's just . . ." He shrugged. "I just have this thing about fire."

Cassie turned herself so that she could block Mark's reactions from Lieutenant Rutherford and Melanie. "Mark, if you need to beg off, I'm certain that Harry or Ed can help me with this case."

"No. You're my partner. It's a silly childhood fear of mine. I thought I'd grown out of it."

"Not necessarily. Besides, I still owe you for that episode at Holcomb Tower."

Mark thought about her statement. Their first case together required her to chase a suspect up Holcomb Tower, a tourist attraction near downtown, something she had been adamant against doing. That was when he leaned of her fear of heights. He wondered how she could come to work and ride the elevator to the seventh floor where their precinct was. Then again, he realized that she did everything she could not to remind herself, like making sure to take a desk that faced the wall instead of the windows. He smiled. Cassie returned it. Then she directed his attention toward the photos. "Look at this."

She handed him the photograph with the symbol. His curiosity and his obsession to do his job until the very end pushed back the haunting memories. He turned it sideways and upside down, attempting to make something out of it. "I've never seen anything like it. What do you make of it, Lieutenant?"

"I don't," Lieutenant Rutherford replied. "It's the first time we saw it at any of the scenes. I sent some people back to the other sites to see if that symbol showed up there, but I doubt it."

"Not a bad idea." Mark returned his attention back to the photo. "If we can figure out the meaning behind it, we're that much closer to the killer."

"Tracing the accelerant would help us a lot more," Melanie countered. "It's not like it's kerosene or gasoline. This was specially made."

"It doesn't explain the reason for him being here late at night," Mark murmured.

"Maybe his dad sent him here for a file?" Cassie suggested.

"No," Lieutenant Rutherford disagreed, "he was brought here. This weird symbol seems to back that up."

Mark didn't respond. He refocused his attention on the photograph. Then he forced himself to look at the human outline on the floor. All the bantering they had been doing about the best attorney in town, and one of the best in the nation had him thinking something else. "You know, Anthony may not have been the target. Della Torre himself might've been."

Cassie crossed her arms. "What makes you say that?"

"Instinct, I guess. I know that anyone who's ever had to deal with him would be celebrating if it had been the father that died, and not the son."

Melanie frowned. "Why's that?"

"You're not aware of Della Torre's reputation?"

Melanie's face twisted in thought. She looked at Lieutenant Rutherford, who had finished his cigarette, and was in the process of lighting another one. "Only what I'm hearing from you," she admitted. "I've only been here since February. I take it he's not a popular guy."

"That would be putting it mildly. He's good . . . damn good. He cross-examined my partner Charlie McKenzie during a preliminary hearing. Granted, it's rarely done, but Della Torre's known for it. We had the suspect cold, and Della Torre got him off. On the stand, Della Torre twisted Charlie up worse than a pretzel. When he was done, Charlie told me he felt more like a rookie than a 17-year veteran of the force."

"So he's got a lot of enemies," Melanie concluded. "It makes you wonder what he did, that would cause someone to do this to his son."

Mark nodded, and forced himself to look at the outline left by the body of Della Torre's son.

"Whatever the reason for this, there's one thing that is certain: Anthony Della Torre was betrayed by the person who brought him here, and that betrayal cost him his life."

V

Mark and Cassie walked the site with Lieutenant Rutherford and Melanie for another half hour, asking questions and trying to become as knowledgeable in the techniques of arson investigation as quickly as they could. The longer they stayed, the more Cassie regretted her initial enthusiasm. "I doubt I'll sleep well after listening to how Anthony Della Torre suffered while he died," she admitted to Mark as they made their way back to his vehicle.

"Neither will I," he agreed. "Are you hungry?"

"No." Cassie sniffed the air and grimaced. She tried to figure out where the scent was coming from. When she sniffed her coat sleeve, she reeled. "Geez, we smell awful! Can you drop me off at home?"

"I know, Cass. I want to go home, scrub down, and burn my outfit too, but we have work to do."

On their way out, they stopped to speak to the owner of the complex. He gave them copies of the log showing who visited over the last 24 hours. It confirmed that Della Torre's code was entered at 11:13 p.m. Mark spotted the camera at the corner of the large storage facility. "Do you have any film?" he asked, gesturing to it.

"They're just there for show, Detective. It gets me a break on my rates, but they're not wired."

"That's a shame," Cassie said, as she grabbed the documents. "Maybe now you should."

Within an hour, they were back at the precinct. The arson squad's investigation labs were in an annex connected to the county complex, but their desks were two floors above Serious Crimes. Cassie bit her tongue and gripped the elevator railing. It was all she could do to make the trip to her workplace without fainting when she stepped off the elevator. Mark stood to the left of her, watching her carefully. His gun hand gave hers a reassuring pat.

They exited the elevator. Cassie avoided looking out the hallway windows, and fought back the urge to run to the bathroom and vomit. Like downstairs, it was hot and humid, but the air appeared gray and dusty, and carried the scent of soot. Melanie met them at the entrance. "Most people don't come up here," she explained. "It's rare for us to get involved with another department. That, and a lot of people think we're a little off our gourd anyway."

"So the cleaning bug hasn't hit you?" Mark teased.

"Hey, I don't even clean my place. I'm not about to start with these guys." She turned to the approaching lieutenant. "I'm heading back to the lab. Maybe the boys have come up with something."

"Mel, don't get your hopes up. I doubt there was enough of anything there for us to test."

"Lieutenant, haven't you figured it out after all this time? I'm an eternal optimist."

She gave him a playful punch in the arm and headed toward the door. When she had disappeared around the corner, Mark turned to the lieutenant. He caught the tone of voice the lieutenant used when he went to caution her. "How long did you say she's been at this?"

"Not long enough to realize that we may never find the culprit. Statistics aren't on our side."

He gestured to a desk toward the back of the room and the trio headed toward it. He sat down in a wooden office chair that Mark and Cassie had not seen used since either of them were in high school. Its red leather cushion wrapped itself around his buttocks. He yanked the handle on a long, deep file drawer on its left side and pulled out a series of folders. He opened up the thinnest one, filled with just a few photographs and sheets of paper bolted down on the left side. "This is site number one. It burned down in the middle of February," he explained. "It was a condemned house on the southwest part of town. According to the county records, the last owner was a woman named Judy Samuelson. She died in 1999 with no heirs. The city took the property on tax sale, but never could find anyone to buy it. It needed a hell of lot of work just to bring it up to code. They decided to rip it down last fall. Demolition was scheduled for the beginning of March."

"How was that one torched?" Mark asked.

"Kerosene. Our tests show it was typical of what you find to light lanterns and heaters in peoples' homes, which means it's untraceable. According to the neighbors, it was a haven for homeless people. They were also several reports of teenagers and drug users hanging out in it, throwing rocks at the windows, dumping trash and stuff there. My guess is that someone burned it down on a dare or some strange gang initiation thing."

"What about the other sites?"

Lieutenant Rutherford reached for two more files and opened them. "This is the second site, torched a few weeks after the house. It was a manufacturing plant for small electronics parts down on Taft. It hasn't been in operation for a few years. The owner, a Lloyd Branson died about five years ago. The company's board of directors bled the assets dry trying to keep it afloat, including the pension fund. The plant shut down about a year thereafter because the heirs got into an argument with all those employees who lost their retirement pensions."

"And the third site?" Cassie inquired.

"A doctor's office over on Smith. A pediatrician named Hubert Raich used it. He moved to a more modern building in 1991, and stayed there until he retired and moved to Colorado in 2002. I managed to track down his stepdaughter. She told me he died last year, in a house fire, ironically. They're still in the process of liquidating his assets, and they were about to put it on the market."

"How were these burned? With kerosene?" Mark asked.

"No, gasoline, which was the same accelerant used at the plant. We thought there might be some sort of connection, but nothing has turned up yet. The plant had a lot of remaining equipment, and a few of the heirs and their former employees are desperate for cash. It wouldn't surprise me if one of them torched it for the insurance money, but we haven't found any solid proof. Since the fire, everyone's clammed up."

"So you really think there's no connection between any of these sites?"

Lieutenant Rutherford leaned back in his chair and propped his feet up on the desk surface. "It's highly doubtful. So far, we've found no connection, and outside of Branson's squabbling heirs and employees, no sign of enemies or bad debts owed. Although they were still insured, the buildings were basically not being used, plus there were too many reports of other people near them that shouldn't be. We've already asked to close the files on them."

"What about Della Torre's place? What's your feel on that one?"

Lieutenant Rutherford squirmed in his chair, but it wasn't because of their questions. He felt the urge coming on. "Detectives, whoever did this was one sick person. Just before you arrived, our Forensics people found the shed's locking device. It was fully engaged, and padlocked to boot. There was no way for him to get out. They murdered him, and they didn't seem to mind if he suffered as he died."

Mark and Cassie exchanged glances. "So where do we go from here?"

"Well, once Melanie returns from the lab, we should sit down and go over the results. Maybe we'll find a lead there, if there is one."

"Oh? I hope you plan on including me in that meeting," a new female voice piped from behind them.

The trio turned toward the main entrance. A woman about Cassie's height stood just in the doorway, her arms crossed and a clipboard tucked under her right arm. The black thick-rimmed glasses held even thicker lenses, which blew her brown eyes up to owl-like proportions. Her thin, dirty blonde hair was pulled back tight in a ponytail that just grazed her shoulder. The off-white polyester shirt she wore stuck to her chest, advertising her starch-white bra, and her stick-straight black skirt did nothing to emphasize anything feminine about her. She tapped her low-heeled shoe on the ground in an impatient rhythm. Mark instantly detected something governmental about her. "I'm sorry," he said in a cordial tone. "We haven't met."

"No, we haven't."

Mark stole a glimpse at Cassie. Her jaw was locked and her arms crossed. Cassie had a strong disposition, and tended to jump the gun when a person rubbed her the wrong way. He reached out and dug his fingers gently into her shoulder. The tension kept growing. "Don't, Cassie," he murmured.

Cassie gave Mark her "Don't worry, I'm under control" smile. Then she returned her attention to the source of intrusion. "Who are you?" Cassie snapped.

Unfazed, the woman approached, reaching for a business card as she did so. "Heather McCade. I work for the state's insurance fraud division."

Figures, Mark thought, taking the card, working to keep his face as neutral as possible. *She has state stiff written all over her.* "May I ask what interest you would have in a dead man, Ms. McCade?" he asked aloud.

"It's not the dead man that concerns me as much as the property that was destroyed. I've been to Mason City several times checking on the lieutenant's progress." Her eyes shifted to Lieutenant Rutherford. The corner of her mouth lifted up in a sneer. "Or should I say lack thereof."

Lieutenant Rutherford lifted a calloused, ash-stained finger. "You know, I really have to go check with Melanie and the boys in the lab. I'll leave you to become acquainted."

Lieutenant Rutherford made to leave the room via the back door. Heather held up a hand. "Stay, Lieutenant," she instructed him. "You're the person I need to see."

Lieutenant Rutherford turned back. He forced a smile to his tired face. "I would love to stay and chat, Ms. McCade, but I've had more than my share of lectures from you and your office. As I said before, if and when we learn something, we'll inform you of it."

"That's the line that you've been giving me for the past month. From what I can tell, you've given very little thought to it."

"Ms. McCade, as I informed you when you first graced our presence, I don't believe there's any connection with these fires. If anything, they only have value to their owners."

"The state insurance board doesn't see it that way." Heather flipped to a sheet of computerized paper. "We've had four suspicious fires in less than four months, and one involved in a heated estate battle. The businesses still had significant amounts of insurance on them. However, you and your investigators haven't been able to find who's been starting them."

"As I was explaining to the detectives, these fires appear to be random. You know as well as I do that we don't always find the ones responsible for them. Unless the culprit or culprits come forth and confess, we may never know."

"Oh. So you're saying that the state has no legitimate interest in protecting the companies that insure property within this state."

"No; only that perhaps you should stop trying to make mountains out of anthills."

The right corner of Heather's mouth started to twitch. Mark and Cassie weren't certain if they should take a side, if there was one. "Even if this turns out to be individual acts of arson," she continued, "your response to the state's requirements for information has been slow, and the victims' families want answers."

"No, they want the money. You told their providers not to pay them."

"Because I'm certain that there's some type of scam going on. We've had more than our share of them these past few years. Your lack of cooperation only convinces me that another one is brewing. Unless and until you can provide evidence to the contrary, I have no choice but to instruct the insurance companies to withhold those funds."

"Ms. McCade, I doubt that anything of the sort is going on," Mark said.

Heather turned to face him. She stared at him as if seeing him for the first time, but unlike with other women, there was no hint of flirtation in her eyes. "And, you are?"

"Detective Mark Daniels," Mark replied, keeping his tone warm and friendly. "This is my partner, Detective Cassie Edwards."

Heather gave Cassie the once-over. She grunted, adjusted the strap of her purse, and returned her focus back to Mark. "Arson, I take it?"

"Serious Crimes, actually," Mark explained, retrieving his badge from his back pocket. "We're new to the case. We were brought in because someone died in this latest fire."

Heather flipped to a new page, and ran a nail-bitten finger down the sheet. "Yes, a mister Anthony Della Torre." She looked back at the two detectives. "I talked to your Lieutenant Michaels on my way here. It's my understanding that you were brought in at the request of the deceased's father."

"Yes."

"I know of Mr. Della Torre. His reputation precedes him. I also reviewed your file, Detective. Your record is impeccable, although it seemed to lack certain details. Tell me, how many arson investigations have you and your partner handled?"

Mark pulled his lip in a thin line. Heather was the perfect example of why everyone hated government bureaucracy. Give them the proof in triplicate and they will still find a way deny what you're telling them. "This is our first one. However, if you want to find out whether we're qualified to investigate murders, I'm sure Lieutenant Michaels can help you there."

Heather tapped her foot faster. She gave an icy stare to Cassie, who gave her one in reply. Then she returned her attention to Lieutenant Rutherford. Cassie stuck her tongue out at her. Mark gave her a stare. At that moment, the door behind Heather opened. Lieutenant Rutherford's face fell. Melanie entered the room, her nose buried in the report she carried. She somehow managed to sidestep Heather and made a beeline for Lieutenant Rutherford. "Lawrence, there you are!" she said in breathless tone. "I have something to show you!"

"In a minute, Inspector," Lieutenant Rutherford mumbled.

"No, you really need to see this!"

"See what, Inspector Keegan?" Heather asked in an overconfident tone.

All the occupants saw Melanie stiffen. She slowly turned back. She couldn't hide the shock fast enough. She shut the folder she carried and pulled it closer to her chest. "Oh . . . hello, Ms. McCade," she greeted her in an overly cheerful voice. "How are you?"

Heather stuck out a hand and pointed to the folder. Melanie glanced down at it and then over at her superior, who could only shrug. "See what, Ms. Keegan?" Heather asked again.

Melanie made to hide the folder in her hands. "It's . . . it's nothing. Just some . . ."

Heather walked over to Melanie, yanked the folder out of her grasp, and returned to her spot in room. Cassie made to swat Heather, but Mark gripped her shoulder again. "Let me hit her, please!" she hissed.

"Cassie . . ."

"Think what you wish of me, Detective Edwards," Heather snapped. "It doesn't matter to me. I'm not here to win friends and influence people."

She opened up the report and began to read. The wrinkle lines on her forehead only deepened. Finally, she let out a huff and handed it to Mark. He took it and opened it. Cassie leaned in to read over his left forearm. Inside was a diagram of a chemical breakdown and several big words they could not pronounce. They looked up at Melanie and Cassie gestured to the report. "I could use a little help here," Cassie admitted.

Melanie shoved her hands into her pockets. "It's my breakdown of the substance that was probably used to speed up the fire."

"Speed up the fire?" Mark asked.

"An accelerant, Detective," Heather explained. "It's not uncommon to find one in fires such as these."

Mark handed the folder to Cassie. "Did you find this at the other sites?"

"Definitely not. I've never seen anything like it. It's almost as if it were custom-made."

Mark caught the note of awe in her voice and the spark of light that came to her eye when she talked about it. He gave her a comforting smile. "You seem pretty excited about it."

She caught the look on Mark's face and blushed. "Chemistry was one of my favorite subjects in high school," she admitted. "It comes in handy for this job."

"I don't doubt it, Inspector Keegan," Heather interjected.

Heather's frigid mood made Melanie pull back. Cassie went to hand the folder back to Melanie. Heather snatched it away and tried to reread it, but she couldn't make sense of it either. She shut the folder. "Do you have any conclusions, Lieutenant Rutherford?"

"It's too soon to say. The fact that a different accelerant was used could mean nothing, or that the arsonist is turning to new methods to attack his targets, or our arsonist targeted Anthony specifically. If that's the case . . ."

"These fires are not linked at all," Mark finished, turning to look at Melanie.

Melanie nodded. "Anyway, if we can trace the chemicals used to make it, then we might be able to find who purchased them and possibly, the arsonist themselves. Of course, it's just a preliminary report . . ."

"That you didn't bother to forward to my office," Heather interrupted.

Melanie swallowed hard. "Ms. McCade, as I said, it's just a preliminary report. I'm working as fast as I can, but sometimes, there's nothing there."

"Or there is something there, and you're trying to hide it."

Melanie bit her lip. Once again, the hint of accusation carried in Heather's voice. Was Melanie the only one who heard it? "I *am* new at this, Ms. McCade," she whispered.

"And you have a lot to learn." Heather's eyes moved from Melanie to Lieutenant Rutherford, who shifted his weight back and forth. "You'll be so kind as to forward me a copy of this lab report with your latest incident reports. Also, in light of the death that's occurred, I want to make sure that I'm kept apprised of what's going on. If you wish to reach me, I suggest that you call my cell phone. In the meantime, I'll leave you and . . . Lawrence alone."

Heather turned left the room. The foursome stood there in silence until they heard the elevator doors close. Then Lawrence leaned forward and grasped the chair in front of him. Its legs began to rattle against the floor in a staccato rhythm. Melanie sank down in the chair next to him and laid the folder down in front of her. Cassie let out a low whistle. "Talk about someone who needs a hobby," she muttered.

"Cassie, she's just doing her job," Mark reminded her.

"It doesn't mean she can't be a little nicer about it." Cassie walked over to Melanie and put a hand on her shoulder. "Are you all right?"

Melanie managed to nod. She looked up at her boss. "Lieutenant, I'm sorry. I didn't know . . ."

"It's all right, Melanie. Let me take a look at what you found."

Melanie handed him the file. He perused it and then handed it back to her. "Get the lab boys on this ASAP. Find out how long it'll take them to trace those chemicals. I'll bet that some of them can't be bought at your local grocery store." He gave her a broad smile. "Good work, Mel."

"Obviously Heather doesn't think so." She looked as if she were trying not to cry. She slapped her hands palm down against the table. "God, she's just so . . . irritating!"

"She could use an enema; a whole day's worth of them," Cassie quipped.

Everyone turned to look at Cassie. Cassie gave them a stare. "Oh, c'mon, folks, I wasn't the only one thinking it!"

The men chuckled. Melanie smiled. "Thanks, Cassie."

"No problem."

Lieutenant Rutherford winked at Cassie. Then he turned his attention back to Melanie. "C'mon," he encouraged her, "let me go pollute the atmosphere, as you so affectionately call my habit, and we'll go down to the lab to see what else they found."

Lieutenant Rutherford guided Melanie by her elbow out the back door. Once they were gone, Cassie turned to Mark. "So, what's our next move?"

Mark checked the time. "Seeing as we're still flying somewhat blind, let's take a look at what they found in the other fires and make an appointment to see Della Torre. If there's time, let's also try to go look at the other sites and talk to those people who saw Anthony Della

Torre last. I doubt we'll find anything, but at least it'll give an idea of what we're dealing with here."

"Sounds like a plan to me, and let's try to avoid Miss Sunshine while we're at it."

"You're never at a loss for words, are you?"

"I have my moments."

VI

Attorney Michelangelo Della Torre sat in his burgundy high-back leather chair. He stared blankly out the window of his office suite, the expanse of downtown Mason City in front of him. His wife insisted that he stay home today, but he couldn't stay there. He wouldn't stay there. Someone out there killed his son. They incinerated them as if he were a piece of scrap wood. "Whoever did this, you will truly burn in hell. That I promise, with every fiber of my being," he murmured.

His intercom buzzed. He turned his chair toward his desk and pressed on the speaker button. "Yes?"

"The detectives are here to speak to you, sir."

Della Torre took a deep breath. He had put off talking to them long enough. Any longer and they might begin to treat him as a suspect. He spun his chair around toward the credenza behind him. An array of photographs greeted his eyes. They were of his family: his eldest daughter, Marlena and her triplets, his eldest son, Michelangelo Jr., with his wife and daughter; and Anthony. He picked up the picture of his youngest, dressed in his college graduation robes from just over a year ago. Would he ever come to grips with the fact he would never see him again? Sighing, he placed the picture back in its place and smoothed out the front of his jacket. A hard look crossed his face. He spun his chair back toward his desk and hit the intercom button again. "Send them in."

A few seconds later, the dark cherry double doors opened and Wendy Bailey, his head administrative assistant appeared. "Attorney Michelangelo Della Torre, Detectives Cassie Edwards and Mark Daniels," she announced.

Michelangelo Della Torre stood and approached them. He made a striking impression, standing about 6'6". His cobalt blue tie stood out from his crisp white shirt. His dark gray suit complemented the snow-white hair on his head, and the silver glasses that rested on the edge of his broad nose. To Mark, he looked about the same as he did when he played basketball for the Mason City Timbermen more than 30 years ago, before a career-ending injury sent him to law school. Now he owned the most prestigious firm in town and he had the reputation of not being afraid to take on any case or anybody.

Cassie held out her hand and he shook it gently. "It's nice to meet you sir," she told him.

"A pleasure," he said, smiling broadly.

"May I introduce my partner, Detective Mark Daniels."

Della Torre grabbed Mark's hand with both of his. His grip was so tight, Mark thought Della Torre was going to break a bone in it. Mark would bet that he could still palm a basketball. Della Torre raised an eyebrow as he studied him. "Daniels? Any relation to Robert S. Daniels, the lawyer in Seattle?"

"He's my father."

"I thought so. You look just like him, except for the eyes." He stared at Mark for a moment longer. "How's your old man doing?"

"Fine, sir."

"Good. Well, no doubt he's disappointed that you didn't follow in his footsteps, but if you're anything like him, you're the best at what you do." He gestured to the open chairs. "Have a seat."

Mark and Cassie sat down in the luxurious black leather chairs stationed in front of his desk. Mark took in the details of Della Torre's office. Cassie focused on a section of Della Torre's desk. She twitched a little. Mark put an understanding hand on her forearm. She glanced at him quickly. *I'll help you through your phobia, you help me through mine*, he thought, giving her a short nod and a smile.

"I understand that this has become a murder investigation," Della Torre said, leaning back in his chair.

"Yes, sir," Cassie responded, as she opened up her notebook. "Based on our findings, it appears that your son was lured to that storage facility."

"Lured? By who?"

"We're not certain, sir. We were wondering whether you knew of anyone he might have met recently who may have been aware of the place."

"Met anyone? Probably half of the young women who live in town, and a few that don't. Any one of them could've been the one to take him there, although I don't know why. It's a storage facility, for Christ's sake. Peanuts?"

He held up a glass candy jar filled with shelled peanuts. The detectives declined. They waited and watched as Della Torre filled a small bowl with them and started eating them one by one. "What can you tell us about Anthony and the work he did here?" Cassie continued.

"As you already know, he is . . . was . . . my youngest," Della Torre said with a sigh. "I must admit that Anthony had the name, but not necessarily the brains for law. He barely finished his first year at Stanford Law. He was here to intern for the summer, but he wasn't here very much."

"Where was he then?"

"At the nightclubs or the courthouse, not so much working as much as he was trying to pick up women. I think he thought he didn't need to work. Anthony thought that all he had to do was mention his name, and the women and the money would come to him."

"Did he have a particular place where he went, when he wasn't working?"

"He visited a variety of places. His favorite seemed to be some club called the Pulse. Lord knows there are enough matchbooks from that place around here. He was there nearly every weekend. It wasn't unusual for him to not come home those nights, and sometimes on Monday mornings, he wouldn't show up for work."

"Did he make mention of meeting anyone while he was there?"

Della Torre thought about her question. "No one outstanding comes to mind."

"What about you, sir?" Mark asked.

Della Torre gave Mark a questioning gaze. "Me?"

Mark leveled his interrogator gaze at Della Torre. "You're pretty well known, Mr. Della Torre. There are more than enough people, both here and outside of the city who have ill feelings toward you. Have there been any unusual threats made against you lately that perhaps the police should be made aware?"

Della Torre laughed and relaxed back in his chair. "Unusual would be when I or a member of my family didn't receive a threat to our life. I believe some people have made a sport of it. As for those who actually try, my security people handle them most adequately."

"Just like they did up in Puget Sound sir?" Cassie interjected.

Della Torre turned from Mark to Cassie. "I'm sorry?"

"There were several reports of encounters between your security staff and the victims of that oil spill a few years ago. A few people wound up in the hospital as a result."

"What does that have to do with my son?"

"A great many victims are still trying to recover what's left of their lives. What they managed to win from the oil company will do little to repair the damage caused. Perhaps someone among them decided to exact their anger out on your family."

Della Torre sat up in his chair and placed his hands on the desk. His gaze bore deep into Cassie's stoic face. "I was hired to do a job, a job that I'm damn good at, Detective Edwards. It doesn't make a lot of people happy, I know, but I'm not in this business to make people happy. I win cases, and I do it the best way I know how. If someone wanted me dead, they've had more than enough opportunity." He sat back in his chair. Mark studied his face. For a moment, Mark thought he saw that façade Della Torre wore fade long enough to reveal the grieving father behind it. "There are many ways to hurt me. They didn't have to kill my son to do it," he added in a whisper.

Cassie made to respond. Mark reached out to restrain her. She looked down at his hand. She didn't need to look at his face to know that she had crossed the line. She chomped down on her tongue until she was certain she had bit through it. Mark regarded her, and then returned his concentration toward Della Torre. "Sir, do you have any idea why Anthony would go out to that storage facility at that hour of the night?" Mark asked.

"Not a clue. I haven't been out to that facility in more than ten years. According to the logs, Anthony went out there to retrieve a file for one of the junior partners, but that was weeks ago. I planned to have the unit shut down and the files destroyed."

"Do you know what was inside of it, or how old the files were inside?"

"I couldn't really tell you. My old secretary could. That woman had a mind like a steel trap. She could remember dates, places, names, peoples' faces. She always made sure that I made it to court on time, and reminded me of every dance recital and football game, and my wedding anniversary. My new girl's good, but nowhere near as good as Cathy."

"Cathy . . ." Mark asked, as Cassie started writing it down.

"Catherine Tinnon. She lives in Parkview. Tell her that I sent you. She'll be more than willing to help you out. Ms. Bailey can give you the address."

Della Torre stood up and extended his hand to the both of them. "I thank you for meeting me here today. However, if you need to talk to anyone else in the family regarding this, please contact me first. They're a little upset about how all this is being played in the media."

"We'll do our best not to infringe on them," Cassie told him. "However, we will need to speak with them at some point."

"I don't know what they can add."

"Neither do we, until we talk to them."

Della Torre nodded. "Point taken, Detective. I will have them contact your precinct to set up appointments. If there's anything else you need, please let me know."

"Thank you, sir," Mark said, as the detectives rose to leave.

"You're welcome. Oh, detectives?"

The officers paused. Della Torre's face turned somber. "Since you didn't ask, I'll tell you where I was. I was with my wife, daughter and her family in Seattle, watching the Mariners get ripped to shreds by them damn Yankees. Monetarily, the materials in that facility weren't worth that much to me, and my insurance policies are paid and up to date."

*   *   *

That afternoon, the detectives grabbed a quick bite to eat at Louie's Deli, and then headed for Parkview, a suburb of Mason City. Catherine Tinnon lived in a small home set back from the street. She greeted them warmly. "Mr. Della Torre called to tell me that you were coming. I have fresh iced tea waiting for us."

They sat outside on the porch, under the shade of a huge red maple tree. She shuffled toward them, carrying a tray with a pitcher and some glasses. Her head was wrapped in a colorful scarf, and she wore a simple lightweight, off-green housecoat and fuzzy green slippers. "I read about what happened in the paper yesterday morning," she said, as she began to fill their glasses. Her brown eyes filled with tears and she fought them back. "It's such a shame about Anthony."

"You worked for Della Torre a long time?" Mark asked.

"Twenty nine years. I was his first secretary when he worked for Clark, Putney, and Dennison as an associate. When he went out on his own, I went with him. He's a taskmaster, but when you did your job and did it well, he rewarded you for it."

She eased her way into her chair and her eyes took on a distant look. Sighing, she reached out an arthritic hand to pick up her glass. "Those were rough days then. He took on the cases that no one else wanted, and most of the time without pay. He knew that those were the kind of cases that you had to take if you wanted to make it anywhere as an attorney."

"Are there any cases that stand out in your mind from those early days?"

"Quite a few. The ones I remember most were children."

Mark and Cassie were stunned. "Children?" Mark said.

"Yes. When he worked at Clark Putney, he handled a lot of the cases where children lost their parents, either by violent deaths or by court order," she explained. "It seemed like there were so many of them. When he went solo, he continued that work. After a year or so, he turned to defense instead. I think it took a toll on him emotionally."

"Were there any cases that were particularly troublesome for him?" Cassie inquired.

"All of them were at one point or another. Take Maggie Sinclair, for instance. Her parents died when she was seven, in a fire, coincidentally. Her parents were heavy smokers. One night, their bed caught fire while they slept. She barely escaped with her own life."

"What do you remember of her?" Mark asked.

"I just remember those haunted green eyes, staring back at me. She suffered burns to her neck and chest and lost nearly all of her hair. That only made them stand out even more. It was one of Della Torre's first cases when he opened up his own practice. He did everything that he could for that child. At first, it was all she could do to be near him. In the end, she didn't want anything to do with him."

"Why's that?" Cassie asked.

"I don't know. I remember that he made such a big fuss over her. She needed to be loved so deeply. She craved the affection and he gave it to her, although he knew better. I don't know. Maybe he gave her too much." Mrs. Tinnon sighed. "I think that she thought she would be going to live with him. When she discovered she wasn't, she was deeply hurt. However, she seemed to bond well with the family that adopted her."

"Do you know what happened to her?" Mark asked.

"No. After her adoption, her new parents moved out of the state, probably to distance her from the trauma she had suffered, and the anger she held for him. In the end, I think it was for the best." Mrs. Tinnon paused to think again. Her expression grew dark. "Then there was Walter."

Cassie looked up from her note taking. "Walter?"

"Walter Jefferson. He came from a broken home; his father deserted his family, and his mother beat him pretty badly. He lived with his grandmother for a time or two. According to his juvenile records at the time, he had this particular fascination with fire and anything to do with it. You couldn't leave any type of match, candle, or lighter around him. If you did, he was liable to set something on fire. He burned down two of his previous houses. It got to the point that nobody would rent to his grandmother while he was still with her. She eventually petitioned to have him taken away from her."

Despite the heat and humidity, they saw Mrs. Tinnon shudder. "The detectives studied her reaction. "You seem frightened by him," Cassie pointed out.

"I was. I still am. You could see it in his eyes. He would get this look. At first, I thought it was if he had a secret that no one else knew. Then I realized that it was malice; cold, hard, unflinching malice. Afterward, he would giggle, as if the fire was some sort of practical joke. Nothing seemed to sway him from setting them."

Mark understood some of what Mrs. Tinnon said. Those who cared for him, but especially Jessie and Tyler, would tell him of the expression that would come across his face when he focused on one track of thought, and would not sway from it. They called it the Look. "Do you have any idea what happened to him?" Mark asked.

"He's probably in jail, or dead. You don't want to wish death on people, but I think the only peace Walter will ever find will be in the grave."

"You said that he attacked Della Torre. When did that happen?"

"It was about 15 years ago. He attempted to torch Mr. Della Torre's last home. His wife spotted him setting the fire and called the police. That was when Della Torre bought the home he has now. It's better protected, and has security on it 24 hours a day."

The detectives paused to take in some liquids before continuing their questions. "Della Torre told us that you recently retired. Does anyone stand out from his more recent cases?" Cassie inquired.

"Only one, a client named Katie Lynn Cetera. She was arrested for allegedly torching her ex-boyfriend's home just before I retired. It never went to trial. He cleared her of all charges. She had it bad for him."

"Bad?"

"She wanted him in a way that not attorney and client, Detective Edwards," Mrs. Tinnon quietly explained. "The outfits she used to wear when she came to see him would make anyone's hair curl, and those stiletto heels! How could anyone stand in them, let alone walk? When his representation of her was over, and he rebuffed the last of her advances, she threatened to torch him and his office like she did her boyfriend's."

Mark and Cassie nodded. Yesterday, Lieutenant Rutherford had them believing that solving this case would be impossible. Now they had two potential suspects. "Anyone else, Mrs. Tinnon?" Cassie asked.

"No. Mr. Della Torre is always very careful with whom he represents. Like with Ms. Cetera, he's handled a few defendants who probably wanted to see him burn alive when he was done, but they're walking free right now because of him. Besides, with the security that surrounds him and his family, it would be a wonder that anyone could get near him."

"But not Anthony?"

"Anthony was always a wayward. He thought it was funny that his dad was a target. I doubt he even dreamed he'd be targeted, and if he did, he would've been part of the joke." Mrs. Tinnon's eyes fell to her glass. "However, what happened to him the other night wasn't a joke."

The detectives waited for Mrs. Tinnon to compose herself. Then Mark asked, "What about that storage shed? Who would know about it, outside of the members of the firm?"

"Nobody. When I read where the fire took place, I was shocked. I made the initial arrangements, and I boxed those files up nearly 15 years ago. They were old files from his early days on his own. The only information in them that would be worth anything would be social security numbers, and we made sure to take those out before we put them in there."

The detectives glanced at each other, and then stood. "Thank you for talking to us," Cassie said to her.

"You're welcome. I do hope you find who did this." Tears fell silently against Mrs. Tinnon's cheeks. "That boy had problems, but that's what comes with being the son of someone who's not well liked. Many people may not like Della Torre, or his occupation. That doesn't give you the right to try and kill him or his family."

* * *

After their visit with Mrs. Tinnon, Mark and Cassie drove over to the Pulse, the club that Anthony had frequented. Anthony had made the rounds, the head bartender told them. He always came to the club with the same group of friends, but he could not recall anyone making any type of threat toward him. The bartender also told them that Anthony had been with any number of women over the course of the past few weeks, and in the darkness, it was hard to tell one from the other. As they interviewed the staff, they came across the same response. No one saw Anthony with anyone in particular, or arrive at the club the night he died. Forensics had already examined Anthony's car. They discovered nothing. Mark could only conclude that the murderer drove Anthony there, or paid someone to do it. How did they know how to get there, unless Anthony gave them directions?

When they returned to the precinct, Lieutenant Michaels and Dr. Xavier Foster, the chief medical examiner greeted them at the door. He handed them Anthony's autopsy report. Dr. Foster had a thin bead of sweat on his forehead, and he did not linger long. "I have air conditioning in my place," he chuckled, as he walked toward the elevator. Cassie headed inside. Mark stood in the hallway, reading. Though the body had been badly burned, Dr. Foster found a contusion on Anthony's brain. The impact was consistent with someone struck against the head with a heavy object. There was no question now: Anthony Della Torre's horrific death was a murder planned down to the minutest detail.

After reading the autopsy report, Mark and Cassie went to see Lieutenant Rutherford and Melanie. The final lab reports were in. "We're lucky that we even got a sample of it," Melanie told the detectives. "Whoever created it is a real genius. Somehow, they've found a way to have it burn completely and leave virtually no trace."

"So this isn't some fly-by-night arsonist?" Cassie asked.

"Nope," the lieutenant agreed. "It would take someone with an advanced chemical degree or exposure to flammable products to produce it."

"But how can it be transported? Wouldn't it be unstable?"

"That's a good question. I have inquires in with my friends at the local chemical labs to see if they can come up with anything. I also have them checking to see if any of their supplies have gone missing since these fires started."

"What about the symbol?" Mark pressed. "Any luck with that?"

"We only found it at the factory site, and that's only because it also burned into the concrete. We sent pictures of it over to the university. We're hoping someone there might be able to crack it. However, I have tracked down two more potential suspects: Troy Deacon, a local arsonist who tends to use his version of accelerant whenever he does a job, and Adam Wurtz, who's under arrest in Seattle for an alleged arson there. We're trying to track down their whereabouts on the nights in question."

Mark took all of this in, but something gnawed at him. When he didn't find what he wanted in the records on the third floor, he decided on a different approach. He trooped downstairs to the subbasement. He wandered the maze of hallway to a small, windowless room, more of a closet than an office. At least a dozen black boxes hummed and flashed green and orange lights on their silver shelves. More black and gray cables snaked their way in and out of the boxes, through holes in the wall, and under the desks. Tyler was where Mark expected him. Mark heard his fingers tapping the keyboard. He rapped gently against the wall. "Hey Ty," Mark said in greeting.

Tyler paused in his typing long enough to see who had greeted him. Then he returned to his typing. "Mark! Are you sure that you should be down here? Last I heard, you had a violent allergic reaction to anything that looked like a computer."

"You know, one of these days, I'll master that device up on my desk."

"Yes, but not today, which is why you're here. I haven't found out anything new about your tenant, if that's why you're down here."

Mark stood behind him with his arms crossed. With this new investigation and his fear that his childhood nightmares had returned, his obsession over Julie had all but disappeared from his thoughts. "No. I do want you to do some case research for me."

"Sure. What do you need?"

"I'm looking for someone; a Walter William Jefferson, formerly of 21471 Blatchford, Mason City. Can you see if he's still alive? He's not showing anywhere upstairs."

"Sure. What's he done?"

"He may be behind the arsons that have been plaguing the area. Allegedly, he has a thing for fire."

"Well, to each his own," Tyler remarked, turning his attention back to the screen. "It may take a bit, but I'll let you know if I find anything. Got anything to go on?"

"Well, according to Della Torre's former secretary, he was arrested as a juvenile for setting fire to some warehouses near the river, and to Della Torre's home."

"I'll search the newspaper archives. You have a date?"

Mark double-checked his notes. "June 6, 1974."

"June 6, 1974," Tyler repeated. His fingers stopped moving across the keyboard, and his expression turned thoughtful. "Isn't that the same day that your mom died?" he asked in a low tone.

Mark stared at Tyler's screen. That had been the first thing he realized when Mrs. Tinnon mentioned the date. His mother's face drifted into his thoughts. "Yeah."

Tyler turned. Mark. "Look man, I'm sorry. I didn't mean to bring up . . ."

Mark placed a reassuring hand on his best friend's shoulder. "Don't worry about it."

Tyler took one look at Mark's face and realized that the subject was closed. Tyler knew not to press it. He knew of the fire, because Mark had told him about it. Tyler did not know any of the details. Mark had never told him, and Tyler had been too much of a friend to run the search that would. Tyler turned back toward his screen, turning back to the original topic: "So what makes you think this guy is your firebug?"

"Apparently, he had a beef with Della Torre and the way he represented him during that time. I'm thinking that it really hasn't gone away. I still think Della Torre was the original target, but Anthony was the one who died. Look, I know this is a long shot at best. Do you think we might be able to track this guy down, and get into those files?"

"Probably, if he's still alive, in the area, and the records haven't already been destroyed."

"Destroyed?"

"As you know, juvenile records are only available until the person turns 18. Then they're sealed. No one can touch them, not without cause. Even still, records that old are probably still on paper. A good researcher would know where to go to get the goods on someone, if they really wanted to."

"Like you?"

Tyler took a small bow in his chair. "Like me."

"Good, but what if they're still on paper?"

Tyler stopped typing and looked at Mark with disdain. "You're kidding, right? You actually want me to go through paper, and risk getting a paper cut, or exacerbate my allergies?"

"No. I wouldn't want you risking those lovely fingers of yours on some paper research." He thought for a moment. "What if the person doesn't have a criminal record?" Mark continued. "Say it's just a standard court proceeding, to award guardianship or something?"

"You'd probably have to check with family court on that one, and I probably know the answer to that question."

"Which is?"

"Their computer records only go back to 1983." Tyler sighed. "I set up their database."

Mark tucked his notebook into his pocket. He had been curious to know what had happened to Maggie Sinclair, the other child Mrs. Tinnon had mentioned. It was a curiosity more than anything related to the case. How had she handled the fact that she survived a fire, but not her parents? He dreamt about his fire again last night. He jogged the neighborhood for the remainder of the night, asking the questions he always asked himself whenever he thought of his mom. "Well, it was a thought. Thanks, pal."

"No sweat. Hey." Tyler turned around again. "You're not still thinking about taking that trip to San Francisco, are you?"

Mark frowned. Was he that obsessed with finding out all that he could about Julie that he was willing to go to the corporate offices for information? "Not right now, but I do want to go. After seeing that land, you have to wonder what's on it that they'll do anything to protect it."

"What makes you so sure something's there?"

Mark thought to all he had seen and heard today. He stared Tyler in the eye. "The same instinct that tells me that our arsonist knows exactly what he's doing, watching everything we're doing to try and find him, and laughing at us."

VII

"State your name for the record, please."

Kate Cetera, the first of their multiple arson suspects, did not answer. Instead, her pale green eyes moved quickly up and down Cassie's body. She noted the slightly impatient look in her eyes and on the corner of her lips, and the way she tapped her pen against her folder. Maybe the men who worked here were attracted to her, but Kate could not see how. Next, Kate perused the bare, gray wall to her right, dominated by the dark-stained door and the huge window. She paused to study her reflection in it. She reached up and with a practiced hand, tucked back an escaped strand of wavy brunette hand. In her mind, she pretended she was making eye contact with the people on the other side. She assumed that the duo she saw standing on the other side were still there; the mousey, bookish-looking girl with her hair tied in one long braid, and the older man who looked like he hadn't slept in days, and showered in at least a week. She recognized him. She saw him last year, when they accused her of torching her ex-boyfriend's home. At her pre-trial hearing, he testified to the evidence he found there. His presence there meant only one thing: they were trying to pin another fire on her.

She turned her attention to the male leaning against the far wall. His presence made this experience worthwhile. Her entire body tingled when she first saw him. He was strong, lean, and had a mysterious air about him. Even in the dim light of the interrogation room, she felt the sensuality of him, just barley revealed by those brown eyes of his. She caught a glimpse of gold on his left ring finger. In her experience, married lovers were the best, probably because they still felt they had something to prove. She wanted to chat with him one on one, preferably in front of a roaring fireplace in a cabin near a lake somewhere, so that she could reach out and run her fingers all over his body.

"Ms. Cetera?"

With a great reluctance, Kate steered her attention back to Cassie. Cassie tapped her pen against her tablet. Kate pursed her lips. "Apparently, you already know my name," she said in a sensual tone tinged with anger.

"It's procedure, ma'am, nothing more."

Kate let out a sigh. She flung her right arm over the chair and crossed her legs. "Katie Lynn Cetera, 1827 North Blackmun Avenue, Unit 47, Mason City," she rattled off in a non-caring tone. "Satisfied?"

Cassie leaned forward slightly to begin writing. The move was more to re-evaluate Kate's outfit. The tight black miniskirt she wore barely covered her derriere, but allowed her observers to view the fishnet stockings that clung to her skin. Seeing her in them made Cassie wondered what kind of dress code her employer had. She wiped at the thin layer of sweat that had formed on her brow. The air conditioning was out for at least another day. Cassie came prepared, dressed in a lightweight yellow T-shirt and khaki slacks, and felt as if she was sweating buckets. Cassie darted her eyes downward to steal a look at Kate's black stilettos. She now understood Mrs. Tinnon's comments about them. They made Cassie's calves ache just looking at them. When she walked in here, her hip movements caught the eye of nearly every male within the precinct. They made no effort to hide their leering gaze. Cassie studied her hair, and saw a strand of stick-straight hair in a color that did not match that on her head. Then she thought she saw the faint outline of cloth covered by black hairnet. *A wig*, Cassie thought with delight. *So, she's just as mousey brown as I am, huh? I can't wait to tell Mel.*

Cassie returned her attention to Kate's face. "Ms. Cetera, I want to thank you again for coming down," Cassie said aloud.

"I didn't have a choice."

"We did inform you of your right to have counsel present, if you wished it."

Kate straightened in her chair. The move brought Kate's head level with Cassie's. "Like that would've made a difference."

Cassie made sure not to shift her body posture in any way. She looked up at Mark. He gave her a quick shake of his head, his indication that she should stay her course. She refocused herself. "As I explained to you earlier, Detective Daniels and I have been brought in to assist the arson investigation team in a case they're working. Their latest fire claimed the life of someone that you knew."

"That I knew?"

"Anthony Della Torre?"

"Oh. Yes, I heard about that." Kate dropped her eyes to the table. She made a lazy circle around the top of the Styrofoam cup. "It's such a shame. I really should stop to give Mickey my condolences."

"Mickey?"

"You know him better as Michelangelo Della Torre."

Cassie made some notes. Her pen scratching and their breathing were the only sounds in the room for about 20 seconds. Then Cassie spoke: "We'd like to ask you about Anthony and your relationship with him and his father. You don't mind, do you?"

Kate sat back in her chair. Her left foot slipped out of its shoe. With her toes, she gently slapped it against her heel. "No. Why should I?"

"We've been informed that Della Torre represented you at one point. We may touch on things that may have arisen during that time."

"I doubt it." She brought her left hand up to stifle a yawn. "However, I guess I can entertain them, under one condition."

"What's that?"

Kate turned to face Mark. The look of seduction in her eyes deepened. She leaned forward, giving all watching a better view of her cleavage. She pointed a manicured finger in Mark's direction. "I would like Detective Daniels to ask the questions."

Cassie turned back to Mark. In their short time together, Mark rarely asked questions. He preferred to observe how their interviewee acted vocally and physically. Cassie immediately appreciated the subtlety of this act. Within minutes, a third of their suspects just began babbling, and then tried to get the charges dismissed because Mark "intimidated" them. They all failed because they could never pinpoint for the judge exactly what Mark said or did. Meanwhile, Mark kept studying Kate. The minute she strolled into the precinct, he dismissed her as their arsonist. Women like her have far more vindictive ways to gain their revenge for whatever wrong they may have suffered. However, she gave Lieutenant Rutherford's theory of an accomplice more merit. A young male like Anthony Della Torre would not have been able to keep his eyes or hands to himself if Kate had entered his radar.

"Detective Daniels?"

Mark's eyes drifted toward the one-way glass opposite them. Then his eyes shifted to his partner. She gave him a shrug of frustration, but there was a touch of whimsy in her eyes. He sighed inwardly. If dealing with Kate's overblown sexuality was what it took to get her to talk, fine. He nodded toward the notes in front of Cassie. "Do you mind, Detective Edwards?"

"Not at all."

He unfolded his arms. In three strides, he reached the table. He pulled out the other chair and sat down across from Kate, still studying her. His movements stirred the stifling air, and within it, he caught the scent of Kate's perfume; a lavender scent, tinged with something else. Nevertheless, he welcomed it. Last night, he dreamt of his mother. This time, he could see and smell what happened to Anthony as well. Rather than go back to sleep, he ran ten miles, pummeled the punching bag hanging in his basement, and shredded his targets at practice. His actions did little to shake the stench of that place, or the memories it rekindled. Meanwhile, Kate was quite delighted over the change. Now she could really stare into those eyes of his, and think of them tonight and every night for the rest of her life. She leaned forward and rested her chin on top of her left hand, while her right hand danced again along the top of her cup. She watched while Mark shifted a few pieces of paper, and then raised his gaze. "Ms. Cetera . . ."

Kate held up a finger, and positioned it as if she were pressing it up against his lips. "Please, call me Kate," she whispered.

Mark did not miss a beat: "Ms. Cetera, we understand that Michelangelo Della Torre represented you in court last year, when you were accused of torching your former boyfriend's house."

Kate gave Mark a slow blink of his eyes. "He did."

"We also understand from his former secretary that you weren't necessarily pleased with the way he represented you."

"Well I don't understand why. I told everyone that I didn't torch my boyfriend's place. He proved it."

"So you bear no ill will to him?"

"None at all."

Mark went to make a notation, when he felt the table vibrating underneath his hand. Thinking it was an earthquake, he looked down. Cassie's right leg shook in a nervous rhythm. He cleared his throat. Cassie startled and looked at him. He nodded to her shaking leg. She smiled an apology at him and tucked her leg back underneath her. He finished writing his thought, and then turned his attention back to Kate. "Mrs. Tinnon and a few others in Mr. Della Torre's office also stated that you made a few unwanted advances toward him in that time."

Kate rolled her eyes backwards. "Oh, that. It was nothing. My mother used to follow the Timbermen when Della Torre played with them. She told me a few stories about him." A sly smile came to Kate's face. "I guess I just wanted to know if any of the stories were true."

"And the threats you made to his life the last time you were in his office?"

At that phrase, Kate sat back. She looked at Cassie, then back at Mark. "What threats?"

"We have it on good information that you threatened to torch Mr. Della Torre's home, while he was still in it."

"And who was your source on that? If it's that old bat of a secretary, Mrs. Tinnon, I wouldn't give it too much weight. She thought anyone who came near Mickey was a threat. Then again, he was threatened so often, she probably felt a little paranoid."

Mark pulled the file toward him. He began to flip through a few pages, pretending to be reading. He knew exactly what he planned to ask her next. Right now, he wanted to give the others an opportunity to study what

Kate was doing when he wasn't talking to her. Cassie fought back the urge to puke. Kate was still ogling Mark. Cassie wanted to do the same, but since they were partners, it was a little tough. "Ms. Cetera, it's our understanding that you work for Pennelton Chemicals, correct?" Mark continued.

"Yes."

"They're based out of Seattle."

"Yes."

"What exactly do you do there?"

"I'm a sales rep."

"And who do you market your products to?"

"My main clientele are manufacturers of non-flammable materials."

"These are companies that produce and sell flame-retardant clothing and bedding?"

"Yes."

"Your job requires you to have a background in chemistry."

"Yes. Why's that important?"

"No reason, Ms. Cetera. We're just trying to verify our facts."

Kate straightened and looked from Mark to Cassie. For the first time, the sex kitten façade disappeared. Her face took on a hard look. "Wait a minute. I get it now. Your shit-ass arson investigators out there can't pin me for the arson I didn't commit, so you're trying to pin Anthony's murder on me. That's slick."

"No, ma'am. We're trying to discern who may have had a motive for killing Mr. Della Torre, or members of his family."

"Really? You must sleep under rocks. Della Torre's just an ass. I can see why anyone might want to kill him, and as for Anthony? From what I heard about his reputation, that would be any woman who's ever been screwed by him, and I don't mean literally."

"You didn't answer the question, Ms. Cetera," Cassie interrupted.

Kate looked at Cassie, the disdain plain on her face. "Which was?"

"That you have a background in chemistry."

Kate sat back in her chair. "I have a degree in chemistry, yes," she admitted. "It doesn't mean I know how to make accelerants."

"We didn't make any mention of accelerants, ma'am."

"Oh I'm no moron, Detective. I know that most arson fires use one. Besides, any bozo can just get the information off the Internet nowadays, provided you know where to look. Even so, why bother? Gasoline does the same thing, it's a lot easier to come by, and harder to trace."

"Unless you specifically wanted to be remembered," Cassie murmured.

Kate flung her hair out of her face. "Trust me, Detective Edwards, I'm already remembered by many people. I don't need to set fires, nor do I have a reason to."

"Except maybe to avenge a wrong committed by Anthony or Michelangelo Della Torre."

"Perhaps. Then again, I never really knew Anthony. I only saw him a time or two at his father's office."

"And maybe outside of the office, like at a local nightclub," Mark suggested.

Kate smiled. "And which night club would that be, Detective Daniels?"

"The Pulse, down on Lincoln, say between 7 p.m. and midnight on Sunday?"

Kate paused to think. She ran her fingers through her hair, refreshing it for the detectives. "I visited a few clubs that night." She looked at Cassie. "Something it appears you haven't done in quite some time."

Cassie went to respond. Mark placed a hand on her shoulder to stop her. "Did your travels take you anywhere near the Pulse?" Mark asked Kate.

Kate held up a finger and pointed it toward him. In her mind, she imagined it just tickling along Mark's jaw line. Cassie stole a quick gaze at Mark. He didn't blink or move. "I know of it. I might have stopped there," Kate told them. "What about you? Would you like to go with me sometime? I'm certain your wife wouldn't mind."

"No, thank you."

"Pity. Then maybe you should take your partner. She could use a little loosening up."

"We're getting off the subject, Ms. Cetera. Did you visit the Pulse that night?"

Kate gave a half-hearted shrug. "As I said, I could have. Then again, my mind was on other things. My date for one."

Mark made a checkmark near one their notations. They had already shown Kate's photograph to the staff. Nearly all of them recognized her, but none could tell them if she had been there that night. "Then would you mind telling us what you did after that?"

At first, they were not certain if she was going to say anything. Finally, Kate leaned forward. The detectives thought her breasts were going to tumble out of her blouse, her cleavage had spilt forward that much. They sat back a little. Kate slid her right foot out of one of those stiletto heels. Her legs were just long enough to reach Mark's feet extended out under the table. She ran her manicured big toe along the outside of Mark's left calf. She gave him a sultry wink. "Come over tonight, and I'll show you."

Cassie slammed her notebook shut and stood up. "That's it. We're done here."

Mark could not have agreed more. He pushed himself away and followed Cassie out of the room. He caught the looks on Melanie and Lieutenant Rutherford's faces, who still watched them from the observation room. The lieutenant looked like he was ready for a good belly laugh, and was holding back out of respect. Melanie's face had a startled expression. Mark jerked open the outer the door and headed toward the hallway. Cassie was tight on his heels. The arson investigators followed. He made for the windows and stared out at the vista before him. Melanie approached him cautiously. "Mark? Are you all right?"

"I will be, once she's out of here," Mark assured her.

Melanie turned to look back into the squad room. "Well, one thing's for certain. She does have a way of attracting men."

"You aren't kidding." Mark remembered each movement of her eyes while she memorized every part of his body. He did not even want to think about what sort of fantasies she envisioned during their too-long encounter. He had not been that ogled by a woman since junior college. Then again, maybe he had been, but never conscious of it. He stared out the window, seeking his house amongst the rooftops hidden by the trees. He shuddered. "God, I need a shower!"

"Can I join you?"

Everyone turned and looked at Melanie. Mark began to turn bright red. At the group's sudden look of fright, Melanie realized what she said. She turned a deeper shade of red than Mark and raised her hands up to cover her face. "Not literally, I mean!" she apologized.

Lieutenant Rutherford chuckled. "I think we get the picture." He gave Mark a reassuring pat on the back. "You did help establish one possible angle, Detective. She does make a credible accomplice. I'm curious to know the type of perfume she's wearing. It smells a lot like what Melanie found mixed in the accelerant."

"Wouldn't it be easier to just hit the perfume counters?" Cassie asked.

"No. Perfumes, like people, have their own signatures to them. That's what makes them unique, and why they smell different on each wearer. Until we can get a more specific breakdown, we'd have to sift through every perfume that carries that scent."

"How long would that take?"

"Weeks," Melanie admitted. She turned to Mark. "Couldn't you get a warrant to search her house and workplace?"

"It's doubtful," Cassie told her. "We don't have enough to tie her to crime, except that she knew the victim, and his father."

"But there's no question she has the background." Mark turned to the veteran investigator. "Did you uncover anything when you investigated her the first time?"

"No, but Ms. Cetera is right. Gasoline and kerosene are harder to trace. Accelerants like this one require a special touch, and the right chemicals. Nevertheless, with her position, I'd like to know what her access is to those chemicals and the lab in general. I'll get our guys on it."

Lieutenant Rutherford turned to head toward the elevators. Melanie turned back to Mark and Cassie. "What about the other man who makes his own? Troy Deacon?"

Mark raised an eyebrow. "Deacon professes himself to be a ladies' man. Maybe Kate knows him?"

"I'll check it out," Cassie volunteered.

She turned to head back to her desk. Mark turned to look at Melanie. She couldn't meet his stare. She was still bright red. "No offense taken, Mel," he assured her. "Honest."

Melanie nodded, too afraid to speak. He gave her a playful punch on the shoulder. "C'mon. Let's finish up with Ms. Cetera. Then we'll sit down and you can teach me how to pronounce the names of those chemicals we'll be researching. Deal?"

Melanie smiled. "Deal."

* * *

Walter Jefferson was also alive and still into the area. Tyler's brilliant research located Walter's residence, an apartment on the west side of town. When Mark and Cassie arrived, he was not there. His landlord told them to go look for him at the Last Shamrock, a bar down on Rowan Street. Walter sat on his usual stool throwing down whiskey shots and screaming obscenities at the television screen. They approached Walter and quietly asked him to stop by and see them first thing in the morning. Walter was sober enough to make sure to contact his attorney, and let him know of their visit.

Promptly at 9:00 a.m. the next day, Walter sat in the precinct's main interrogation room, his attorney beside him. He hadn't wanted to come, but his attorney had been insistent. "They have nothing on you. Just go, find out what they want, and we'll get you the hell out," he assured him. Three officers were in the room with them, none of whom he recognized. However, he was happy to see that two of them were attractive women. He barely glanced at Mark, who stood off in the corner, his arms and legs crossed, leaning against the wall. He gave each woman a sultry wink, his somewhat detoxified brain lapping up the images before him. "So, which one of you want at me first?"

Cassie ignored the remark. "I'm Detective Cassie Edwards. That's Detective Mark Daniels," she said, pointing to Mark. She gestured to Melanie. "And this is Inspector Melanie Keegan of the arson squad."

At the sound of the word arson, Walter straightened. He ran a calloused hand through his long, greasy brown hair, and leaned forward. Cassie caught the scent of his sweat, stale alcohol, and she thought, kerosene. He was wearing the same ragged jeans and torn plaid shirt they had seen him in last night. "So, you like playing with fire, too?" he asked Melanie, as he slicked his tongue over his dry lips. "Sounds like my kind of woman."

"Not in the way you do, sir," Melanie retorted.

"Why not? I'm the reason why you even have a job." Walter glanced over at Mark, who said nothing. He settled back into his chair. "You're the ones who invited me here. What do you want from me?"

"We just brought you down here to chat," Cassie explained.

Walter propped his feet up on top of the table and crossed his arms. "Yeah? About what?"

Cassie straddled a chair next to Walter. "About you, your fascination with fire, and your feelings about Michelangelo Della Torre."

At the sound of Della Torre's name, a glint of anger came into Walter's eyes and his shoulders stiffened. He glanced over at his attorney. His attorney eyed the detectives. "What's this all about?" Walter's attorney asked.

"It's about a series of arsons that have plagued the city this last few months," Melanie informed Walter's attorney, who sat in a chair opposite of Walter. She opened a manila folder and pulled out photos of all the arson scenes. "A death has occurred at one of them. We're trying to find out whose causing them and why."

"What does this have to do with my client?"

"It has come to our attention here that Mr. Jefferson here likes fire in a big way," Cassie calmly explained.

Walter looked up at Mark again. Apparently, he was going to let the women do all the talking, which was fine by him. Walter refocused his attention on them. He had checked each of them out carefully when they walked into the room. Both of them had the body type he liked in his women, but never could land; strong and athletic, without being too masculine. In his mind, he began to undress each of them. He also let a few brief fantasies drift into his thoughts. They all involved the two women, him, and a pair of handcuffs. A sneer crossed his scarred face. "You think I'm doing it?"

"Two of the fires fit your M.O., Walter."

"And one of the facilities that burned was a storage unit for Michelangelo Della Torre," Melanie added. "His youngest son died inside of it."

"And I'm supposed to be upset at this?"

"It has come to our understanding that you had some issues with Mr. Della Torre."

"Issues?"

"Walter, wait," his attorney began, putting a restraining hand on his client's shoulder.

Walter glared at Melanie. He wrenched his shoulder away, pulled his legs down from the table, and pulled the chair closer to it. "The man's a lying, two-faced, soul-sucking pig," he retorted. "I would use harsher terms, but seeing as there are females present, I won't."

He smirked at the women. Melanie thought of ways she could wipe that look from his face. They all involved a high-pressure fire hose and a lot of water. "Why do you say that?" Cassie asked.

"He's a greedy shark. His only ambition is to line his own pockets. Of course, that is the mentality of most attorneys, isn't it?" Walter turned and smiled as his own attorney, who crossed his arms and gave him a cold stare.

"May I inquire as to what it is about him that you don't like?"

"What don't I like, besides the fact that he has gobs of money and a higher than God attitude? Trust me, Della Torre may believe that he started out with good intentions for me, but he's caused me nothing but grief."

"Our understanding was that he got you out of an abusive household," Melanie pointed out. "He put you with people who tried to help you turn your life around."

Walter turned his attention to Melanie. "Yeah? Look where's it's got me."

"So you're saying that Della Torre's counsel didn't benefit you?"

"He's good at making something seem wonderful, when it's already been burnt to a cinder. With Della Torre, whenever you see smoke, there's definitely fire, and he should know." Walter sat back in his chair again, a goofy smile crossing his face. "I gave him a houseful of it one time."

Cassie smiled at Walter. "Funny you should use that metaphor. Let's talk about those fires, like the ones you set as a youth."

"Those records are sealed, Detective Edwards," Walter's attorney retorted.

"Yes, I know." Her gaze fixed on Walter's face. "You set those fires as a juvenile."

"So I tried set fire to his house when I was 16 or so. Big deal. That was a long time ago. I did my time for it."

"And now?"

Walter propped his feet up on the table. "I don't get the urge as often. As you probably know from my records, I've been through therapy."

"It doesn't look like it's helped much." Melanie retorted. "You've had two arrests for suspected arsons in the last three years."

"What's that comment supposed to mean?" Walter's attorney asked.

"Nothing. We're just curious to see if his so-called therapy has truly helped him. If it has, he has nothing to fear. However, if the evidence shows that your client was in any way responsible for any of these fires, I'm certain that the D.A. will have no problems getting them unsealed, will she?"

"You better watch yourself, Investigator," Walter's attorney retorted, "and, if you're going to arrest him for this, you better have some good proof, or harassment charges against the three of you is going to be the least of your problems."

"Fine," Cassie said, "let's lay it all on the line, Walter. Where were you between the hours of 7:00 p.m. and midnight on Sunday?"

Walter turned his gaze back toward Mark. He hadn't moved, and Walter was certain that Mark hadn't even blinked. Walter shifted in his seat. He didn't like the look on Mark's face. Walter could tell that there was a major dark side to this cop, and he didn't want to go anywhere near it. His eyes were the most unsettling part. They looked innocent and sincere, yet at the same time, hauntingly evil.

"Sir?"

Walter turned his gaze back toward Cassie, feeling Mark's gaze boring into his soul. He sat back in his chair. "I went drinking."

"Where?"

"Where you found me. Then I went home. I would love to say that I was with someone when I did. Unfortunately, I was alone."

"About what time was that?" Melanie asked.

"Midnight, give or take." Walter pulled a pack of cigarettes and a lighter out of his pocket. He pulled one out of the pack and tapped it lightly against it. "I don't know anything about what happened to his son. Even if I did, I know one thing's for certain."

"What's that, sir?"

Walter leveled his lifeless gaze at her. "If I wanted to go after Della Torre, I would've torched his house, while he and his family were in it, instead of his son in a storage unit. I also would've stuck around and enjoyed every moment of it, and probably brought some friends along for a picnic."

Mark watched as Walter placed the cigarette in his mouth and brought the lighter up to light it. "This is a non-smoking facility, sir," he said quietly.

Walter looked at him through his beady eyes. He made to light it. Then he caught sight of the flame. The three of them saw the look that crossed his face. It was one of pure anticipation and delight. He looked up at the people questioning him. "Barbeque, anyone?" he cackled.

His attorney dropped his head into his hand, shaking it in disbelief. Mark stared at him for a moment. Then he motioned to the women. The women collected their papers and photos. Mark followed them out of the room to the observation room on the other side. He waited until the door closed behind them before speaking: "Well, what do you see?"

Cassie smiled. The question Mark asked the women was the way Mark and Cassie began all of their investigations. It was a carryover from a technique used by Mark and Charlie. The goal was to orient themselves, look at everything simultaneously, then dissect the picture and analyze every piece. They had done this each time they gathered more information about these fires. With their interview with Walter concluded, Mark asked it now to see if any of Cassie's original conclusions had changed. Cassie looked over at Melanie, who stood there watching Walter through the observation glass. She shuddered. "Creepy," Melanie said.

"I have to admit, he's up there in my book," Cassie agreed.

"In mine too," Mark answered, "but, he also brought up an important point."

Melanie turned to look at him. "Which is?"

"If our arsonist really wanted Della Torre dead, why didn't he just torch Della Torre's house? Why kill his son and take him to some unimportant storage facility to do it?"

"Because he would've been caught the minute he tried," Cassie argued. "There's no way he could've made it to the house or to Della Torre himself, not with Della Torre's security system and bodyguards around. It would've been suicide."

"But our arsonist didn't even try. If this person had such a beef against Della Torre, why didn't they, and what does it have to do with any of the other places that were torched?"

Cassie went to say something, but took a step back. She looked at Melanie. Then the women looked at Mark. "You really don't think these cases are related?" Cassie asked.

Mark stared back at Walter through the one-way mirror. He ran his fingers through his hair. "I'm not certain. I mean, what really ties these fires together, other than the burn pattern?"

"The symbol," Cassie answered.

"And the accelerant," Melanie added.

"But not the same accelerant," Mark countered. "You said it yourself, Mel. Two were gasoline fires; and one was kerosene. Only Della Torre's was the special accelerant, and the symbol was only found at the storage facility and at the factory."

"Mark, I'll give you that, and I admit, I'm still new at this, but it takes someone with a really strong chemistry background to make the accelerant that that burned down Della Torre's place. Kate fits that description to a T."

"Also, Kate knew his son," Cassie reminded him. "She has access to some of the chemicals, and she does have a chemistry background."

"But the method used to carry out the other three fires fits Walter and Deacon's M.O," Melanie added. "Plus, Walter already has issues with Della Torre."

"I know, Mel, and I'm not counting them out, either." He smiled at Melanie and her expression softened. "We'll ask Lieutenant Michaels to keep our suspects under surveillance, and we'll look into all of their alibis. If they check out, we're back to square one." He sighed. "How long has it been since the last one?"

"About three days," Melanie replied. "Why?"

"And the time frame between all of these fires has been a couple of weeks, right?"

"Give or take. It doesn't mean anything."

Mark stared back at Walter through the one-way glass. "True, but if any of our potential suspects are our firebugs, our talking to them should let them know we're on to them. Maybe it'll be enough to convince them to stop or at the very least, find another way of getting whatever's eating them out of their system.

*   *   *

At midnight, Christie parked her car near her next target. She made sure to park well away from the streetlight. She climbed out, then opened the back door and removed several one-gallon containers with clear liquid. It was probably more than she needed, but she wanted to be certain that it burned to the ground.

She made two trips from the car to the back of the house, staying on the walk so as not to step in any of the precision-laid flowerbeds that surrounded the property. Their leaves and petals glittered from the watering they had received a few hours prior. She stared up at the overcast sky. The wind had picked up slightly. A rumble of thunder rolled through the atmosphere, but there was no lightning. She heard the steady humming of air conditioning units going full blast. She drove through the neighborhood a few times over the past few nights to determine when everyone went to bed. She had no fear of observation. The houses were dark well before 10:30 p.m.

In the corner, Christie spotted her first objective: the phone box. When she first saw the place, she visited the library to study its blueprints. She also checked its security system. She smiled with menacing delight and retrieved a pair of wire cutters from her back pocket. She snipped the lines in one pass. It would be the first thing the arson and insurance investigators would check. It would deepen their suspicions about their other suspects, or even better, put the blame on the homeowners.

She carried all the jugs to the back porch and then pulled out the key her friend Stuart had made for her. He lifted the house keys from the unsuspecting tour guide two weeks ago and made a mold of it in one of the upstairs bedrooms for her. *There had been some advantage to dating Stuart*, she thought, as the lock clicked and the door swung open. He was a master at showing people how to break into things. He thought she was going to burglar this place. He would never tell anyone. He died a few weeks ago when one of his cigarettes fell on his mattress while he slept, so the arson investigators concluded. She chuckled at the memory. They found no trace of her at that fire, either.

Christie walked through the white kitchen into the spacious dining room toward the winding staircase. "Don't look at it. Don't look at any of it," she kept telling herself. It only served to remind her of what she had done without. The children who once lived here probably got new toys every Christmas. In fact, they probably got whatever they wanted whenever they asked for it. There had been no new toys for her at Christmas. She was lucky if her parents even remembered that it was Christmas. She felt the sting of her mother's hand cut across her face and she flinched a little. Then she felt her father inside of her. She fought back the urge to vomit. *Soon*, she thought, *soon, this place will be a memory. There'll be no happy homecoming for the owner of this house. I'll make sure of that.*

Christie left half a dozen containers by the stairwell and carried four up the stairs. She reached one of the bedrooms. Giving one final contemptuous glance at the pine-stained four-poster bed, she uncapped the first bottle. She started to pour it out slowly, in a specific pattern. Then a fierce anger enveloped her. She started throwing the liquid over everything. She made sure to leave some in every room, but with each pass, her actions became more flamboyant. She didn't just want this place to burn. She wanted it destroyed, just as her life had been.

She made her way down the stairs, leaving a liquid trail on the royal purple runner rug that covered them. Then she made her way to the dining room, coating all the ornate furniture, the rugs and the parquet flooring until her supply was exhausted. She collected her empties and stored them in the back of the car, then returned to the back door. She retrieved a small, white candle, fashioned out of the accelerant and generic beeswax to slow its burning time by about five minutes. She placed it in the center of doorway and lit it. She smiled, watching as the flame descended toward the floor. Then she locked the door again.

Christie was back at her car by the time the candle burned down to the liquid below it. A bright spark of light lit up the kitchen. Within seconds, the whole room was ablaze. The flames followed the liquid food laid out for it. They raced through to the dining room, seared the heavy oak dining room table in half, and enveloped the hand-carved hutch in the corner. Then they entered the remainder of the home. The sudden wall of heat began to blow out the windows. Within ten minutes, the structure's glow illuminated her car mirrors. She stopped at the end of the street and admired her handiwork. She thought back to her mother's screams and smelt her burnt flesh, yet all she felt was clean and new again. She breathed deeply, rounded the corner, and disappeared into the darkness.

A few minutes after Christie departed, Harriet Nesbin shuffled into her dark bedroom, a glass of water in her left hand and a pill bottle in her right. "Leave it to her to forget to take my angina pill like I'm supposed to," she scolded herself. She set the items down on her nightstand. That was when she noticed the orange tint to her wall. She turned toward the window. An unusual glow tinted her ivory curtains. "That was funny. The streetlights don't usually glow like that."

Curious, she walked over to the window and parted them. She gasped as the light lit up the entire bedroom. She stumbled back toward the bed and groped for her husband. "Harold?" she screeched. "Harold! Wake up! Call the fire department! Old Malachi Wallace's house is on fire!"

VIII

Mark got word of the fire early the following morning. He was grateful for the call. It woke him from another wrenching nightmare. By 8:00 a.m., he and Cassie were driving down Harlan Avenue in the city's historical district, heading toward the site. He remembered driving areas like this with Jessie whenever she felt like redecorating. Many of the houses here had stood at least 100 years. They were sprawling structures of wood and stone masonry, some of them with Victorian architectural additions like elegant wooden lattices, cupolas, and wrought iron gates; others in a neo-Classical design, complete with Ionic columns and Roman arches. He didn't remember passing these houses on their sightseeing tours. Then again, they had seen so many, it was a wonder Mark could think straight afterward.

"Oh my God," Cassie murmured.

Mark pulled over to the curb and they exited the vehicle. He caught glimpses of what the place once looked like before they left the station. There was no evidence of that beauty now. Part of the kitchen fireplace, the frame around the front door, and a corner of the north wall were all that remained of the structure. Mark saw something that looked like the remains of a hutch or armoire within the surviving corner. The earth all around it was black, save for a few flowers that managed to escape the fire's wrath. One fire truck was still at the scene, and firefighters and evidence technicians walked the perimeter, gathering up the last of their equipment and anything they thought would help them find who or what caused the blaze.

While the detectives stared at the remains of the home, Lieutenant Rutherford walked over to them. He wore the same uniform they had seen him in for the past three days. A few of those carefully placed hairs stood straight up. "You made good time," he commented, stomping out his cigarette. "I talked to the fire chief. The place was engulfed by the time they got here. All they could do in the end was prevent it from spreading to the neighboring houses."

Mark looked around. "Where's Melanie?"

"Right here," they heard her voice call.

Melanie emerged from behind the remaining wall. She wore a firefighter's jacket over her uniform, now smudged with soot and dirt. She also held a silver metal canister. Strands of hair stuck out of her braids, and smudges of ash stained her cheeks and forehead. She looked like she had a sleepless night. Her facial expression was intense, and she moved ever so carefully so as not to lose her prize. "What are you doing?" Mark asked her.

"Collecting evidence, I hope."

"What is it?" Cassie inquired, pointing to what Melanie held in her hand.

Melanie paused to push her glasses back up her nose. "A couple pieces of the dining room wallpaper. I'm hoping that they might have traces of the accelerant on them, if one was used. Based on how fast this place went up, it's the most logical conclusion. I'm taking them to the lab for analysis. Maybe we'll get lucky."

"Good luck," Mark encouraged her.

Melanie nodded and headed toward her car. Lieutenant Rutherford watched her thoughtfully. "Better her than me," he muttered. "I hate lab work, but she seems to like it."

He lit another cigarette and led Mark and Cassie to the now-destroyed front porch and the tottering door frame. Cassie looked at it, her expression a mix of awe and disappointment. "French doors, I bet," Cassie muttered as they stepped on the first stair.

Mark stopped and turned to her. She caught his amused smile and shrugged. "I like to study interior design," she admitted. "Someday, I want to own a house with huge French doors." She sighed and stared at the blackened frame. "I bet they were gorgeous ones, too."

Mark chuckled. "You and Jessie would've gotten along well."

Cassie blushed. It was the first time he mentioned her and his wife in the same sentence. He hardly talked about her, nor did Cassie broach the subject. Cassie only knew that Jessie had been a painter, and that her illness and death were sudden and unexpected.

Mark and Cassie took another step onto the wooden porch, but as their feet landed, they heard the porch floor creak underneath them. The detectives stopped walking. Lieutenant Rutherford turned to check on their progress. He saw the uncertain looks on their faces. "The engineers have already been through this place. Don't worry. It's solid dirt underneath it."

They looked down. There was a plank missing, showing that it was dirt under them. They glanced at each other, and then followed Rutherford through what was left of the foyer. Mark reached out to touch the doorjamb. It crumbled under his fingertips. There was no smell of burnt flesh this time. He trembled, but not as much as when he had been at the storage facility. He focused his attention toward the ceiling that no longer existed. "What a waste," he lamented.

"Yeah," Cassie agreed.

Warily, they ventured into the structure, stepping where Lieutenant Rutherford stepped. "Do you think this house was selected at random?" Cassie asked.

"Nope. We found what remained of the alarm box. Our arsonist snipped the wires before entering. Preliminary forensics found not sign of forced entry on any of the locks, meaning he probably had a key. We found traces of wax residue just inside the back door, which indicates that a candle was used as the trigger; all clues that lead me to believe that someone was hired to burn it to the ground."

"Any chance it's our same arsonist?"

"We haven't found the symbol anywhere."

"So you're ruling it out of our circle?"

"Who knows? Granted, it's the first true residential property. We'll know more if Melanie and the boys can find traces of accelerant on what we gathered. Based on what I see though, I'm not holding my breath. I bet we'll be charging the owners with insurance fraud in a few days."

As they walked deeper into the gutted home, Mark and Cassie heard the steady dripping of water in the corner, like a metronome ticking away the beats. The air had a hard charcoal smell to it, tinged with something sweeter. In the remaining corner, an elaborate paper pattern of red and cream curled away from the wall. Mark imagined Jessie's heart-crushed reaction if he had brought her here to see the damage. "It must've been a really nice place."

"It was." Rutherford flipped to a page in his notebook. "It's listed on the county historical registry. Malachi Wallace, one of the early timber lords, built it sometime around 1860. When he first moved in, he found it was too small, so he sold it and built himself a bigger place." Lieutenant Rutherford looked around at the walls that no longer existed. "I called the county historical society president. She's in shock. She told me the owners let them give tours of it. It was a real popular home for people to visit, especially antique lovers."

"Why's that?" Cassie asked, walking over to a corner and staring at the burn pattern on the remaining wall.

"According to their records, there were some Oriental rugs in here that were in near-perfect condition. The walls had centuries-old silk wallpaper imported from

China, and it housed an Austrian crystal chandelier that used to hang in the main palace in Vienna. A lot of the furniture dated back to the fifteenth, sixteenth, and seventeenth centuries. From what the president told me, they were some really nice pieces too; most of them one of a kind."

Cassie whistled. "Had I known this place existed, I would've loved to tour it. It also makes you wonder."

"Wonder?" Mark asked.

"Whether the owners hired someone to burn it? I mean, if you're that short on money, why just make it the sensible way, and sell a few pieces?"

She treaded carefully into what remained of the dining room. In front of her was the hull of a huge hutch. It stood about eight feet tall. A part of its decorative top paneling managed to survive the fire. It seemed to depict some type of scene from Europe or early America. She went to examine it. What remained was covered in scorch marks. Pieces of china littered the floor, and she bent down to retrieve some. She saw traces of gold leaf trim and blue on soft white. She was no expert, but she bet that this stuff was the real thing, not the manufactured stuff so common now. "I hope these people had a boatload of insurance on it," she said, staring up at the smoke and water damage caused to the remaining wall. "Of course, if they did order this, they won't see a penny of it."

"Who does own this place?" Mark asked.

Rutherford ran his pudgy fingers down the page and a puff of smoke came out from his mouth. "The property is registered to some place out of San Francisco called the Foundation."

The detectives turned and looked at him. "The Foundation?" they chorused.

"Yeah." Rutherford looked up from his notes. He blew out another puff of smoke and squinted at Mark through droopy eyes. "You two know of the place?"

"Yes," Mark replied, "but more important, I know one of the officers. I don't think they'll be too pleased at the news."

Cassie stood. Her face took on a curious expression. "You know one of the officers?"

"Julie Warren."

Cassie gave him an incredulous look. "Wait a minute. Not only is your tenant the daughter of the CEO, she's an officer?"

"Yeah." Mark stared up again at the sky, which now formed the house's new ceiling. If Cassie thought that was a shock, wait until she heard the money it had at its disposal. Tyler never found this during his search. Then again, Mark realized that he had barely scratched the surface when it came to Julie and the world she lived in.

"So, she's a corporate officer, and could have stayed here in the lap of luxury. Instead, she rents an apartment from you. Talk about trying not to make yourself look like a trust fund baby."

"She must have her reasons, Cass."

"Yeah, I know."

Cassie walked over to him. She joined him in staring upward. Then she sighed. "You better call her. She might want to see this for herself."

*   *   *

"The whole house is destroyed?"

"It's been totally gutted."

"And you have no clue who or what started it?"

Mark shook his head and set down his forkful of macaroni salad. He called the Foundation's office in San Francisco shortly after leaving the crime scene. Jennifer Tatum McIntire, the Foundation's director tracked down Julie, who had just returned from her three-week humanitarian mission in Beijing. Julie agreed to meet him for lunch in the complex cafeteria. He met her at its entrance. She looked like she had come straight from the airport, dressed in a gray business suit, her briefcase in her right hand, glasses on. To Mark, she looked exhausted, as if she had run back-to-back-to-back marathons, but didn't bother to rest in between. He waited until they had their food and were seated before breaking the worst of the news. The pain it caused was evident in her deep brown eyes. "What does this mean?" Julie asked in a soft voice.

"What we know for certain is that it's definitely arson. They cut the alarm wires and they used a candle to trigger the fire. The arson investigators also found scant traces of a possible accelerant on some of the wallpaper that didn't burn. The lab's running an analysis right now."

Julie stared at him, her expression one of shock. For a moment, Mark thought she might cry. Then her attention dropped to her mug. She picked up her spoon and absentmindedly stirred her hot chocolate, dissolving what was left of her whipped cream into the watery mixture. Mark watched her. Around him, he heard what remained of the lunch crowd complaining about the heat. Thankfully, the building's air conditioning was working again. It dawned on him what she was drinking. He remembered the meteorologist saying that it was going to get up above 90 degrees today and tomorrow. How could she drink hot chocolate? "Julie? Are you all right?"

She nodded. "This isn't news that I wanted to hear after coming back from a trip like mine," she murmured.

"I'm sorry, Julie. I thought you should know so that you could file your insurance claim. It's going to be a bit before we can let your adjusters in, though."

"Why?"

"It's part of a criminal investigation. We need to make sure no potential evidence is damaged or destroyed." Mark drank some of his water and picked up his tuna sandwich. He thought about whether he should say the other thing on his mind. The police officer within him instructed him that he needed to. "I hope everything was well covered."

"Yes, everything was, but that's not the point. There were many original pieces in that place. Money won't replace the sentimental value they held."

Julie put her spoon down, rested her chin in her left hand, and began to watch the people milling in and out of the cafeteria. Mark chewed on his sandwich, following her gaze. Outside of their lunch date her first week here, this was the first time they had sat down and talked. He turned back to look at her, his police vision on. Sitting there, she looked younger than her years, yet she also seemed so much older. He studied her dark hands and the long elegant fingers, tipped by short, manicured nails. *Artist's hands*, Jessie would have called them. Jessie loved studying people's hands. She could tell what type of work they did just by looking at them, and she was rarely wrong. Julie's did not have a mark on them. They were as youthful looking as her face, which indicated she never performed physical labor as a child.

His observations moved to her clothes. Once again, her suit look custom tailored, and it hugged her curves without exaggerating them. He had seen more than a few of the men in the place glance over their direction, checking her out. She did not seem to notice or care. Her short jet-black hair was styled in a manner that was attractive, yet maintainable. She wore very little makeup, an inexpensive watch on her left wrist, and fake pearl earrings. She said that she came from a little money that day she treated him to lunch, Mark recalled. *Right, when the truth of the matter is that she* is *a trust fund baby, who didn't want people to think she's a trust fund baby.*

He relaxed back in his chair. He thought about all the information that Tyler had found out about her. Some things still made no sense. "Julie? Can I ask you a question?"

Julie turned to look back at him. "You just did."

Mark balked and then chuckled. "Funny. I forgot you have a sense of humor."

Julie smiled and nodded. "What's your question?"

"I thought you told me you didn't have a place to live here."

Julie ran her left index finger down the side of her water glass. "I didn't, at least not until I agreed to move into your wife's studio."

"But why are you living above my garage when you could live there? You own it, don't you?"

He bit into his sandwich again, watching her carefully. Julie picked up her mug. "No, I don't own it," she corrected him. "The company that I work for owns it."

"You mean your family's company? You're the CEO now, are you not?"

Julie stopped mid-sip. She stared at him over the edge of her glasses. He saw a flicker of something flash in her eyes. She set her mug down. "You've been checking up on me."

"I'm not going to deny it. I'm a cop. It's second nature. Besides, any good landlord does and should." He set his sandwich down and leaned forward. "I don't want to be renting a place to someone who winds up being a deadbeat," he told her in a low voice.

Julie leaned toward him. "But I paid my rent in full for the year."

Mark shrugged. "You didn't answer my question."

"Which was?"

"Why live with me?"

Julie sat back and picked up her mug again. "As I told you when we met, I travel a lot and I don't need a lot of space. An apartment is much easier to maintain than a house. Besides, I don't like having to watch what I run into, or that I don't break anything. There're a lot of regulations you have to follow when you own a home that's on a historical registry."

She took a sip and looked into Mark's face. She sensed that Mark didn't believe her. Frowning, she set down her mug and met his gaze. "My guardian's great-grandmother bought that house from its original tenants," she explained. "Before she died, she deeded it to the Foundation. We let clients stay there when they're visiting this part of the Pacific Northwest. Most of them aren't in a rush to leave and like historical houses with fancy antiques. It makes them feel important or something." Julie looked to her right and picked at her uneaten blueberry muffin. "I wanted something a little more convenient for me. Is that a crime?"

"No, it's not, but it does make me wonder."

"Wonder what?"

Just then, Cassie walked into the cafeteria. Spotting Mark, she joined them at their table. "Melanie's traced the accelerant," she informed him, barely acknowledging Julie's presence.

"That was fast."

"It's because she didn't have to look very hard. Read this."

She handed Mark a few pieces of stapled paper and slid into the chair next to his. Mark began to read. A third of the way down, his brow furrowed. "Melanie says the accelerant found at this place had the same chemical make up as the last one. It still doesn't mean it was the same person. Besides, except for the condemned place, they were all commercial structures."

"No, but look here." Cassie pointed to a spot toward the bottom of the first page. "Both the lieutenant and Melanie said that there's something odd about the way the accelerant was spread out. Everywhere else, it looks like it was evenly distributed. Here, it looks like it was spread haphazardly, as if someone was throwing a tantrum."

Julie looked at Cassie, then at Mark, confused. "What does that mean?"

"Maybe it's the same person," Cassie replied, "and maybe not. If it's a copycat, then there's a chance that it was targeted for the insurance money."

"But that doesn't make any sense."

"No. A lot of things don't make sense." Cassie looked from Julie to Mark. "Hey, I'm just the messenger," she added, holding up her hands. "I'm heading back upstairs to let Lieutenant Michaels know what's going on. I'll catch you later."

Cassie took the report from Mark's hand, got up and headed out of the cafeteria. Mark watched her go. Then he turned to look at Julie. He picked up his fork again. "So? Made any new enemies of late?"

"Not that I'm aware of. Why?"

"What about the insurance policy on that place? I take it from what was in there, it was a pretty hefty policy."

"Yes, it was."

"Is it paid up?"

"Why? Am I a suspect in my own fire? Do I have to provide proof of where I was when it happened, too?"

"No, Julie. I just . . ."

"If you've been checking up on me as you claimed, you would know that I have no need for the money," Julie said in a loud voice. "My family's company has more than enough to spare. Therefore, I have no reason to burn down any of the properties the Foundation owns, especially that one. That place meant a lot to me, more than you'll ever know." She fought back a sob, picked up her briefcase, and stood up. "If that's all, Mark, I have to go," she continued in a barely controlled voice. "Like you said, I need to call the insurance company and get started on my claim."

She made to leave. Mark reached out and grabbed her free arm. She glared at him. Mark stared into her hardened face. He saw the tears in her eyes, but he did not relinquish his hold on her. He felt no guilt for asking. The question would be asked eventually; if not by him, then by Cassie, Lieutenant Rutherford, Heather, or Melanie. For him, it went deeper. For him, that place just served as more proof that she was hiding something. Still, he tried to be contrite about it: "Julie, I didn't mean anything by that question. I have to ask. I need to know."

Julie jerked her arm away. "If you need me for anything else, Detective, call me. You have my numbers."

Julie stormed out of the cafeteria. Mark watched her go. He rested his chin on top of his chair. The Look came to his eyes. There was no doubt that the questions he asked touched more than a few nerves. Perhaps touching a few more might get him the answers he sought.

IX

The destruction of the Foundation's house sparked a new surge of determination within the investigators. Through phone calls or personal visits, they talked with the surviving relatives, and tried to retrace Anthony's last steps with little luck. Cassie and Melanie went back to the Pulse that night to talk to some of the patrons, all of who remembered Anthony being with any number of women in the weeks leading to his death. Mark and Lieutenant Rutherford re-interviewed Della Torre, and reviewed his case files over the last ten years. They yielded nothing.

The next morning, Mark suggested a new approach. He commandeered the Serious Crime Unit's large conference room. Armed with plenty of water bottles (as the air conditioning had started acting up again), they located some rolling dry-erase boards. Then they plotted out everything known about each fire, starting with the condemned house, and ending with the Foundation's house the night before. Three exhausting hours later,

Lieutenant Rutherford, Melanie, Cassie, and Mark sat at the table. Each of them hugged a water bottle, staring at their work. Finally, Cassie sighed and rubbed her eyes. "I don't know about you, but that just looks like gibberish up there."

The others nodded. Their attention went to the table. Everything they had was in front of them. Nothing made sense. Yesterday, Mark and Cassie were inclined to take the condemned house out of the picture, since the other destroyed buildings were commercial buildings, and heavily insured. Then the arsonist torched the Foundation's house. Mark sat back in his chair, flipped to a fresh sheet of notebook paper, and picked up a pen. "Let's start from the beginning. What do we know about arson in general?"

"Well, the most prolific arsons are done either for profit or to cover up a crime of some sort," Lieutenant Rutherford explained. "I don't think we have either of those types here."

"Why do you think that?"

"Only the condemned house had no insurance." Lieutenant Rutherford pointed to the line dealing with the insurance and financial status of each party victimized. "The other buildings were well protected, and the owners were current with their policies. Only one of the owners was financially unsound."

"So what's left?" Cassie asked.

"Fraud, kids playing with matches, revenge," Melanie commented, "or someone who just like to start fires because it's a turn on for them."

Mark and Cassie looked at each other, and then back at Melanie and Lieutenant Rutherford. "Come again?" Mark asked.

"We call it pyromania. These people like to set fires because it excites them. It gives them a feeling of being in control of something, usually because they have no control over their own lives."

Lieutenant Rutherford nodded in agreement. "What Melanie says is true. At least, it's been the usual cause of most arson fires in the 20-odd years I've been investigating them."

"No control, or a turn on. That's the method of William Jefferson," Cassie muttered, recalling Mrs. Tinnon's conversation.

"Revenge is a strong possibility, also," Mark noted. "After all, we're still trying to track down that odd symbol found at two of the sites."

"But revenge for what, and why not leave it at the other sites?" Melanie asked.

"Are we certain that they didn't?"

"Well if it's revenge, that leads us back to Katie or Walter," Cassie argued. "He still carries strong feelings for Della Torre, and three of our fires fit his M.O."

"Yeah, but his alibis also checked out," Melanie countered. "What about Deacon? He's the homemade accelerant type of guy."

"True, and we haven't traced his whereabouts for the last two fires," Mark realized.

"Wasn't he also linked to Kate at one point?" Cassie asked.

"For a one-night stand," Mark reminded them.

"It doesn't mean that he didn't have a part in it," Cassie argued. "He could've had someone else do it. Taught her some of his methods?"

Silence greeted her last comment. Cassie looked at the veteran investigator. "Setting our suspects aside, if you were to write a profile of our arsonist, what would it say?"

Lieutenant Rutherford turned to his trainee. "Melanie? Here's your chance."

She took a deep breath, pulled off her glasses, and rubbed her eyes. "More likely a male," Melanie said. "I'd say he's somewhere in his twenties, not more than his mid-thirties." She looked at Lieutenant Rutherford, who nodded his assent. "He's definitely intelligent. He'd have to have a major background or experience with chemicals, seeing as he seems to be creating his own accelerant, or has access to the materials needed to make it."

"What about the perfume?"

"Probably to throw us off, or leave a signature. I'm learning that every arsonist has one."

Mark continued to make notes. "What about background? What kind of life did he have, or what is his life like now that's causing him to act like this?"

Lieutenant Rutherford's facial expression turned somber. "More than likely, he suffered some sort of physical or emotional trauma in his life, Detective."

"What makes you say that?"

"Physical or sexual abuse is the most common trait found in the backgrounds of the arsonists I've arrested. It seems to be part and parcel."

"But why do it in the first place?" Cassie asked. "What's the point in it?"

"From what I've been taught, most arsonists find that fire is something that they can dominate," Melanie answered. "They know that if they start it, they control what burns and how long it burns. They don't necessarily want someone to die." She shrugged, and slipped her glasses back on. "Who knows? Maybe Mr. Della Torre's son was a mistake."

Mark picked up a folder. "Maybe. Personally, I still think Della Torre himself was the target, and like you, Lieutenant, I'm pretty certain these fires aren't being set for money. The Foundation's place by far was the most expensive. According to the policy, it was insured for more than 20 million dollars, and the policy was renewed this past April the first."

"That won't make Heather happy," Melanie commented. "She's just dying to keep the money away from the victims, and make sure that the lieutenant and I are the reason why."

"It still doesn't explain why her house was targeted," Cassie said. She had seen some of the Foundation's financial information that Mark saw a few days prior. It only reinforced her theory of Julie being a true trust fund baby. It also made plain that whoever their arsonist was, they didn't care what they burned, so long as it did. "You know, you'd think for that much protection, her family's corporation would have a better security system in place."

"It should have, but it also had a lot of foot traffic in it because of the tourists," Melanie explained.

"They wanted to keep the security system as simple as possible."

"I don't think the best security system in the world would have swayed our arsonist from destroying that home," Lieutenant Rutherford interrupted.

"Why's that?" Cassie asked, looking at him.

"Arsonists live for the feel of that burn, Detective Edwards."

Lieutenant Rutherford pulled his lighter out of his pocket. He flicked it and the orange flame shot up to the ceiling. Cassie, Mark, and Melanie watched him as he stared at it, as if entranced. His face however, did not have the same manic insanity that Walter's had two days prior. He looked like he was fighting the urge not to be ill. "It's a sickness, Detective, a perverted sickness. To them, fire is their nicotine, their cocaine, their pornography. Seeing something burning is to feel something. It takes away some of the frustration and pain that they're experiencing, until it comes back, and they need the fix again. If they couldn't have gotten into the place, they might have burned something else, or they would've torched it from the outside."

He extinguished the lighter and returned it to his pocket. He looked at Mark and Cassie. "You two seem a little cynical that Ms. Warren would choose a cheap apartment over living there, but you should thank the Lord she did. If she hadn't, she'd be dead right now, and personally . . . ." He looked at Melanie. "I don't think that our arsonist would've cared."

* * *

The blazing summer sun cut a path through the cloudless sky. Julie pulled up in front of the blackened remains of the Foundation's house and parked it near its front walk. She ignored the scene before her, so that she could continue her telephone conversation. "Jennifer, it's all right if you can't find the duplicate furniture list," she said to the speakerphone mounted in her rearview mirror. "I'm certain it's around somewhere."

"Julie, that's not the point," Jennifer replied in disgust. "I know I filed it. I just can't remember where I filed it."

"The last time the insurers reviewed it was more than five years ago, when you were still Jack's assistant. You've had a lot of responsibility since. Now go home and relax. I don't need you going into labor over this."

"Julie, I have at least six more weeks."

"Still, you don't need the stress of this weighing on you. Have Elise look for it first thing in the morning. In the meantime, I'll review what the insurance adjusters concluded today, and we'll take it from there. Okay?"

There was a heavy sigh. "Okay. I'll see you tomorrow."

Julie waited until she heard the second click, indicating that the connection had been terminated. She checked to make sure she wasn't being observed. "NIK?" she asked aloud.

Yes, Ambassador?

"Send a message to Elise to keep an eye on Jennifer. We don't need her going into labor sooner than we expect."

As you wish, Ambassador.

Julie shut off the engine and sat in her vehicle for a moment. Then she leaned on the steering wheel and stared at the yellow crime scene tape that surrounded the property. It still stunned her that some human had burned it down for no reason at all. "Perhaps the Eldar are right," she said. "This planet's humanoid society really has changed, and not necessarily for the better."

Dejected, she grabbed her handbag and made her way up the front walk. Once the police gave them clearance to enter, she met with insurance adjusters, and came with them to see for herself what had occurred. What she found horrified her. She had lived nearly 65 million Earth years, and to this day, still could not understand violence like this. "What did I do?" she whispered. "Was it you, Eldar? Was this your doing, and not the human they're blaming in their media? Is this your way of telling me to give up on my dream to be like them?"

She stopped before the front steps, staring at what remained of this once stately home. During her earlier visit, some of her neighbors visited to express their sympathies. A quick reading of their minds informed her that they saw nothing odd over the past few days. The historical society's president also called, expressing her grief and hope that the Foundation would rebuild it.

Julie slipped off her suit jacket and flung it over her bare forearm. She forced herself to walk up the driveway alongside the destroyed hull of the house. She paused to examine the now-trampled flowerbeds. Even they had paid the price. The firefighters had no choice but to walk through them as they worked. She squatted down and touched the stem of one of the geraniums. She heard it squeal in pain. "I'm so sorry," she told it, "but there's nothing I can do for you, or your cousins."

She abandoned the plants and stared up at the remaining wall, struggling to keep her mind focused on the task in front of her. It wasn't easy. The situation on Anichia also weighed on her mind. She had just begun to earn their trust when one of their warriors stabbed the premier of Dogin Prime, right in front of her. Leaders from four islands neighboring islands watched in fear while the relations between the Beata and Quartan disintegrated into chaos. When Julie received word of what had happened here, Simon took her place. His reports back to her were not very encouraging.

Julie turned right and headed toward the back of the house. Her thoughts shifted again; this time to her conversation with Mark in the cafeteria the other afternoon. She knew he was only doing his job when he quizzed her about the insurance, and any other relevant information regarding this place. However, she knew that part of the reason for his curiosity was because he knew so little about her. Mark and the rest of the planet could never know that she was actually immortal. So far, she had been able to keep her secret. NIK and the Illani kept her informed of Tyler's ongoing research. The discovery of this place only raised new questions within Mark that Julie could not and would not answer for him. "The Illani were right about his obsessive nature when there was a mystery that he could not readily solve," she concluded. "I hope he'll apply some of it to this investigation."

She took a few steps back from the burnt-out structure. When Julie conducted her initial walkthrough with the adjusters, she thought she sensed something unusual. With the insurance people there, she hadn't been able to take the time to delve into it. She felt certain it was her humanoid fatigue causing it. She studied the charred stone facing. Then she scanned the ground for any signs of footprints, debris, or anything that the investigators might have missed.

Ambassador?

Julie paused in her wanderings. NIK spoke to her now. NIK was the voice to a vast computer database on Narcalonia, several thousands light years away from Earth. Their lead scientist Molin developed a special processing chip and implanted it into her. It allowed Julie to telepathically link to NIK. Julie used the same link to maintain contact to the Illani and with all that was happening in the places she traveled, and obtain information without having to resort to trolling the minds of whom she was helping. Although NIK was a machine, Julie could tell when it was concerned about her. She noticed a slight change to NIK's "voice." Julie always wondered if Molin deliberately programmed it that way so that to Julie, it had some semblance of personality. Then again, Julie had been referring to NIK as a "she" since she first met it. "NIK, what is it?"

I have been analyzing your thought processes. They seem random and disjointed. I conclude that you are perplexed about something. May I inquire as to what you are looking for?

Julie stared up at the vacant space. Even NIK noticed her thoughts were churning non-stop. They alternated between the events on Anichia, what had happened here and everything else occurring in her life—if one could call it such. "I'm not sure. It's just . . . there just has to be a reason why this house was targeted."

I have reviewed the information gathered by the humans. Their investigation was most thorough.

"I know. Maybe I'm just hoping they missed something."

You realize, Ambassador, that this crime may go unsolved. According to the statistical data that I have studied, the closure rate for these types of cases is under fifty percent.

Julie frowned. "I didn't know that. "Thanks, NIK. Let me know if anything changes."

As you wish, Ambassador.

Julie stopped at the back of the house and sighed again. It wasn't really the loss of the house that bothered her as much as what was inside. Julie had many fond memories of the human men and women who built the furniture that once decorated its interior. She remembered wandering through their workshops, marveling at their ability to change their resources into a functional piece of art with their bare hands, their tools, and their imaginations. Julie could duplicate their work with just a thought, but it was never the same. To Julie, it was as if a part of their life essence had transferred itself into each piece. Julie felt it every time she touched one. Now the last part of each of their creators had finally died as well.

She walked up the steps that used to lead to the back door of the structure. As she approached it, she thought she smelled something odd. She reached the top step. A flash of something shot through her head. Julie looked about trying to discern what had triggered it. She took another step forward. It hit her again: an instantaneous image of a girl, screaming. She stared at the empty space. "What caused that? What did I see?"

"Unfortunately, staring at it isn't going to make it come back."

Julie straightened, and then turned to face the strange voice that spoke. A woman she did not recognize stood at the foot of the stairs. Julie stared into the owl-size eyes behind the thick plastic lenses. "I'm sorry, but did you say something?"

The woman gave her the barest hint of a smile. "I apologize for startling you, but to me, it looked like you were trying to will that house back into existence."

"If only that were possible." Julie descended the steps, and her expression turned serious. "Who are you?"

"Heather McCade. I work for the state insurance fraud office." She retrieved her clipboard and tugged a business card out from under the clip. She handed it to Julie. Her eyes narrowed even further. "And, you are?"

"I'm Julie Warren. My family's company owns . . . owned this house," Julie heard herself say.

Heather gave a curt nod. "So you're the elusive woman Detective Daniels told me about."

Julie took the card Heather offered her. "Not that elusive, Miss McCade. Obviously, you found me."

"That's because I called your office. A Ms. Carpenter told me you were on you way here. I'm glad that I did find you. I thought it would be best to talk to you out of earshot of the arson investigators." Heather took a step toward her. "Detective Daniels seems particularly intrigued by you."

"Oh? What would give you that idea?"

"Perhaps it's the interesting lifestyle you were raised in, your occupation or the money at your disposal. Perhaps it's the fact that you rent out the place that his deceased wife used as her art studio instead of living here, or the fact that this is the second time in less than three months that you've made an appearance in his case load." Heather scrutinized the look Julie gave her. Only a slight flicker in Julie's eyes gave Heather any indication that her dogged research had served its purpose. "You are quite something, I must say."

"It's coincidence, Miss McCade, nothing more. I doubt that our paths would've crossed in this matter if circumstances were different."

"Perhaps. If I may ask, what are you doing here so late, and without your insurance people?"

Julie turned back to look at the remains of the destroyed structure. "I'm just here to try and find a reason for why someone would want to destroy such a beautiful place," Julie answered in a wistful tone. She returned her gaze back to Heather. "And since we're in the mood to ask accusatory questions, may I ask why someone from the state's insurance fraud division would want to talk to me?"

"It's standard procedure whenever there's a suspicious fire. We just want to make sure that no one profits from this disaster any more than they should."

Julie thought back to everything lost inside, and the void within her began to expand. "No one stands to profit from this, least of all me or my family's company. If there were a way for me to reverse what happened here, I would."

"I'm certain that you would. However, it doesn't change the reality that stands before you, or the circumstances that led to its occurrence."

"I don't understand. I thought this house was targeted at random."

"That hasn't been completely ruled out. As you're new to the area and constantly traveling, I doubt that you're aware of what's been happening. There has been a rash of arsons in the city these past few months. This house seems to be the latest one. The state wants to make sure that these fires are simply random occurrences and not some pattern designed to make people rich."

"What do you mean?"

"I met with your agent. He went over your policy and its coverage with me. From what I've seen, it's quite . . . large."

Julie didn't like the way she had emphasized the last word. She kept her face stoic. "There were quite a few antiques in this place, Miss McCade, and as my agent probably informed you, this house is on the historical registry. My family's company needed to keep a high policy on it to protect its contents in the event of damage caused by people touring or living in it."

"Yet your security system was easy enough to be foiled. The reports claim that the alarm wires were cut, and the arsonist probably had a key to enter it."

Julie looked over toward the corner of the house where the phone box once stood. The security could be thousands of years ahead of what any human had ever seen, had the Illani had their way. Julie declined it. First, there would be no easy way to disguise it. Second, it meant that an Illani would have to live here at all times to monitor it. Third, the humans who worked for the historical society had protected it from potential thieves and vandals for more than 20 years. A deliberately set fire never occurred to them. "We were working on upgrading it. Unfortunately, events overtook us."

"Yes. It seems they did."

Julie stiffened. "What are you hinting at, Miss McCade?"

"I need to ask you Ms. Warren: Where were you between the hours of 9:30 p.m. and midnight last night?"

"I was in Beijing, Miss McCade, watching a children's play with the British, Norwegian, and North Korean ambassadors to China. My left shoulder could confirm it, if it could talk. I kept jerking it away from the Norwegian ambassador's grip throughout it. I'm certain that each of their offices would forward you sworn affidavits to that effect, if at the end of your investigation, I'm still considered a suspect."

Heather eyed her over her glasses. Then she dropped her gaze back to her clipboard and made a few notes. Inside, she fumed. Heather already confirmed Julie's whereabouts with the Foundation's Beijing office, and the offices of the ambassadors she just mentioned. She also contacted their insurance carrier, Lloyds of London. In more than three hundred years of representation, their records showed that this was the first major claim the Foundation ever filed. She stopped writing and looked back at Julie. "I take it you'll be in town for the next few days?"

The tension Julie felt did not ebb. She reached into her bag and retrieved one of her business cards. Heather took it, read its face, and chuckled. *She's the CEO and President, and she still lists herself as a "consultant,"* Heather thought. She placed it with hers on her clipboard. "If I have any more questions of you, I'll call."

"I'm certain that you will."

Heather gave her a nod of acknowledgment, turned, and walked away. Julie watched her as she climbed back into her vehicle and started the engine. She eyed Julie one more time before dropping the car into gear and pulling away from the curb. Julie walked to the curb, watching until she saw Heather's vehicle disappear around the bend. She rubbed at her temples, willing away the Eldar's attack away before it began. She did not need them to remind her that now two people were suspicious of her, albeit for entirely different reasons. "I need to do something to curb their curiosity," she told herself. "The trick is how to do it."

Ambassador?

Julie closed her eyes. "Yes, NIK?"

I must remind you that you have not rested in 77 Earth days. According to my latest readouts, I estimate your humanoid strength is down to 68.4 percent.

"I know, NIK, but need to find an answer for all of this."

I apologize for not being able to assist you further, Ambassador. However, I cannot perform any additional analysis without additional data.

Julie squatted down to the ground to pick up a charred piece of wood. She closed her hand around it, felt it crumble beneath her fingers, and then brushed her hands off on her skirt. Heather's appearance had broken Julie's concentration. The imagery she had seen before her arrival had vanished. Now there was nothing outside of burnt wood, crumbled brick, shattered glass, and misery. *I can heal people with a touch. I can know how someone feels from a hundred miles away, but I can't change this reality. I can bring the things back that make it look like it once did, but it won't be the same. It can never be the same.*

She fought back tears and turned toward her vehicle. "Maybe you're right, NIK. Just let me know if you find out anything else. In the meantime, I think I'll just head home."

X

That evening, Mark pulled into the driveway of his home. He sat there for a few moments, savoring the last bits of the cool interior. His head pounded slightly, from the heat, this case, and because he hadn't slept well these past three days. With everything about work competing with his childhood nightmares and the loneliness he felt not having Jessie there, he wondered how he was sleeping at all.

He exited his truck and headed into his home. The wall of heat that greeted his arrival made him reconsider going back to his vehicle, or to a hotel. He thought about the money sitting idle in the bank. He knew he should use it to pay the bills. Now, all he wanted was to sleep, and a cool place to do it. Whenever he caught a break, he called every heating and air-conditioning company in Mason City, asking how soon he could have central air installed. The earliest someone could perform an estimate was two weeks. By then, Mark figured he would have melted.

He stowed his gun and badge in the safe. Then he trooped upstairs to shower, take a couple of aspirins and change into a fresh T-shirt and a pair of shorts. As he made his way back down, his stomach rumbled. Once again, the craving for oatmeal raisin cookies hit him. He pushed the thought out of his mind, concentrating instead on what was in the refrigerator. It didn't make him feel any better. Tyler cleaned out the last of his leftovers a few nights ago. The one thing he knew was edible he would never touch. It was a jar of pickles from Louie's Deli, tied with a sunlight yellow ribbon. Knowing it was hopeless, he walked over to the fridge and opened it anyway. He stared at the near-empty shelves. "What's for dinner?" he asked himself, "Chinese, Southwest, or Louie's?"

The doorbell chime rippled through the air. He thought for a moment. Julie had returned to San Francisco, and Tyler was busy on a case for Vice. Therefore, it was not either of them. His bare feet pattered against the hardwood floor as he went to welcome his visitor. Melanie's bright smile greeted him from the other side. She had on a yellow halter, short denim shorts, and white wedge sandals that showed off her athletic legs, and her tan, trim body. Her glasses were gone, and her hair was out of its braids and flowed down below her shoulder blades. She looked radically different when she was out of uniform. "Hi!" she said breathlessly, flinging a strand of hair away from her face, her green eyes twinkling.

Mark was a little startled. "Hi, Melanie, how are you?"

"I'm hungry."

She held up a white casserole dish. Mark caught the smell of the bubbling tomato sauce. He heard his stomach gurgle. Melanie heard it, too. She also saw the ways his eyes bulged in anticipation, and how his nostrils flared. A shy smile crossed her face. "Care to share with me?"

Mark looked at her for a moment. "Sure," he stammered.

He opened the door wide and Melanie walked in. She glanced around to make sure that no one was around. "I hope I'm not disturbing you," she commented, as she made a beeline for the kitchen.

Mark closed the door, scratching his head as he followed her. "No. Actually, I just got home."

"Well then, I'm just in time."

Melanie set the casserole dish down on the kitchen table and made her way to the sink, pulling dishes out of the drainer. She started to set the table, laying all the silverware in place. She walked over to the refrigerator and rummaged around inside it for a few moments. She clicked her tongue, and then reached in to find a bag of wilting ready-made salad mix, a tomato, and some carrots. She carried the items over to the sink. Mark stood in the doorway, arms crossed, watching. Granted, he didn't mind much. He did the cooking after Jessie proved to him that she could burn water. Only Jessie's mom and his maternal grandmother had cooked for him since Jessie died. He pushed back the lump that had suddenly appeared in his throat. "So, how did you find my place?"

"I asked Cassie, and she gave me directions."

She poured the lettuce mix out of the bag and into two matching bowls. She picked out the wilted and brown pieces. She expertly diced up a tomato and some carrots, and sprinkled a little of each on top of the salads. She carried the bowls to the table and set them by the plates. He thought back to their workload. "Given what we've been going through these past few days, how did you find time to make this?" he asked.

"I do a lot of it on the weekends and freeze it. Today, I just had to have some, so I set the timer this morning, threw it in the oven, and here it is. I don't know about you, but I hate eating Italian alone."

"Don't we all?"

Melanie flashed him a quick smile. She walked over to a drawer near the stove in search of a spoon. She rummaged through it for a moment, and then pulled one to that was to her liking. She walked back to the table and lifted the lid off the casserole dish. Mark glanced inside. The cheese on top was the perfect color brown. He could see little bubbles around the edge where the sauce had broken through. He could already taste the delicate layers of cheese, tomato, and pasta. His mouth watered. Melanie watched his reaction, a grin on her face. "I hope you like lasagna."

Mark smiled and then offered Melanie a chair. His eyes danced. "I love it."

They sat down and Melanie began serving. Mark took a bite and his eyes closed, as the savory tastes delighted his taste buds. "This is heavenly. Where did you learn how to cook like this?"

"Believe it or not, at the firehouse I worked at in Seattle. It's amazing what you can pick up from a group of guys. Some of them are pretty good cooks, but don't tell them I told you so."

"What about your family? How do they feel about you being a firefighter?"

"I think they'd be proud. Well, at least that's what I hope they'd think."

"Why? Where are they?"

Melanie looked down at her plate. She dipped a lazy fork into her salad. "They died in a car crash when I was seven," she murmured.

"Oh. I'm sorry."

"Yeah. However, being a firefighter is something that I've always imagined. My Aunt Gertrude thinks it's pretty funny. She says I was chicken of just about everything when I was little." Melanie sighed, and then looked at him. "What about your parents? Are you close to them?"

"Well, my mom died when I was six. My dad worked a lot back then, so his mom pretty much raised me." Mark picked at his salad. "She passed away shortly after I got married."

"Where's your dad now?"

"He lives in Seattle. We don't talk much."

Not liking the turn the conversation had taken, Mark put down his fork, stood, and went over to the refrigerator. He pulled a bottle from the bottom shelf. "Wine?" he asked, holding it up for her to see.

Melanie's eyes lit up. "Yes, please!"

Mark walked over to the glass cabinet and pulled down two glasses. He popped the cork and poured, then walked back to the table and handed one to her. "So, what do I owe this honor?"

Melanie took a sip. "Excuse me?"

"I'm being treated to a homemade meal by a firefighter. I must've done something good." Mark sat back down and took a sip from his own glass, watching Melanie carefully. She truly was an attractive woman, when you set aside the reality that she loved playing with fire.

Melanie blushed. "Well, technically, I'm no longer a firefighter. I haven't been for the last 18 months."

"Do you miss it?"

"A little. I think it's the adrenaline rush I miss the most. You know, walking into a dangerous situation, not knowing if the beam above your head is going to come crashing down on you, or the floor's going to give way? Then there's the 'saving someone's life and being a hero' bit."

"Trust me, I understand that completely." He sighed. "I really feel bad for Julie, though."

"Julie?"

"Julie Warren. Her family's company owns the house that was torched the other night?"

"Oh? Why?"

"The other buildings were abandoned or unused. That place was giving back to people and to the community. When I told Julie what happened, her reaction was as if someone close to her had died. I think that house really meant something to her. She seemed devastated by what happened, as if someone had torn out a piece of her soul."

They ate in silence for a few more moments. Then Melanie put her fork down, and gazed about the kitchen. She adored the yellow color palate and the ivy border above the windows. It gave the room a cozy, homey feel without being overpowering. Everything she had seen of his place was functional and beautiful, perfect for a young couple just starting out. Her eyes swept the counters. She spotted the white cat-shaped cookie jar in the corner near the fridge and giggled. "I have to ask. Who did your decorating in here?"

"My wife."

"She has great artistic taste. Where is she?"

Mark picked up his wine glass and took another hard swallow. "She's dead."

"I'm sorry, I didn't mean to . . ."

"It's okay."

She saw the pain in his eyes. "She died recently, didn't she?"

Mark closed his eyes, picturing what his beloved looked like when the doctor pronounced her death. "Seven months, three days, eleven hours," he murmured.

Melanie gasped, and then covered her mouth. "Oh, Mark, I'm so sorry. Perhaps I should . . ."

Mark reached out and put a hand over hers. "No, it's okay," he told her. "I'm glad for the company, and the meal. Every little bit helps to ease the burden."

Melanie gave him an uneasy smile and gripped his hand tight. They finished their supper, making small talk about the weather, their musical interests, and some of the more interesting cases Mark had worked. Then they wandered into the living room. With the sun now at the back of the house, the room had cooled slightly. Mark gestured to the sofa and Melanie sat down. He had brought the wine bottle with him, and he refreshed both of their glasses. Melanie stared at him with the same gaze he had seen her give him when they had first met at the storage facility. He tried to ignore it. "I noticed that you haven't mentioned the case," he said, as he sat down beside her.

"I try not to talk about work when I'm socializing, but since you brought it up, I have noticed something."

"What?"

Melanie dropped her gaze. She wasn't sure that she should say anything. After all, she was still the junior officer. "I've talked to the other officers in Serious Crimes and to Cassie. I've heard that you're an excellent detective. You've proved it more than once since you joined us. I mean, you've seen things that I never would have considered."

"You probably will in time. You're still new at this, but what's bothering you about me?"

"It's just that it still seems to me that you don't want to be a part of it."

"What makes you say that?"

She shrugged and ran her finger along the rim of the glass. "It's your reaction to them, especially when you first came on board. It just seems to me that these cases are getting to you, and I mean in more than a professional way."

"You don't think I'm going the right way with it?"

"Oh, no. The approach we took today? Lieutenant Rutherford told me afterward that you highlighted some things that Lieutenant Rutherford and I might have overlooked otherwise."

"Lieutenant? Not Lawrence?" Mark teased, taking a sip of wine.

Melanie blushed, recalling Heather's scathing taunts from that first afternoon. "Oops. I really did say that, didn't I?"

"Don't worry about it. From what I can tell, it's purely platonic. Lieutenant Rutherford is probably one of the best. He's the one who found the arsonist torching the southeast waterfront district a few years back. They were nasty."

"I know, although I think of him more as a dad than my trainer. The guy I was training with in Seattle was a total jerk. He had more fun watching me fall flat on my face than training me. Lawrence is so much the opposite. I've learned so much from him. He doesn't see me as a trainee. From day one, he's treated me like an equal, someone he can learn from as well. He doesn't laugh or chide me when I make a mistake. He just encourages me to keep going." Her voice drifted off and she stared into her glass. "More so than Heather, at least."

"Just keep in mind that Heather's only doing her job. She has to think about the millions of dollars to be distributed. Once it's gone, it'll be impossible to get back. In the end, she'll see that you're doing your job, and doing it well. If it wasn't for you, we wouldn't have the accelerant to trace."

"I know. I just wish there was something else to go one, something that we could connect these arsons together."

"There is, Melanie. We'll find it."

Melanie couldn't help but smile. He was so hopeful. She wished she could have just a fraction of it. Then her expression turned serious again. "We got off the subject, you know?"

"We did?"

"Yes. My question dealt with your reactions to these cases."

"Oh. Well, just so you know, they're not really my forte, Mel. Fire doesn't give me the same adrenaline rush that it gives you."

He smiled. She nodded, but the look in her eyes remained serious. He tried to keep his attention focused on it, but found he had to turn away. There was a lingering silence. Finally, he relented. "All right, I'm not a big fan of fire in general, Melanie," he admitted. "Fires tend to bring up some painful memories for me about my mom and how she died."

"Why? How did your mom die?"

Mark stared into his wine glass. "In a fire."

Melanie sat back. "That explains your reaction the other day at the storage facility. You were remembering it, weren't you?"

Mark swirled the remaining wine in his glass. He didn't really hear Melanie's comment. Parts of his dream slid into his thoughts. She studied him. She sensed that there was something that he wasn't telling her. "It must've been pretty traumatic for you, to lose your mom that way."

"It's more than that, Melanie. I started it."

Melanie's eyes widened with shock. "Oh, no! How did it happen?"

Mark sat his glass down on the table and leaned forward. He let loose a heartless chuckle. "Playing with matches in the living room. I was trying to stop my mom from smoking, only my plan backfired."

Immediately, she realized what he was about to do. She reached out to take his hand. "Mark, please don't. You were young. It was an accident. You didn't intend to hurt anyone."

He jerked his hand away from her, abandoned his glass, and headed for a nearby bookshelf. An array of pictures looked back at him. Most of them were of him and Jessie, either by themselves, or with friends. There was one of him and his mom, taken just before she died. He picked up the cherry wood-framed print, wishing his mother's eyes looked at him now instead of Melanie's. He traced a finger over her face. He had inherited her eyes, the family claimed. His began to burn. She should be here now. She should be home with Dad, rubbing his shoulders, listening to him talk about how the day went, calling to check on her only child, dropping off his favorite cookies. At least if she were still alive, he would never had to deal with the look that came to his father's face every day since then. "Yeah, I know," he mumbled. "I've heard it all, Mel. It doesn't change the fact that it was my fault."

Melanie rose from the sofa, set her glass down and walked over to him. She reached out and caressed his shoulder. "Mark, it wasn't deliberate. You didn't mean to hurt her. You have to believe that she knows that."

"But I did it, Melanie. If I had thought about what I was doing, if I hadn't been so obsessed with trying to stop her from smoking . . ."

She gently took the picture away from him and set it back on the bookshelf. Then she turned him toward her. "You were young. You didn't plan it. You did what you thought was right so that you mother wouldn't continue hurting herself."

"That doesn't mean that it makes missing her any easier, or feeling guilty about what I did to cause it."

"Mark, we're all gifted with 20/20 hindsight. So many things happen in our lives that we wish we could undo, but we can't. Your mom's death was a tragedy, but if what you learned from it helps you to save a life in the here and now, then her death wasn't in vain."

Mark looked into Melanie's eyes. Some of the pain had eased, but not all of it. "I wish it were that easy."

She slipped her left hand into his right, linking their fingers. Mark gazed down at it, then at her. He couldn't tell if the smile on her face was one of concern and conciliation, or one of seduction. She moved closer and reached up to tuck away the lock of hair that blocked his eyes. She cupped his left cheek with her right hand and pressed her forehead against his. "Then let me help ease some of the burden that you're carrying."

She leaned forward. The fingers of right hand left his cheek to tickle the back of his neck. He sensed the desire she felt for him, desire that he did not feel in return. He made to say something, but before he could, she drew him in and pressed her lips to his. Just as they did, Mark's doorbell rang again. Somehow, he managed to break the kiss and wriggle free of her. He gave her an apologetic smile. "Excuse me. I should get that."

He sidestepped Melanie and ran his fingers through his hair. He waited until he was around the corner and out of her sight to exhale. Silently, he thanked whoever chose to bother him at this time. He opened the door. Julie leaned against the outside doorjamb. Ash marks decorated her cheeks, hands, the collar of her shirt and her sheer hosiery, and her suit and shoes were coated with a fine gray powder. She looked hot, frustrated, and sad. "Hi, Mark," she greeted him in a tired voice.

Mark smiled and leaned against the door. "Julie, it's good to see you, but I thought you were heading back to San Francisco."

"I am in the morning."

"I see you've been to the site."

"Yes." She stepped inside the hallway and glanced about. "Look, about what happened in the cafeteria . . ." she began in a low tone.

Mark shook his head. "I was out of line, Julie. I should've waited to ask you about all of that."

She sighed and rubbed her dark forehead as if trying to ward off a headache. Mark watched with amusement while more faint black soot marks formed on it. "No, you were just doing your job, and I failed to appreciate it at the time. I apologize for snapping at you. I've had a rough few days of it lately. This situation isn't helping any." She looked past him toward the kitchen door. "Actually, I also stopped by to ask a favor. Do you have a measuring cup I could borrow? I can't find mine because I think it's still packed, but I'm too tired to look for it, and I'm too stubborn to go buy a new one."

"Sure. It's in the kitchen."

Mark turned and started back toward it. Julie made to follow him, but stopped as soon as she reached the opening to his living room. Melanie stared out at her from the center of it. Julie took a step back. "Oh, I didn't realize you had company."

Mark returned from the kitchen, a one-cup measuring cup in his right hand. He stared at the two women. Melanie stood there, her arms crossed, glaring at the source of the intrusion. "Julie? I don't think you formally met Melanie Keegan. Melanie, this is Julie Warren, the woman whose house fire we're investigating," Mark said by way of introduction.

"Miss Keegan, it's nice to meet you."

Julie held out a soot-covered hand. Melanie glanced at it, but she did not take it. Her eyes glittered like sparkling firecrackers, and she wore a stony look on her face. Julie didn't like the feeling she was getting from her, but she was too exhausted, and her mind too confused to try and read her thoughts. "How did you come by this investigation?" she asked in a cordial tone.

"Melanie's on loan to us from the Seattle Fire Department," Mark explained. "She's volunteered to help us try and find out who's committing them." Mark gave her an appreciative smile. "She's been a big help."

"That's good." Julie took the measuring cup from Mark. "Thanks," she whispered.

"You're welcome. Anything else?"

"No. Look, I didn't mean to interrupt. I'll just head back to my place." She pointed to the front door and held up the measuring cup. "I'll make sure you get this back."

"Whenever, Julie. I know where to find you."

Mark smiled at her and Julie tried to smile back. She turned and nodded to Melanie. "It was nice to meet you Miss Keegan."

"You too, Ms. Warren, and I'm sorry to hear about your place," Melanie replied.

"Thank you." She turned to Mark. "I'll see you later."

She made her way out of Mark's house, clutching the measuring cup close to her chest. As they heard the door close behind her, Melanie turned to him. "She lives around here?" Melanie asked, trying to keep the hostility out her voice.

"Yes. Actually, she's renting the apartment above my garage."

"Wait a minute. Didn't you say that she works for her family's corporation?"

"Yes."

"Then why is she renting a place here? Wouldn't it be more convenient to rent a place in San Francisco, or Seattle, for that matter?"

"Apparently, she doesn't like big city life."

He glanced out his window, watching as Julie made her way up the steps. Melanie gave him an uneasy gaze. She didn't like the look on his face. She wasn't certain if it was one of admiration, adoration, or curiosity. "You seem to know her pretty well," she commented.

Mark returned his attention back to Melanie. "Who, Julie? Actually, I don't know her that well at all," he admitted. "She's only been able to stay at her place a few days since she's moved in. Her job keeps her busy, and she's on the road a lot."

"So, you two aren't close?"

Mark chuckled. "No, Melanie, we're not. I can barely even call us acquaintances."

"Oh." She gazed at him again. "So is there anyone?" Melanie took a step toward him and slid a hand around his waist. "Since your wife's passing, has there been anyone special? Anyone at all?"

He raised his head and met her gaze. He saw the look in her eye again. He saw it with nearly every female who had come into his life since Jessie died. He knew what Melanie wanted, but he also knew that he could not give it to her. He ran his right thumb along the band of gold on his right pinky finger. Jessie's wedding ring pressed into it, as if her hand were there squeezing his. It didn't matter. He felt Jessie all around him and within him. He steeled himself. "No, and I don't think there will be anyone. Ever."

Melanie caught the finality in his last word. A frown touched the corner of her lips. She blinked her eyes as if to clear her thoughts, then released him, and flung her hair back. "Well. I think I've overstayed my visit. I should be getting home."

She picked up her purse, straightened her clothes, and Mark escorted her to the door. "I'll get your casserole dish back to you as soon as possible," he assured her.

"No hurry, Mark. I'm going to be in town for quite a while, and it's not like I don't know where to find you."

Mark saw the hurt he caused in her face. The gentleman in him wanted to apologize, but the freaked-out, grief-stricken widower held him back. She stood on her toes to give him a peck on the cheek, before turning and walking toward her car. He made sure to wait until he saw her get in and drive away before he shut the door. He leaned against it, breathing a sigh of relief. He went back to the living room, collected their glasses and dishes, and deposited into the sink. Then he made his way to the office to tackle some of the dreaded paperwork, and deal with the newest wave of creditor calls that filled his answering machine.

That night, as Mark tried to sleep, he thought back on the conversation he had with Melanie. He recalled the look of seduction and wanting in her eyes, and the emotions he had generated in her, but did not feel in return. Since Jessie's death, he had not felt desire for anyone. Two questions repeated in his head: Could he ever fall in love again? Did he want to? He knew that Jessie did. She made that plain to him those last few weeks of her life. "You will find love again, Tigger," she begged him. "Promise that to me." More than a year after the delivery of her death sentence, he was no closer to fulfilling her last wish of him.

He turned to his side and saw Jessie lying beside him, her head resting on her hands, her blue eyes glowing in the darkness, the blonde strands of hair falling into her face, the way they used to when she slept. He reached out to her, but grabbed nothing but air. How he ached for her presence. He longed to be holding her now, and to stare into those eyes one last time. He shut his eyes tight and willed back the tears. "No one will replace your spot here, Jessie," he whispered, reaching up with his right hand so that her ring covered his heart. "That I promise you."

XI

"Mommy? Mommy!"

Six-year-old Mark Daniels crawled along the sidewalls, groping for the baseboard that led to the stairwell. He knew it had to be close. He had already passed the doorway that led into the big room they only ate in when they had a lot of people visiting, or during Christmas and Thanksgiving. Behind him, an orange glow engulfed the living room. It was moving closer to him. He started to cough. He hadn't meant to do what he did, but now the fire was growing. Now his only instinct was to find Mommy. She would know what to do. She would get them out. She would keep them safe.

He reached out frantically and his hand landed on the first step. His heart leapt. There it was! He pushed up, climbing as fast as he could until he felt his hand reach the top one. As he grabbed at it, his hand hit something. It tumbled down the stairs into the growing inferno. He crawled on his stomach along the floor, staying below the smoke, just like his teacher Mrs. Jones had taught him during fire safety month. Mommy's bedroom door was the first one, and it was slightly open. He shut it behind him and felt around in the smoky darkness for her bed. He found her lying face up on the blankets. "Mommy!" he screamed.

She didn't answer. He coughed again, covering his face with his shirt. "Mommy! Mommy, wake up!"

There was no response. Tears streamed down his face. "Mommy!" he screeched.

He shook her as hard as his little arms could. She wasn't moving. She looked like an angel to him, lying there in that white dress, her brunette hair flowing down her back. Smoke started to fill the room. Mark groped his way around to the other side of his mother's bed. He wished that Daddy would come home, but he was working late again, like he always did. Mommy never liked it. "Mommy! Mommy, wake up!"

He pushed her again, but she didn't move. Mark stared into his mother's face. Her eyes were open, but she didn't blink. He thought he saw her chest moving up and down, but in all the smoke, he wasn't sure. "Mommy! Wake up! We need to get out!"

The floor underneath him felt hot. The smoke grew denser. It was becoming harder to breathe. He coughed harder. He tried to shake her again, but he felt so tired. Far away, he thought he hard the sound of a siren approaching. He had to get Mommy out, but she wouldn't wake up. Why couldn't he wake her? "Mommy!"

"Mommy!"

Mark jolted awake, his breath coming in hard gasps. His heart thumped against his chest. Once again, he found himself entangled in his bed sheets, drenched in sweat. He heard the echo of his screams inside his head, as he rubbed his face and gazed about, trying to recover his bearings. Reluctantly, he turned to look at the clock radio. It read 2:37 a.m. "Damn!" he muttered and threw a pillow across the room.

He slumped back onto his remaining pillow, groaning. Then he sat up. He stared out into the darkness. Somehow, he untangled himself and made his way to the bathroom. He turned the faucet on full and splashed some cold water on his face. In the darkness, he stared at his reflection. The imagery from his dream would not leave his mind. He couldn't recall ever dreaming about his mom in the time Jessie had been in his life. Now it seemed the dreams wouldn't stop. He felt himself shaking and he gripped the basin. "It's these cases," he mumbled. "They're getting to me. I need to solve them and quickly, before I lose my mind."

He made his way back toward his bed. He should try to go back to sleep, but knew it was pointless. He considered making his early morning jog. It would help a little. As he passed by his bedroom window, he glanced out. Through the barely rustling maple leaves, he saw light shining in Julie's windows. He looked at the clock again. He wondered what was keeping her awake. Was it the heat, or her job, or her thoughts about the fire that destroyed one of her childhood homes?

He reached out for the nightstand phone, intending to call Tyler. Mark knew that he would still be awake. Tyler claimed he did his best work between the hours of 2:00 a.m. and 5:00 a.m. Mark needed to talk to someone, anyone, just to hear another human being's voice and know that he wasn't going insane. As he punched in Tyler's number, he thought better of it and hung up. His mother's serene face entered his thoughts again. Again, Mark found himself asking the same questions he had tortured himself with since childhood: *Why didn't she wake up? Why did she die, and why did I live?* His attention drifted across the way toward Julie's window. Despite all that he knew so far, this woman remained a stranger to him. How he wanted to talk to someone about it, but would she listen? Would she even care?

Mark groped around for his discarded shorts and T-shirt and slipped back into them. He headed downstairs, out the front door, and crossed through the yard. His bare feet grew wet from the dew on the grass. He deftly climbed the stairs to her apartment. Through her open window, he heard the sound of a single cello playing. He also thought he heard her talking aloud to someone named Nick. When he reached the landing, he thought about what he was going to do. He was supposed to be finding out who torched her house, not coming to her place, bemoaning about his problems. He hesitated, and then rapped on the door. "Just a minute," he heard her call.

The music stopped. A few moments later, the outside light clicked on and Julie opened the door. She was barefoot as well, and had showered and changed into a pair of cropped pants and a T-shirt. Her glasses were gone and for the first time, Mark saw how deep in clarity her eyes were. "Mark? What are you still doing up?" she asked in a startled tone.

"I couldn't sleep," he admitted. "The heat's getting to me, I think."

"I think it's getting to us all. Please, come in."

"Thanks."

He stepped inside. Her place felt hotter than his did. The ceiling fan he had installed for her whirled above her dining room set. There was a box fan in her kitchen window, making a futile attempt to exhaust out some of the heat. The air carried the faint scent of cinnamon. He glanced around. It dawned on him that he had no clue if she was seeing anyone. She had said that she wasn't that day at Scordalia's, but maybe things had changed. Maybe it was this fellow Nick. "I'm not interrupting anything, am I?"

"No. I was just catching up on some paperwork." She closed the door, and then gestured behind her toward the kitchen. "Would you like some lemonade? I just made a fresh pitcher."

He thought to ask her who Nick was, when he realized his throat was parched. His eyes lit up. "That sounds great."

She pointed to the large black couch in the living room. "Have a seat. I'll be right back."

Julie disappeared into the kitchen and Mark wandered into her living room. Since the last time he had been here, she had added two black side chairs and a glass-and-wood coffee table set to the room. "You still haven't found any artwork?" he asked, as he eyed the bare space above her sofa.

"No, but I really haven't had a chance to look. I'll find something."

He wandered over toward the entertainment center, set against the opposite the sofa. He perused her music collection, and concluded he wouldn't be over to "borrow" anything. They were all classical titles. He could tolerate it, but given the choice, he'd take Bruce Springsteen or the Stones every time.

He looked over toward the side window that faced Mrs. Johnson's home. She had positioned her desk underneath it, and the banker's lamp atop it glowed. Her laptop computer lay open on it, although the screen was blank. There was a blue folder beside it and her glasses rested on top. Her briefcase leaned against the left leg; her black messenger bag was to its right. There was a half-full bookcase in the corner with a few of the latest bestsellers sitting on it. He took a few more steps and peeked around the corner. There were still unopened boxes stacked in the hallway leading back to the bedroom, but he liked what he saw. "I'm surprised you're still up, too," he called out to her, as he walked around the room.

"That's because I'm still on Beijing time," she explained between the ice cubes dropping into glasses. "With the amount of traveling I do, I usually sleep better on planes than in a bed."

He made his way to sit down, absently playing with his keychain emblem. Like Cassie's pendant, he received the charm from the Amendu a few months back. After a bit, he laid his keys down on the table, and plopped his tall frame on her sofa. He stared down at the plush blue area rug underneath her living room furniture. He hadn't had a chance to look at it when the movers were laying it out. He tilted his head to study it closer. It had an intricate pattern in it made with silver metallic floss. It looked like it made out something. As he studied it, he heard her footfalls. He looked up. Julie came cautiously around the corner. In her right hand, she had a plate of cookies perched on top of a pitcher. Pinwheel lemon slices floated about inside the translucent yellow mixture. She held two ice-filled glasses in her left. He took the plate of cookies from her and placed it on the coffee table. The scent of cinnamon wafted through the air and he stared at them. *I don't believe it. Homemade oatmeal raisin cookies.*

She sat down across from him in one of the chairs, poured one glass, and handed it to him. "I hope you like it," she said, an anxious look coming to her face.

He gave her a silent salute of thanks and took a sip. He smiled and smacked his lips. It was the best glass of lemonade he had drank in a long time. "This is great!"

"Really?"

He downed the glass and gave it back to her. "Yeah. You need to give me the recipe."

"Oh, no. I can't do that."

"Why not?"

"Because," Julie told him, as she took his glass to refill it, "I promised the lady that I got it from that I would never share it with anyone else. It would ruin her legacy."

"I didn't realize that recipes come with conditions."

"No. Just this one."

Julie smiled mischievously while she poured herself a glass. Mark took another swallow and reached for a cookie. They were still warm. He was a little hesitant. Would he still have the same reaction to them as an adult that he did as a child? He bit down into it. "Mmm! These are delicious! Did you make these?" he asked, cramming more of it into his mouth.

"Yes." She reached for the plate. "It's the reason I needed the measuring cup, and why it's so hot in here, I'm sorry to say."

"Wow! You're on the road so much. Do you get to cook often?"

She took a bite of her cookie and settled back into her chair. "Not as often as I would like. I find it to be good therapy for me when I'm troubled about something."

"Like the fire?"

Julie's thoughts drifted back to Anichia. She stared at her cookie. "Among other things."

Mark sat back in the sofa, savoring the last bite. He studied her appearance now, so different from when he had seen her yesterday and earlier this evening. Without her glasses on, she looked so much younger, except in the eyes. To him, her eyes seemed that much older without them. Whose eyes did she inherit? Her mother's? Her father's? What did they look like? What about her guardian? He saw no photos of anyone around her place, and there were no diplomas or photos on her walls. Then again, she hadn't been here much. They still could be packed away. What was she thinking right now, seeing him sitting here in her living room this late at night, drinking lemonade and chomping down on homemade cookies as if this was a regular thing?

"So, what's the occasion?" Julie asked suddenly.

Mark smiled. *I guess she was thinking that.* He reached down and stuffed another cookie in his mouth. "Who says that there has to be an occasion to come visit a neighbor?"

"Well, no one, but . . ."

"But?"

"Well, I may be new to the renting thing, but from what I've heard, when a tenant gets a 2:30 a.m. visit from her landlord, the police are usually with them." She gazed at him, her expression thoughtful. "Something's troubling you."

"What do you mean?"

"I haven't known you for long, but I've noticed that there's a shadow that comes over your face when something's bothering you."

"A what?"

"I don't know how else to describe it. It's like a curtain that gets drawn across your mind and no one can see what's going on behind it, except you." She smiled at his baffled expression. "Sorry. I've had way too many courses in how to read body language."

"It looks like they're paying off."

She sipped her lemonade and licked her lips. It was the perfect blend of sweetness and tartness. She had to make sure that NIK cataloged this exact mixture in her database so that she could replicate it. "In all honesty, you seem bothered by something." She stared at the liquid inside her glass and then set it down on a coaster. "Do you want to talk about it?"

Mark twirled his glass in his hands. The condensation had formed rapidly, and he wiped it from his hands to his shorts. "It's these cases. I'm not quite sure how to proceed, or where to go."

Julie pondered this statement. "I won't claim to be an expert on police procedure, but aren't you supposed to go wherever the evidence takes you?"

"Yeah, but it seems to be taking it in five different directions."

"How so?"

"Well, from what we can tell, it doesn't seem to be any type of insurance scam."

"I bet Miss McCade isn't happy to hear that."

Mark smiled. "So you've met Miss Congeniality, huh?"

Julie didn't understand the reference. NIK gave her an explanation and Julie correlated it to the tone of voice Mark used when he said the words. He meant the exact opposite, she realized. She nodded. "She visited me at the site today, I mean yesterday. She seems convinced that I'm responsible for my own fire."

"She's just doing her job, Julie. Granted, she could smile when she did it, but she has a legitimate concern."

At that phrase, Julie turned away from him. She buried her chin in her chest. The disheartened look Mark saw cross her face that day in the cafeteria returned. She shook her head. "I wouldn't have done that. I could never have done that, no matter what she wants to believe," she mumbled.

Mark took another bite of his cookie, watching her. He wanted to understand why she was reacting the way she was. It was only a building, yet Julie acted as if she had lost a parent, a sibling, or a close friend. He wondered what had been inside of it that made it so special to her.

"Mark?"

Mark snapped out of his trance. Julie's focused gaze had returned to his face. "Yeah?"

"Why would someone do it? Why burn something down that's not yours?"

Mark shrugged. "Because they can. Because it's there." He noticed the look of confusion on her face. "I learned today that arsons happen for a variety of reasons. I think once we find out why your place was targeted, we can figure out who's behind it."

"Miss McCade told me there've been a series of these fires. Is that true?"

Mark nodded. She looked up toward the blank space above her sofa. "I remember Cassie saying something in the cafeteria about there being other fires, and that you were looking for a connection. Do you think they're related? Is it possible that it's more than one person, or could it be the same person committing all of them?"

"It's hard to say. The evidence has too many inconsistencies. That's why were sort of stuck. Cassie, the arson investigators and I are at a loss as to where to go next, or what to do."

"Well, I'm sure that you'll figure it out. You're a good investigator, Mark. You don't seem like the type who just reaches a conclusion without examining everything, or give up until you find out the truth."

Mark felt warmth rush into his cheeks. It was the nicest compliment he had ever received. "Thank you."

Julie sipped her lemonade and reached for another cookie. "You're welcome, but this case isn't the reason for you being here."

"Oh?" Mark swallowed the last of his lemonade and set the glass down. He too reached for another cookie. "What makes you say that?"

"A hunch. I heard you screaming a few minutes ago."

Her gaze drifted toward dining room table, and the open window beyond. Mark frowned. He had forgotten that his were open too. He looked back at her. She wore a serious, but concerned look on her face. In the busyness that surrounded this investigation, he never asked her about her trip. Based on their conversation in the cafeteria, it hadn't gone well, yet she seemed willing to set aside whatever problems she had to listen to his.

He turned away from her and bit his bottom lip. For days, he had been looking to get what was bothering him off his chest. He came here with that same intent. Now that he truly had someone who was more than just curious, he found he couldn't speak. He wasn't sure if he should tell her, but he felt that if he didn't talk to someone, he would collapse under the weight. He stared at the cookie in his hands. They reminded him of his mother's cookies; the ones she made for him the day she died. He sighed and rested it on top of his empty glass. "I'm having this recurring nightmare. I've had it for the past few nights." His gaze fell to his clasped hands. "It's about my mom."

"Your mom?"

"She's part of the reason why I became a police officer and not a firefighter." Mark paused and he looked at the floor. "The anniversary of her death was this week," he added. "She died in a fire, when I was six."

"Mark, I'm sorry. I didn't mean to . . ."

"No, it's all right."

Mark stood up and began to pace the floor. Julie watched him. She noticed that his neck and shoulders looked tense. He shoved his hands deep into his pockets. A troubled expression crossed his face, far deeper than anything that she had seen or sensed from him. She waited patiently for him to speak again.

"She was always sad," Mark began. "I don't really know why. I think it was because my dad was gone all the time. He was working sixteen to nineteen-hour days, trying to make partner at the firm. Every day, it just seemed to be case after case and client after client. She drank a little, and she smoked, too. The longer he was gone, the more she smoked and drank. She was up to two or more packs a day at one point. She didn't get violent or anything like that. She would just withdraw. She knew it was bad for her, but she couldn't quit. I never liked it. I remember that I used to try to hide her cigarettes and matches from her, hoping that it would stop it, but she would just go out and buy more.

"Then, one day I hit on this brilliant idea: I decided I would just light all the matches in the place. If she didn't have one to light, then she couldn't smoke. One day, when she went upstairs to lie down, I took all the matchbooks into the living room. Then I put them into the ashtray along with her cigarettes, and I lit them. It worked, until I realized I forgot about something."

Julie picked up her empty glass and twisted it in her hands. "You accidentally started a fire," she whispered.

Mark felt a lump growing in his throat. He stopped pacing and stared at her bare living room wall. "I went to stand, and I kicked the ashtray. The rug caught fire. I stood there for what seemed like an eternity, not knowing what to do. Then I ran to the kitchen to get a glass of water, but by the time I got back . . . . The flames spread so fast. I could hardly see through the smoke. I didn't want to leave the house without her, so I crawled up the stairs to the bedroom." Mark clasped his hands behind his head. "She was just lying there with her eyes open. I thought she was awake. I screamed her name, but she wouldn't move. I shook her, and I pounded on her chest, but she didn't wake up. I smelled the smoke and I felt the heat from the flames all around me. I knew I was in danger, but I had to get her out of the house. It would be my fault if she died."

Mark swallowed a sob and wiped the tears away from his face. "I don't know what happened next. I just remember waking up the next day in the hospital's children's ward, and my dad sitting there." he whispered.

"She died. To this day, I don't know why she never woke up."

There was silence between them for a few minutes. Julie closed her eyes. In her mind, Julie relived Mark's memories of that day. She had felt a part of it when she had handed him his glass. She experienced the fear and anguish he felt at the time it occurred and the returning guilt he felt now. She opened them and stared at the remaining ice cubes in her glass. "What about your father? What was his reaction when he found out how the fire started?"

"My father? Calm, unemotional, under control. The only thing I'm certain of is that he blamed me for her death. He blames me for everything that goes wrong in his life, and he's never appreciated or approved of anything I've done in mine since."

Julie set down her glass. "Mark, you don't believe that."

Mark turned to face her. His eyes narrowed and his tone turned bitter. "It's the truth, Julie. I know it in my heart. I see it in his face every time he looks at me. He always gets that same look. All the anger, the disappointment, and the hatred of me for what I did to her? It's imbedded right here." Mark pointed to his head. "It's all I see any time I think of him or see him. Nothing I ever do will ever make up for that day when I killed his wife."

"Mark, he doesn't think that."

"Doesn't he? How would you know? You've never met him or talked to him! You didn't grow up in his house! You've never had to watch him come home night after night and year after year to that look on his face! Since that day, he's never given a damn about me or anything that has happened or will happen to me!"

Julie pursed her lips, considering her next few words: "Mark, did you ever stop to think that maybe he's still grieving for her, too?"

Mark stared at her, dumbfounded. "Grieving? What do you mean?"

Julie stood and slid her hands into her pants pockets. She approached him. "People grieve differently, Mark. I've seen my share of it."

"What are you, some expert on death and dying?"

"No, but what I've come to realize is that it takes some people longer to get over a loss of a loved one than others. For the most part, you've been able to move on. There were always people there to help you cope with the guilt you felt, and your loss. This case seems to have brought back some painful memories, but you're an adult now, and you're better able to handle it. I think once the case is concluded, you may finally be able to set aside the blame you've placed on yourself."

"But what does any of this have to do with my dad?"

"Well, maybe your father hasn't found a way yet to cope," she continued. "Maybe your father's still torn apart by the fact that he was away, and that when he looks at you, he's reminded of the fact that he wasn't there for either of you. You told me that you and he don't get along. Maybe his inability to come to terms with your mother's death is what's causing the tension you hinted at when we had lunch my first week in town.

Maybe he's afraid that if he gets too close, he'll lose you, too."

"Robert Sebastian Daniels, the man who fears nothing, who cares about no one but himself and the next case he can win, is still grieving? After 30 years?" Mark let out a harsh laugh. "That's a pretty far-out theory you have there."

Julie fixed her gaze on his face. "Is it? Mark, did you ever stop to think that you two may have a lot more in common than you realize?"

"Yeah? Like what?"

"Well, even though I haven't met him, you both seem to be somewhat stubborn." Julie paused. "Also, both your wife and his wife seemed to have died young, and unexpectedly."

Mark stared at her, his words ringing in his head. It hadn't dawned on him to think of it that way. His mother and Jessie had been about the same age when each of them died. He gave her a reluctant nod. "Yeah, but . . ."

"Now answer this, Mark. Since your mom's death, has he developed any close relationships with anyone female? Has he developed any type of relationship with anyone where he feels a total commitment to them, and a willingness to share all that goes on with his life, including you?"

Mark thought hard. Outside of his father's long-time secretary, Mary Cunningham and Mark's paternal grandmother, Mark had never seen him with anyone. He dropped his arms and toed the plush carpet with his bare feet. "No. His work is his life. Always has been."

She placed a hand on his shoulder. "Not always. He gave part of his life to you, and to your mom. Maybe he's afraid that it'll be taken away, if he gives any more of it."

Mark considered her words. It took a few minutes for him to realize that the tension in his neck and shoulders had eased. He covered her hand with his and stared into her face. "I'm sorry. You're trying to be helpful. I shouldn't have snapped at you."

"Apology accepted. Don't worry. I'm used to it. In my line of work, I get it all the time."

He saw something flicker in her eyes. He couldn't quite place it. *There* is *something special about her*, he thought to himself again. "You know, you speak like someone with a lot of experience at doing this." He recalled Tyler's research on her. He smiled mischievously. "I didn't realize you had a psychiatric degree, too."

"I don't. I've just had years of training in mediation, negotiation, and diplomacy. However, the methods are pretty similar."

She walked back toward the coffee table to collect their glasses. As she did so, Mark remembered what Tyler told him about her past. "Julie? Can I ask you something?"

"Sure."

"Your parents died when you were young, didn't they?"

Julie paused. He saw her bite her bottom lip. It was as if she wanted to answer his question, and yet not want to. "Yes, before I turned three months old."

"If I may ask, how did they die?"

Julie set the glasses down and turned to gaze out at the streetlight. She knew nothing about her true heritage, except that her people were dead. She was the lone survivor, and an immortal to boot. Did she dare tell him the truth? She turned back to him, a hardened look to her face. "They were murdered, Mark."

"I don't understand. When I ran the background check, it said your parents died in a car accident."

"That would by my guardian's way of shielding others from the truth. If you were to ask him why, he would say it was for my protection."

"But who killed them, and why?"

"I don't know. They never found them. I was only an infant at the time. My father worked for my guardian as a gardener. When he found out there were no other relatives to care for me, he took me in and raised me as his own. He taught me to call it an accident, to make it easier for me to explain whenever anyone asked. When I was older, I read the police reports, and eventually found out the truth."

"But why didn't they kill you?"

Julie shook her head. "I don't know."

"But haven't you wondered? Didn't you ever question why they were killed and why you were left alive? Have you ever thought about looking for their killer?"

A faraway look crossed her face. "No. Besides, they're probably dead now, and it doesn't change what happened to my parents, or to me."

"But don't you ever ask yourself why? Haven't you wished to know what your life would've been like, if they had raised you?"

Julie stared at the rug underneath their feet. The pattern within it was Illani scripture, telling of the days of their world before and after Julie came. Would their planet still exist if things had been different? Would hers? Would she be immortal, or would she have died, as humanoids do? "Sometimes," she murmured. "When I travel somewhere and I see a couple with a young child, sometimes I wonder." She brought her head back up to meet Mark's gaze. Her eyes glistened with moisture, but the look on her face was resolute. "But I don't dwell on it. I live in the here and now, Mark. I have to accept things for how they've come to pass, and try to live my life the best way I can. In my heart, I believe it's what they would have wanted."

The ringing of soft chimes caught their attention. They turned toward the sound. The cherry mantle clock on the corner bookshelf read 3:00 a.m. Mark raised his eyebrows. He had to be back at work in a few hours. He also realized that he had taken advantage of her hospitality for too long. "I should try to get back to bed."

She sighed. "Yes. I guess we both should."

She followed him to the door. After he opened it, he turned and gave her a kiss on the cheek. Julie was surprised by his sudden gesture. "What was that for?"

"A quick thank you," he told her. "Thanks for listening and for giving me something to think about."

"You're welcome. Oh and next time, try to make your counseling appointment for a more sensible hour of the day, okay?"

She winked and he chuckled and winked back. She stood in the doorway, watching him as he made his way back across the yard and into his house. She waited until he had closed the door behind him, before closing her own. Unconsciously, she reached up to caress the spot that he kissed. She leaned against the doorframe and gazed back into the living room, thinking about their conversation and grateful for the chance to learn something about him without having to probe his thoughts for it.

Ambassador?

Julie closed her eyes. In her head, she stood in front of NIK, yet she felt like she was in front of the Eldar. "Yes?"

Based on my experiences with you and your relationships to other humanoids, I believe I am to say that you did a very kind thing for him.

"Why, thank you NIK." Julie waited for her to continue. When she didn't, she raised her view to the celling. "I'm sensing hesitation on your part, NIK. What's your question?"

Are you not worried that he will become suspicious?

"Suspicious?"

I believe that is the correct term. Based on the events that have occurred, I conclude he may inquire as to whom you were talking to before he arrived. He may also inquire as to how you know about his father, or about the particular kind of cookies you served.

Julie chuckled. She hadn't planned on making cookies. Granted, it would have been easy for her to materialize herself a measuring cup, but she felt guilty for her actions that day in the cafeteria and wanted to apologize to him. When she took the cup from him, she sensed that part of Mark that longed to taste his mother's cookies one last time. Her cooking skills had done the rest. "Well NIK, if a plate of cookies arouses more suspicion about me, then I'm really losing my touch. Now, give me Simon's latest report on Anichia, if you would, please."

*   *   *

From her car, parked in the shadows of the houses and trees, Christie watched as Mark emerged from Julie's apartment. She saw the kiss Mark gave Julie, and her insides twisted in a jealous fury. He hadn't been inside for long, but it didn't matter. She knew what had occurred. They shared an intimacy she had never known. Della Torre did the same thing. He had made her feel special, but then tossed her away as if she were worse than garbage, just like her parents.

With beady eyes, she observed Mark walk back to his place. The door closed behind him. Her attention refocused on the lights above his garage, and that filthy, disgusting feeling began to fill her. Then just as quickly, she realized the cure. An evil grin came to her face. Her primary target remained out of reach, but that didn't matter. It was time for someone else to die, and she knew exactly who it would be, and how to do it.

XII

Julie did not go to bed that night. Once she knew that Mark had fallen asleep again, she left her home and teleported herself and her vehicle back to the farm. By the time Mark arrived at work, she was back in San Francisco. Jennifer met her at the door, her glowing face made even more so by the triumphant look on it. She waved a piece of paper in Julie's face. "See, I told you I would find it," she said in a confident tone.

"I had no doubts, Jennifer," Julie said, smiling as she took the paper. She glanced over Jennifer's shoulder at Elise Carpenter, who gave her a wink. They spent the next few hours reviewing the preliminary insurance findings, and debating the next steps once the arson investigation was completed. Then Julie shooed Jennifer out of her office. "No need for both of us to face his wrath," Julie explained, while she called her guardian to explain what happened.

"You weren't there, Julie. He can't blame you for it."

"I know, but just in case."

At mid-afternoon, she returned to the farm, where she met with the Illani council and discussed events occurring on the surface. Afterward, she went to the nursery. Incubating there were 387 new members, waiting to emerge. Julie sat alone in the middle of the room. She closed her eyes and immersed herself in their heartbeats, trying to remember all of their names, both human and Illani. For the first time in several days, she felt at peace. Then she realized something. Her eyes fluttered open. "The birthing ceremony," she whispered. "The Illani need to go into stasis before it. I need to prepare myself." She stared out at the next generation of Illani. "I just hope the situation on Anichia resolves itself before then."

She decided to drive back to Mason City. She arrived at her apartment just as the sun began its descent in the western horizon. She noticed that Mark wasn't home and wondered where he could be. She climbed the stairs to her apartment. When she reached the landing, she saw a note taped to her door. Julie pulled it down and opened it:

> *I have information regarding your fire.*
> *Meet me at the old Sullivan warehouse,*
> *on the corner of Webster and Jamison at*
> *10:00 p.m. tonight.*

"I don't understand," she said in a puzzled voice. "If this person has information, why don't they go to the police? It makes more sense than talking to me."

She reached into her messenger bag and pulled out her mobile phone. She caressed the outside case. It was primitive compared to the technology she experienced on a daily basis. She only carried it because the Eldar ordered it. If she was to live there as a human, she had to act as they did. She could not use her powers except in the direst of circumstances, and never in front of a human. She began to dial Mark's mobile number. Then she thought better of it. She checked the time. It was already 9:30 p.m. If she didn't hurry, she would be late. "NIK?"

Yes, Ambassador?

"Give me directions from here to a Sullivan's warehouse, please. It's on the corners of Webster and Jamison in Mason City."

Twenty minutes later, Julie pulled up in front of the warehouse. She parked her vehicle on the dark, deserted street. Off in the distance, she heard the faint roar of the highway, and saw the last touches of sunset disappearing in the west. She climbed out of the truck. The red and white-trimmed lettering that spelled out the word "Sullivan's" were barely visible against the tin-roofed structure. She glanced down at the note in her hand and verified the address. "What was this building used for again, NIK?" Julie asked.

According to the public records, it is some type of facility used to store clothing, furniture, and other wares sold to humans in what they call a department store. It is not in use at this time.

"Then why would this informant meet me here?"

Julie leaned to the right. She spotted a door in the center of the wall closest to her. Seeing no one outside, she headed for it. She reached for the doorknob, and saw it was ajar. Julie pushed on it. The streetlight lit up the doorway to the darkened structure. She stepped inside. Her footfalls echoed in the empty space. "I guess I should have brought a flashlight," she scolded herself.

She stood still and allowed her exceptional eyesight to compensate for the darkness. She spotted some odd lumps and shapes in the darkness, stacks of wood and boxes all around. The smell of sewer waste and garbage hung in the air. She wrinkled her nose. "Why would someone want to meet her in a place like this? Well, whatever the reason, they better hurry up and get here," she muttered.

She took another step and heard a small splash. At the same time, a sweet odor wafted up to her nose. She looked down. She had stepped into some type of liquid. Curious, she bent down to touch it. It had the consistency of mucus. She brought it up to her nose to sniff it. There was a hint of alcohol to it, and something else. It reminded her of a particular cluster of purple plants that grew in the nether space arboretum. Then she realized that she wasn't alone. She made to rise, and thought she heard a match struck. There was a flash of light. It lit up the floor and blazed a trail to where she stood. Julie's eyes opened wide. She dove away from the flames streaking toward her. There were puddles of the liquid everywhere. Somehow, she managed to avoid them. Before she knew it, she found herself surrounded by a raging inferno. Her first instinct was to teleport herself out, but she still sensed a human presence. She couldn't use her powers in front of them. She threw up her arms to protect her face. The note she held floated away from her. The flames swallowed it, and it disappeared into the blaze. She stumbled forward, just stopping short of the flame wall. In the darkness, she caught a glimpse of someone watching her from another doorway. They wore some sort of silver suit. Simultaneously, the image of the little girl screaming returned. Julie blinked and the image vanished. Her observer brought a gloved hand up to their face, blew Julie a kiss, and disappeared.

Julie stared after the figure, almost oblivious to the firestorm around her. The heat grew in intensity. The flames began to leap higher, throwing sparks around. Some of them landed on the discarded boxes and crates. They began to smolder, and then burst into flames. It wouldn't be long before the entire building was engulfed. "I need to put this out, but how without my observer seeing?" Julie asked herself. She looked upward. Above her, she saw pipes and sprinkler heads. Her thoughts followed the pipework toward the far end of the wall, and down into the ground. She found the water turn-on switch, and concentrated on it. Nothing happened. "The system must be disconnected," she concluded, "or my captor crippled it."

The fire kept growing. Soon, the smoke began to thicken. Julie wasn't afraid of burning to death. However, other lives would be in danger if the fire burned unchecked. She reached out with her thoughts to make sure her observer was gone. "NIK!" she screamed

Yes, Ambassador?

"Contact the authorities! Inform them there's a fire at the old Sullivan department store warehouse. Give them the address, and use my mobile number as the reference. Tell them to get here as soon as possible!"

Ambassador? Your stress levels have risen 17 percent.

"Never mind me. Just make the call!"

As you wish, Ambassador.

Julie focused her thoughts and felt a twinge move through her. Her oversensitive eyes caught the flicker of energy surrounding her human form, forming a shield around her body. She walked forward into the flame wall. The bright flames illuminated the protective bubble that surrounded her. She walked through wall after wall of fire toward the door she used to enter the building. When she was sure she was well away from it, the energy shield vanished. She felt a surge of pain and looked down at her right hand. She had forgotten that she had some of the liquid on it. It was burned so bad that the skin above her wrist had blistered, and her finger muscles were peeling away from the bone. She held it up to the firelight. It seemed to glow for an instant. Then her hand reappeared with no damage to it at all. She flexed it and smiled, thankful once again for her body's instantaneous ability to heal itself.

Off in the distance, she heard a car engine revving. She ran toward it. As she approached, she saw the taillights on the back of a vehicle light up. The driver maneuvered away from the scene in a squeal of rubber. Julie watched as the vehicle disappeared into the night.

The sound of metal giving way touched her ears. She turned around. She had emerged from the building just in time. The roof had caved in. Orange-red flames shot toward the sky attempting to touch the darkness overhead. Glowing sparks of burning material fluttered to the ground about her. In all her existence, Julie had never witnessed a fire burn with such intensity. Then the wail of sirens and the flash of red lights caught her attention. She turned towards them. Emergency vehicles were making their way to the location. She backed away from the inferno toward her vehicle. She sat behind the wheel, contemplating what had just occurred. Her mind drifted to the flash of the little girl screaming. It had come when she spotted the person in the silver suit. Were the two linked? If so, how?

Ambassador? You may wish to leave now. The humans are approaching.

Julie looked up. Two fire trucks had made their final turn and were fast approaching the burning warehouse. It was in her best interest to leave the scene, but if she left now, they would see her. They just might begin thinking that she was the one responsible. "No, NIK, I think I better stay here. Patch me through to Mark."

Two hours later, Mark and Cassie stood with Julie beside one of the ambulances. Around them, the noise of water splashing, diesel engines, and firefighters bellowing out orders competed for their attention, as three fire departments fought to subdue the fire. By scanning their thoughts, Julie learned that Mark and Cassie had been at the library engaged in more background research on the buildings destroyed by the newly christened "Mason City Arsonist." Mark was frustrated. Three microfiche tapes they needed had gone missing, but no one knew when it had happened.

Mark paused in his questioning to scan the crowd. The newspaper's crime beat reporter, Renee Blackwell there. She watched the three of them keenly. Her head bobbed up and down as she noted what was happening. Heather McCade was also there. She stood at the front of the onlookers with her arms crossed, watching the three of them with disdain. Julie saw her also, and realized that Heather's observation of her here gave extra credence to Heather's theory that Julie set her own property on fire.

"Julie?"

A set of fingers snapped in her face. Julie returned her attention back to Cassie and Mark. The two of them watched her carefully, although Mark's gaze seemed slightly more concerned than Cassie's. "Yes?"

"So, you were telling me that you got a note from me, instructing you to meet me here?" Cassie asked.

"No. I received an anonymous note telling me to meet someone here who had information regarding my fire," Julie answered for the fifth time, rubbing her forehead. She felt grimy and sooty from the fire. Her clothes smelled of smoke and the liquid she had touched. The scent of it still hung in her nostrils.

"And where is this so-called note?"

"I think I dropped it when I ran out of there. It must've gone up in the fire."

"Did you see anyone?" Mark asked again.

Julie's frustration with them began to grow. "Like I said before, Mark, they were in some kind of silver suit. They had a mask over their face. I couldn't tell who it was."

"And you have no idea why they brought you here?" Cassie countered.

"Well, outside of trying to turn me into a cinder, no, I don't have any idea."

Cassie glared at her. "You know, this'll go better without the sarcasm."

Julie leaned her head back against the ambulance. She struggled to understand the image that she had experienced when she saw the person in the suit. She had not told Mark or Cassie of the image she had seen, nor could she. Julie wasn't even certain that there had been a person in there, but then, someone had to set that liquid afire. She brought her gaze back to Cassie's face and tried to smile. "I'm sorry, Cassie. I guess I'm a little on edge."

Cassie nodded. "Apology accepted."

Mark and Cassie looked at each other and then at Julie. Julie knew what they were thinking without having to read their thoughts. Even at this distance, they all felt heat radiating from the still-burning building and saw the fire reflecting in lenses of Julie's glasses. Outside of some soot on her face and clothing, she didn't have a scratch on her. "How did you get out again?" Mark asked.

"I was only a step or two inside it, and when I saw the flames, I ran really fast."

"Do you remember anything else?"

"I saw a vehicle leaving the scene. I also thought I smelled something when I walked through the door. It was a scent I remember detecting at the house with the insurance adjusters."

"It was probably the flowers surrounding the place," Cassie said.

"No, this was different. It was something sweet and perfume-like."

Mark and Cassie exchanged glances again. "Are you sure?" Mark pushed.

"I'm not certain, but I think I could recognize it again if I was exposed to it."

They heard someone clearing their throat and the three of them turned in the sound's direction. Lieutenant Rutherford and Melanie approached. Melanie was dressed head to toe in fire gear. Her mask dangled in front of her, and she grimaced with the effort of adjusting the oxygen tank strapped to her back. Their faces were covered with grime and soot. Lieutenant Rutherford motioned to the two detectives. The detectives excused themselves and the group left Julie for a quieter part of the street. "Well?" Mark asked when they were out of Julie's earshot.

"It's definitely the same person who set the last two," Lieutenant Rutherford told them in a low tone, blowing cigarette smoke out of his nose. "We're picking up the traces of the accelerant outside the building."

Lieutenant Rutherford's eyes fell on Julie. Mark saw where he looked. Immediately, Mark shook his head. "It wasn't her," he told them in an affirmative voice.

"I think she's telling the truth about what happened in there."

"Then what do you want to do?" Cassie asked.

Mark stared at the glowing orange structure in front of him. Mark lied to them just then. He didn't believe the part of Julie's story about how far she made it inside. He remembered reading Melanie's reports on how fast the accelerant burned once ignited. *Julie should not be alive. How in the hell did she get out?* Then he thought about her comment about the scent she picked up, and Melanie's new discovery regarding the accelerant. He had a wacky theory on that and he wondered if Julie could help prove it. Mark walked back to Julie and touched her arm. "I'm going to need you to come to the precinct in the morning," he instructed her. "We'll need to get a formal statement from you, and I want you to look at something. Can you come by the station first thing?"

Julie stared at him. "Mark, I really need to get back to San Francisco."

"It'll only take a few minutes. You can delay your trip back until the afternoon, can't you, Miss CEO?"

Julie bit her lip. She had so many things to do. She was also due back on Anichia. However, she didn't think it would be a good idea to refuse him. His suspicions about her were already high. She let out a sigh. Then she nodded. "Okay. I'll be there at 10:00 a.m."

Giving the group an uneasy glance, she shoved her hands in her jeans pockets and walked toward her car. Once she was inside, NIK asked: *Ambassador? Is it logical to involve yourself further in this matter?*

I don't think I have much of a choice. Someone already has.

The group watched her depart. As soon as Julie's vehicle had left the scene, Cassie looked at the others. "Do you believe her?"

"She had traces of the accelerant on her clothes," Rutherford said. "You smelled it."

"Yes, but if the warehouse was already covered in it like she claims, she would've stepped into it when she walked inside," Mark countered. "Also, she was in China when at least three of the other fires took place. Besides, why would she burn down her own property?"

"To throw us off the trail? To distract us?" Cassie pointed out.

"No, Cass. That place meant too much to her. If you'd seen the look on her face when I told her, you'd understand."

"Although the 9-1-1 call for this fire came from her cell phone," Melanie mused.

When the other three turned to look at her, she shrugged. "On a hunch, I thought I'd check. You know, to see if there's been any pattern? Some arsonists like to report their own fires. It makes them feel like heroes. Unfortunately, it's been six different people."

Lieutenant Rutherford was impressed. Not too many rookie investigators would have thought to check those. Even he hadn't thought to check. Mark turned to Cassie. "What about Walter? Any word on where he might be?"

"No idea. He seems to have pulled a disappearing act on us since we spoke to him."

"Sounds like a guilty conscience to me," Lieutenant Rutherford muttered.

"What about the other potentials?" Mark asked.

"Wurtz is still in Seattle's lockup because he couldn't make bail," Cassie explained. "Deacon's with his girlfriend getting it on, according to the neighbors. They called to complain about the noise. As for Kate, well maybe you have an idea."

She winked at Mark. Melanie tried not to giggle. Mark's expression turned stern. "Trust me, if she comes around, she'll be in lockup before she makes it to the front porch. Check on her. We need to know where she was."

"It doesn't matter. We now have three fires linked together with the same cause," Lieutenant Rutherford said, lighting up a cigarette to replace the one he smoked in the minute they had been talking. "At least we can give Heather concrete proof that this is no insurance scam, especially since another person almost died."

"Unfortunately, now she'll have Julie in her sights," Cassie commented. "Two fires in three days with her involved in some way? How much you want to bet that she'll ask us to arrest her?"

"But Julie's not the one, Cass," Mark reminded her. "This one, she was almost a victim."

"Do you really think that's going to matter to her?"

"I don't care!" Melanie lashed out. "There's a reason for all of these fires, and we need to find out why they're being set. Once we do that, we'll find out who's behind them."

The others looked at her. She grimaced and adjusted the tank on her back. Its weight reminded her of the accusatory look that Heather gave her every time she came to talk about the investigation. "Look, as it stands right now, I'm ready to confess to setting them so that it gets Heather off of my back," she explained in a more contrite voice. "Aren't you?"

The others looked down at the ground and not the direction of the barricades, where Heather still watched them. They couldn't wait until tomorrow when she graced their presence again. Mark turned to look at the destroyed warehouse. "So tell me the truth people: where do we go from here?"

*   *   *

Once she returned home, Julie contacted Simon to tell him what happened over the past few hours. She paced the living room, engaged in a telepathic dumping of all she experienced. "I wish I still had that note," she said to the empty room. "Maybe I could've gained some more information."

Perhaps, but given your current state, you might have ignited it as well. I understand your need for resolution on this. However, I do need you here on Anichia.

"I know, Simon, but there's something going on here that's deeper than just a series of fires. I just wish I could figure out that image I keep seeing."

You will, Halbrina, once you have rested. I know it's been some time since you last slept. I also know how you get when you don't sleep.

"I'll be fine."

You will not be fine. You'll be cranky. I don't think the Eldar would be pleased if something were to happen while you were in that state.

"When have the Eldar ever been happy with what I do? Never, because they don't know what happiness is, Simon."

As I stated, when you don't rest, you become cranky, as you have so aptly demonstrated.

Julie paused. Simon knew her so well. She plopped herself onto her sofa. "Simon, I need answers," she wailed to the ceiling.

They will come in time. Meanwhile, get some sleep. Things will look better once you have rested, and can see the world with clearer eyes.

"I have vision that's better than anyone in the universe, Simon."

Not when it is clouded with the thoughts that churn in your head right now. Give it time, Halbrina. Then you will find what you're looking for. Meanwhile, I will do what I can here.

Julie sighed. "All right. I promise I'll get some rest, and join you as quickly as I can."

She waited until she felt certain he was no longer eavesdropping on her thoughts. Then she went over to her desk and opened her laptop. "NIK, call up everything known about these fires. I need to see if I can find something that Mark and the others may have missed."

NIK began downloading the information known. Julie coupled it with what she learned from the investigators. Together they made a flow chart similar to the one at the precinct. It was after two in the morning before she took a break. She rose to pour herself a glass of lemonade. As she did, she heard Mark pull his vehicle in the driveway. He paused to gaze up toward her place. "He wants to talk to me about how I got out without getting hurt," she said, as she scanned his thoughts. "I'm sorry, Mark, but I can't tell you that." After a few moments, he went inside his home. She listened for him to scream again, but he didn't. She concluded that either he didn't have the dream, or he didn't go to sleep.

By morning, Mark had already left for work and Julie was no closer to finding a motive for these fires. She stood up and stretched. She heard her stomach rumble, so she walked into the kitchen and opened up the fridge. "I know I should rest, but maybe a little nourishment will help," she convinced herself, while rummaging for an egg and some orange juice. She made a batch of pancakes, fetched her copy of the morning paper, and sat down to enjoy her breakfast. She skimmed the front page. On it was a color photo of the warehouse engulfed in flames, and an article about the fire. The reporter who wrote it made a point of saying there was a witness at this last blaze. Julie winced at the reference. Publicity was the last thing she needed. She didn't need to give the Eldar more proof that she should terminate her stay here. They were still furious about what happened last night, although Julie had tuned out their arguments hours ago.

She turned to watch a squirrel scurry up the maple tree outside her living room window, and tried to recall the image of the screaming girl. "Why am I so hung up on it?" she asked aloud. "What about it has me so confused? Then again, what if it isn't the image, but what I'm feeling when I have it?" She walked back over to her desk to review the list of destroyed buildings. "I wonder if I were to go to these other places, is there a chance I'll see it there as well?"

She heard her mantle clock toll and she glanced at it. To her surprise, it was already 9:00 a.m. She remembered promising Mark of the time she would arrive. She changed into a fresh set of clothes, grabbed her messenger bag and took off toward the county complex. She parked on the fourth floor of the garage and took the bridge that led over Main Street to the main entrance. There, she saw a woman leaning against the wall, dressed in tan slack and a white, short-sleeve shirt cotton shirt. Her auburn hair was tied back with a multi-colorful scarf, and her purse hung casually at her side. She eyed Julie intently. Julie didn't like what she sensed from her. She adjusted her grip on her bag and quickened her pace, hoping to maneuver her way by her. The woman anticipated her movements and stepped directly into her path. "It's Ms. Warren, correct?"

"Yes?"

"I'm Renee Blackwell, Mason City *Journal*."

Renee smiled and held out a hand. Reluctantly, Julie shook it. "I was wondering if I could have a few minutes of your time, before you talk to Detective Daniels," Renee continued.

"How do you know that I'm here to talk to him?"

"I saw you at the fire last night. You must've been there for a reason, and since you're now here, it must be in connection to the investigation he's conducting. Unless of course, you're the arsonist," Renee added teasingly.

Julie frowned. She remembered seeing this woman at the fire last night. Now, she put the article she had read that morning and the woman together. "How can I help you, Miss Blackwell?"

"I understand that you might have seen who's responsible for this rash of unsolved arsons. Would you mind telling me what you saw?"

There was a sudden click. Julie looked down at Renee's hand. Somehow, Renee materialized a tape player and a notebook out of her purse. The red light on the tape player glowed, indicating that it was recording. Julie returned her eyes to Renee's face. "Where did you get that idea?"

"Well, rumor has it that the arsonist may have lured you there."

"Really? Where did you hear that?"

Renee smiled slyly. "Sources. I also saw all the investigators speaking to you last night at the scene, and you're here this morning." Renee's smile broadened and her green eyes sparkled. "I've done a little research. I know that the company you work for owns one of the destroyed properties. I have to assume you have information that's pertinent to this investigation."

"Yes, my employer does own one of the properties, but I'm not certain why that's relevant."

"Ms. Warren, everything about these arsons is relevant. The investigators have said little to the media. One would think that they're hiding something from the public. As a victim of these fires, you should be outraged that there's been no progress."

Julie squared herself to her. "Miss Blackwell, the investigators have done a more than adequate job keeping me and my insurance company apprised of what's happening with my case. As for my presence here, I . . ."

Julie's voice drifted off. In the air, she detected the same scent that she caught at the house and at the warehouse last night. At the same time, she saw the image of the screaming girl, but this time, she also heard her. She stared off in the distance, listening to her. The girl sounded like she was hurt, but it didn't seem like a physical pain of any type. Then why was she crying?

"Ms. Warren?" Renee's voice broke through her thoughts. "Are you all right?"

Julie snapped of her trance. She looked at Renee. "I'm sorry, Miss Blackwell," Julie apologized, "but I really don't have anything to tell you. Now, if you would excuse me, Mark is expecting me."

Renee's smile grew broader. "Mark? Just how well do you know Detective Daniels?"

"We've only just met," Julie lied. "Why do you ask?"

Renee gave her a knowing look. She had seen the way that Mark had touched her last night, and the intense look on his face. She knew that look. She had been covering this beat for more than three years, and his behavior toward this woman was more than the concern of a detective seeking information from a victim, or a suspect. "Oh. I see."

"No, I doubt that. Now, if you would excuse me."

Julie maneuvered her way around Renee, through the sliding doors and toward the security checkpoint. She glanced back over her shoulder to make sure that Renee had not followed her. When she reached the security area, NIK warned her of the security devices before her. She laid her bag down on the conveyor belt and with a thought, blinded the machines to the contents within it. Then she made her way toward the main elevator banks. When she entered the precinct, she spotted Mark in the large room on the other side. She saw him look up and wave her toward the room. Smiling, she walked over and opened the door. "Hi, Mark."

Mark straightened. His smile was cordial, but the look in his eyes was all business. "Julie, thanks for coming."

The door opened again. Cassie and Lieutenant Rutherford had entered. Cassie nodded at Julie and Julie returned it. Lieutenant Rutherford smelled faintly of cigarette smoke and soot. Mark gestured to him. "Julie, this is Lieutenant Lawrence Rutherford the head investigator," he said by way of introduction. "Lieutenant, this is Julie Warren."

"The owner of the historical house." Lieutenant Rutherford held out his hand for Julie to shake. "I'm sorry about what happened."

Julie nodded and gazed behind the couple. "Where's Melanie? I thought she was also helping with this case?"

"She went back to the warehouse to do some follow-up work. She should be back shortly."

Julie glanced about the room. "Mark, what's going on? I thought I was giving you a statement about what happened last night."

"You are, in a way," Mark reassured her. He gestured to the table. "This is what I wanted you to see."

Julie looked to where he pointed. Several bottles of various shapes and sizes sat on the table, filled with different colored liquids. "I don't understand. What are these bottles for?"

"You said that you smelled something at your place and at the Sullivan warehouse," Mark explained. "I just want to see if any of these scents here are similar to it."

"That's an odd request. I'm not certain if I can be that specific."

"Just do your best, okay?"

Julie studied the variety of bottles before her. It wasn't that she couldn't do it. Her powers made her humanoid senses extremely sensitive. She just feared that these same senses would betray to them what she really was. She set her messenger bag down on the floor beside the table and sighed. "Well, I'll try."

She approached the table, studying the bottles before her. Cassie and the lieutenant walked up to Mark. "Do you really think this is going to work?" he murmured.

"Lieutenant, we actually have a witness to one of these fires," Mark answered. "If she can match that scent to what she experienced at the fire, it may be the first solid step toward finding our arsonist."

The trio watched as Julie picked up the first sample, inside a square bottle filled with a liquid the color of virgin olive oil. She scrutinized its contents. Then she uncapped it and sniffed. It was too musky in scent. She shook her head. "No."

Cassie picked up a clipboard and began making notations. Julie was still uncertain as to what they were looking for, but she reached for the next bottle without question. Her response to it and the next three bottles was the same as the first. Mark and the lieutenant watched. After the third bottle, Lieutenant Rutherford wondered how she could tell the difference anymore. Human noses can become confused when exposed to too many stimulants, and Julie wasn't taking that much time between bottles to clear her head.

Bottle number six was hourglass shaped, and filled with a purple colored-liquid. As Julie touched it, the image of the girl came back to her. This time, there was something else attached to it. Ignoring it for the time being, Julie uncapped the bottle and sniffed. All of them saw her eyebrows raise and her eyes light up. She nodded and handed the bottle to Mark. "That's it. That's what I smelled at the warehouse when I first stepped inside."

Mark and Lieutenant Rutherford exchanged glances. "Cassie?" Mark asked.

Cassie looked down at the notes they had made earlier. "*Romantic Interlude*," she read. "It's a scent that most major department stores and drug stores used to carry."

"And it has some meaning to our arsonist," Mark said, turning the bottle in his hands. "The question now is what?"

"I don't understand," Julie interjected. "What's so special about that perfume?"

Mark held the bottle up for Julie to see. "The accelerant you stepped in? Melanie found a trace of a lavender-scented perfume within the residue found at our last three crime scenes. Its chemistry signature matches this one. We're not certain if it will lead us to our arsonist, or just something to throw us off their trail."

Just then, Melanie walked into the room, a clipboard in her hand. She saw Julie before she saw anyone else. Julie nodded to her, but did not extend her hand. "Hi, Melanie," she greeted her. "It's nice to see you again. How are you?"

"Fine, Julie," Melanie replied, her tone guarded. "I'm glad to see that you're all right."

The door opened again. Everyone turned to the new presence in the room. "Heather," Mark greeted her. "It's nice to see you."

"As it is you." Heather's gaze hovered over Melanie. Melanie dropped her eyes to the floor and stepped behind Lieutenant Rutherford. Heather glowered inside. She turned in the lieutenant's direction. "Are there any new developments since last night?"

"We're working on the update as we speak," he assured her. "We plan to have a report to you no later today."

Heather laid the loose sheets of paper she carried down on the table and walked over to the display board.

The others saw her give a nod of approval, something none of them expected. "Hmm. This is an interesting way to approach this case, Lieutenant. Was this your idea?"

"Actually, it was Detective Daniels who decided on this method."

"Has it led anywhere?"

"No, not yet. We're hoping Ms. Warren can help give us some insight."

"Ms. Warren?"

The lieutenant nodded toward the opposite corner of the room. Heather turned in the direction where Julie stood. When she saw her, her eyebrows flew up into her thin bangs. "What are you doing here?" she snapped.

"I'm here to give a follow-up on my statement," Julie told her. "Also, they asked me to sniff some perfume."

"Perfume?"

"It may be a clue as to who our arsonist may be," Mark explained. "Melanie found traces of the same kind in some of the she samples recovered."

Heather's cold gaze landed on Melanie, but it didn't linger long. She rounded on Mark. "Detective Daniels, you are aware that this woman is now linked to two of the fires?" she asked in a harsh tone, pointing at Julie.

"Yes, I am. However, since Julie wasn't even in the country when her place was destroyed, and that someone tried to kill her last night, I'm not considering her to be a suspect."

"Hardly. From the way you're acting, you'd think you already have it figured out." She gestured toward the display behind her. "Trust me, Detective Daniels, it's a brilliant strategy, but you're reading too much into this."

Mark crossed his arms. "I am?"

"I'm certain the lieutenant informed you that the majority of arsonists are those who have contact with fire on a regular basis, probably because of their particular fascination for it."

Heather's gaze landed on Lieutenant Rutherford and Melanie. The tension kept mounting. Julie tried not to squirm. Heather spotted her actions out of the corner of her eye. She smiled. "Ms. Warren, I read the officers' reports on the blaze last night. In it, you allege that you were lured there and that you were caught inside."

"Yes, but I managed to escape, as did our arsonist."

Heather looked intrigued. "The arsonist was still there?"

"Yes, they were."

"Did you see them?"

"No, ma'am. They escaped before I could identify them."

Heather sighed. Then she turned her focus back on Melanie. "What is this about perfume?"

"It's just I keep finding scant traces of the same perfume in the samples I tested," Melanie explained. "We're trying to track down the distributors to determine if any of our suspects may have purchased it."

"How long until you have the results?"

Melanie shrugged. "About a day or two."

Heather clicked her tongue. "Delays. That's the story of your life, it I'm not mistaken."

She walked back to the end of the table and made to gather her pages she laid there. "I'm going to talk to the Sullivans regarding their loss. I expect your updated report no later than 5:00 p.m. today, Lieutenant. If you wish to reach me before then, you have my numbers. Have a pleasant day, everyone."

She turned and without a second glance, exited the room. The door closed behind her, and everyone took a collective breath of relief. Lieutenant Rutherford immediately reached for the pocket that contained his cigarettes. "I'm going for a smoke," he muttered.

"I'll join you," Melanie said.

Lieutenant Rutherford was stunned. "You don't smoke."

"No, but with the way things are going, I'm going to start."

Lieutenant Rutherford gave his protégé a pat on back. "C'mon. Let's see if they've had any hits on that perfume."

The two of them headed out of the room, leaving Julie with Mark and Cassie. Cassie busied herself gathering up the perfume bottles. Julie made her way to Mark's side. Something Heather had said bothered her. "Mark? Is there any truth behind Heather's statement that many fires are started by those who investigate or fight them?"

"Unfortunately, yes, Julie, but I don't think we have that here. Lieutenant Rutherford and Melanie especially have been working extra hard to find out who this arsonist is."

"Which is why she said it," Cassie interrupted. "She's trying to throw all of us off our guard. She hopes that maybe if it is one of them, they'll slip up and reveal themselves."

Julie nodded. She turned and saw the display the investigators had created. She focused her attention on a photograph taken at Della Torre's storage unit, and the symbol burned into the concrete floor. The image of the girl returned as she did so. "Cassie, what is this?" she asked, pointing to it.

"Something the investigators found at two of the sites. What it means we don't know. We haven't been able to find someone who can translate it for us."

Julie turned back to the photograph. She closed her eyes, and sent an image of it to NIK for analysis. She had never seen anything like it, and she knew that she had seen and done more than the people in this room could even imagine.

Julie took a step back and stared at the board. Their display was more detailed than her charts. She reviewed it all of thoroughly, transmitting it to NIK so that she could make her notes as accurate as what she saw here. She thought again of going to the sites, but she didn't know the area well. Then an idea came to her. "Mark?"

"Yeah, Julie?"

"Is there any way you could take me to visit the other sites?"

"I don't see why not." Then his brow wrinkled. He stopped shuffling the papers and stared at her. "Why?"

"I just want to see these places I guess, and gain a better understanding of what's happening."

Mark thought about this. "Sounds like a long shot to me. I doubt you're going to smell anything at the first three sites. Those fires were a few months ago, before you moved here, and before I was assigned to the case."

"I'm not expecting to. I'm just curious, that's all. Even the last site before our fire will be satisfactory. Please?"

Mark still seemed hesitant. Finally, he gestured to the door. "All right. Let's go."

Half an hour later, Mark pulled up in front of the gutted storage unit. The boxes that survived the flames still stood in the back corner. They looked as if they would collapse into themselves any minute. Julie got out of the truck. Mark didn't. Despite knowing that there was nothing here to harm him, he still wasn't comfortable being here. He watched as Julie approached the structure. He saw her chest expand wide. He shook his head. *She had good olfactory nerves, if she could pick up the scent here,* he thought.

Julie stared at the outside of the facility. She took a step inside the gutted frame. As Julie touched the inside of the frame, she gasped. The image returned. It lasted longer this time. It was also different. This time, Julie saw an old house and a little girl sitting on the porch, clutching one of the posts, her face smudged with dirt. She also looked like she had a black eye. Her fingers were long and thin, and her bitten nails had blood around the cuticles. There was another face there, a dark-haired man. He stood next to her. The girl seemed to like him. Who was he?

"Julie?"

She turned. Mark gazed at her. Her facial expression had turned vacant. For a moment, Mark thought she had a look in her eyes similar the one he spotted when she first viewed Jessie's painting. "Are you all right?"

"I don't know. There's such an odd feeling to this place. It's as if someone died here."

"That would've been Anthony Della Torre."

Julie pulled her hand away from the doorway and shuddered. Without wanting to, she felt the agony Anthony experienced before he died. It was like the pain of so many others she had witnessed and had personally inflicted on others. She focused her eyes on the few stacked boxes in the corner. She cocked her head. Then she turned toward Mark and pointed to them. "What's going to happen to those?"

"I don't know. Della Torre was sending someone to get them, last I heard. Why?"

"Just curious."

"Julie, I doubt the answers we're looking for are in there. According to Della Torre, there wasn't anything of value here."

"But what was so special about this place?"

"We think that the arsonist somehow convinced Anthony to come here with them, and then torched it after they locked Anthony inside. Unfortunately, only the arsonist knows why." He leaned toward the passenger door. "So are you done, Sherlock?"

"Sherlock?"

Sherlock Holmes, Ambassador, a fictitious character in this planet's popular literature. He is an investigator in a manner similar to that of Detective Daniels.

"Oh. Yes, Mark, I am. Thanks for bringing me here."

"You're welcome."

She made their way back to his truck. When she had closed the door, she took one more gaze at the burned-out unit. She thought about the boxes inside and the board in the conference room. They found the symbol here, so it must be significant. What about the man that just appeared? Was Michelangelo Della Torre the man she had seen? Julie had read about him in the local papers. NIK had provided her with his dossier. Why would someone want to hurt him or his family? She sighed. Her idea was just as odd as Mark's obsession with the perfume. Would it even be worth it? *NIK?*

Yes, Ambassador?

Contact Russell. Give him these coordinates and have him come here with a scanning device to upload the information in those leftover boxes. Tell him to come after dark, so that no one sees him. I want to examine their contents.

Are you looking for something specific, Ambassador?

I'm not certain. Something tells me part of the answer is inside there.

As you wish, Ambassador.

"A penny for your thoughts?"

Julie turned toward Mark. "I'm sorry?"

"You seemed to be concentrating on something. Want to let me know what's going on?"

"Oh, it's nothing, Mark," she said, as she fastened her seat belt. "The CEO in me just has too much on her mind, I guess. I should be heading back to San Francisco."

"Well, I won't delay you any longer."

Mark headed for the exit. Julie stared out the window. Her thoughts drifted back to the girl. To Julie, the girl thought the stranger was there to protect her. Suddenly, her emotions for him had turned dark and cold. Why? She compared it to the emotions that Mark had for his father. Mark felt neglected and somewhat abandoned by his father, but the girl's emotions were different. She had been hurt, angered, and . . . "Betrayed," she whispered.

"What?"

Julie turned. Mark stared at her. "Nothing, Mark," she said. "I was just talking out loud. I do that a lot."

"Okay. Thanks for the heads up."

They waited for the gate to rise. Julie stared straight ahead. *Betrayal: that's the emotion that I'm feeling*, Julie realized. Now Julie knew that she needed to determine the girl betrayed. Finding her would possibly lead them to their arsonist, and to the reason for the betrayal.

XIII

That evening, Lieutenant Rutherford sat in his home study, reviewing the evidence. He had made copies of everything, including the photographs. In his 20-odd years on the job, he had never felt so baffled by the evidence before him. At first, he wasn't happy when the chief of police suggested that a couple members of Serious Crimes help them after Anthony Della Torre's death. However, the insight that they provided, especially Mark Daniels, had been invaluable. He recalled the meeting the four of them had with Julie Warren. She seemed so young to be CEO of such a big corporation, but hell, youth these days. Give them some money and they'll spend it in a heartbeat, or they might use it to try to make a difference in the world. To him, Julie looked to be one of the latter and from what little he had seen, she seemed to be doing a bang-up job of it.

He put out the cigarette he had been smoking and lit a new one. He took a drag and reread his notes again. He came across a report dealing with Della Torre's storage facility. He didn't recognize the handwriting. He shook his head in disgust. It probably came from one of the junior lab rats, who was so lazy, he didn't bother to pay attention to what he were doing. In some spots, he had written Mickey. "Mickey?" he grumbled. There was no mention of a Mickey anywhere. There was a Maggie. Della Torre's old secretary had mentioned a Maggie. Her parents died in a fire some 25 years ago. Detective Daniels made that notation, with a note to check on it. What did that have to do with anything, and why did Detective Daniels care about it?

Lieutenant Rutherford stood up and began to pace his study. He had solved most of his cases in this room, but the answer to this one eluded him. He puffed away on his cigarette, forming a long ash stick that threatened to fall at any sudden move. What was it? What made these places so significant? It wasn't the properties themselves. The torching of the Foundation's home had proven that. The burn pattern had been too random, too emotional, and it was valued at more than twice that of the other properties. Something told him that it had nothing to do with the other fires, even though the accelerant used had been the same one used at the storage unit, and at the Sullivan warehouse fire. He walked back to his desk, picked up his red felt-tip pen, and scratched it off his list. "One down; a whole host to go," he mumbled.

He picked up another set of notes and let out a puff of smoke. That morning, he had a friend at the county records do a search on them. Their respective families still owned all of them, except for the condemned home, which had reverted to the city. None of the properties had any significant change in value, or were located in areas where there was increased population growth. He tapped the pen against the papers. "It's the victims," he muttered. "The people who owned these places are the key, but there's nothing there. What am I missing? What am I not seeing?"

The phone rang. He put out the cigarette he was smoking and flopped around on his desk, letting its shrill ring guide him. Finally, he found it. "Hello?" he answered in a gruff voice.

"Hi, Lawrence."

"Melanie, please don't tell me you're at the lab."

"Yes, but I'm leaving soon. I just wanted to call and ask you something."

"Not about the case."

"No. It's about Detective Daniels."

Lieutenant Rutherford sat back in his chair. He saw the looks Melanie gave him when she thought no one was paying attention. She had bonded quickly with Cassie, who was also from Seattle. However, he knew Melanie had a lonely go of it since transferring here. She longed to be in a relationship with someone, but the few men she had met here seemed a little put off by the fact that their date played with fire. "He's a keen detective and a good man. He's taking an approach to this case that I probably wouldn't have considered, but it seems to be working."

"It's not just that. He's such a handsome man, and intelligent. Cassie tells me that he's recently widowed. She told me before I went to his place the other night.

I made him dinner, and we talked a little, but I think I overstepped the mark."

Through the phone line, Lieutenant Rutherford saw Melanie's cheeks turn bright red. He shook his head. "Melanie, if it bothered him any, he hasn't let it show, has he? Besides, if anything, he's treated you with kindness. He respects your judgments and the insights that you've brought to these cases, unlike Heather."

"No! Don't mention her in the same sentence with him!"

"Sorry, Melanie, but it does go to prove my point."

"I don't get it Lawrence. Why does she hate me so?"

"I think she hates the world, Mel. You just happened to be this month's punching bag."

He heard Melanie try to laugh. A part of him wished he were with her right now so that he could give her the hug she wanted. "Melanie? Is there something else you want to ask me?"

There was a pause. "Me and Mark? Do you think a girl like me has a chance with someone like him?"

Lawrence's voice turned conciliatory. "You'll find someone, Mel. Don't rush these things. They happen when they happen, and when it does, you'll know."

"Thanks, Lawrence. Look, I'm stopping to get something to eat. Want anything?"

"If you're stopping where I think you're stopping, I'll take my usual."

"Lawrence, your heartburn . . ."

"I'll deal with my heartburn. I'll see you in a few."

He hung up the phone, ran his hand along the top of the receiver, and sighed. Granted, he knew he wasn't

Melanie's real father, but for the last 14 months or so, he had assumed that role. She seemed grateful for it. He too, was grateful. He never found the time to marry or have children. Melanie was the closest thing he had to a daughter. Their time together had been one the most enjoyable of his life in this job, and made him wonder what could have been if things had turned out differently.

He picked up his notes again, trying to recall where he left off. Then he remembered. With the felt-tip pen, he began to trace lines from the names of the owners to their destroyed properties. He picked up another sheet of paper. On it were the contact numbers of the respective owners. Coincidentally, most of them were dead from accidental house fires. Shaking his head, he picked up a ballpoint pen, and wrote "Mickey" on a separate sheet of paper, with a question mark next to it. He wasn't certain why this name bothered him so much. It didn't match up to anything that was in front of him. He stared at the unfamiliar report. Why is it only on Della Torre's? Was Mickey some sort of nickname? If so, who would call a man like him Mickey, outside of those who knew him best, or hated his guts? He studied the handwriting. Something about it was familiar. "Stupid idea, Lawrence," he mumbled to himself, as he picked up his phone again and rifled through more papers. "Stupid, stupid, stupid."

He located Della Torre's home number, dialed it, and waited patiently for him to answer. "Mr. Della Torre? This is Lieutenant Rutherford of the Mason City arson squad. I'm sorry to bother you so late at night, but I have a quick question. Did you ever go by the nickname of 'Mickey' at any time in your life?"

Lieutenant Rutherford listened intently to Della Torre as he danced and wavered. Finally, he answered him. Lieutenant Rutherford raised an eyebrow and stared down at his other notes. "Thank you, sir. That's a big help."

Lieutenant Rutherford clicked the phone off. He lit another cigarette without finishing the one prior to it, and stared at the information before him. He started to make a few more notations on the separate sheet of paper. He paused, and then took another hard look at the stray sheet of paper. Something else about it struck a nerve. He began to write down something else. As he did so, the doorbell rang. Frustrated, he shoved himself away from his desk. "Just a minute," he called out. *Not like there's a fire or anything,* he thought, smiling at his own joke.

He picked up his cigarette and stuck it back in his mouth. Stumbling over the scattered papers and his shoes, he made his way toward the front door. He paused long enough to pull the cigarette from his mouth. He let out a puff of smoke, and then opened the door. Before his brain recognized who it was, his visitor struck him on his right temple, knocking him out cold.

Five hours later, Mark walked the perimeter of the lieutenant's home, careful not to trip over the remaining hose strewn across the yard, as the fire chief walked the house with a structural engineer. Earlier, the fire chief told Mark they found the lieutenant in his now-destroyed bed. He stared at the blackened structure and tried to see the good in what was in front of him. *Good? An arson investigator dies in a fire of his doing, and you're trying to find the good in this?*

"Coming out!" a voice called.

Mark turned. Four firefighters stepped precariously over the doorframe and hoses, carrying out the lieutenant in the familiar black body bag. They placed him on a gurney, and then inside the coroner's van. Mark assumed that they were taking him back to the complex for an autopsy, although the cause of death looked cut and dry.

He turned again to face the front sidewalk. About ten yards away, Cassie stood next to Lieutenant Michaels surveying the damage. The fire had been contained mostly in the bedroom and the back of the house, with smoke and water damage to the front living areas. The next arson investigator in line had left town for a funeral, and wasn't due back until the following day. Lieutenant Michaels was the first available senior officer. They turned as Mark approached. "Damn," the lieutenant whispered. "Just our luck that he had to die before your case broke. Given his profession, why the hell did he smoke in the first place?"

Mark and Cassie shook their heads. Their boss regarded them. "You think his death is related to your case?"

"I doubt it, Lieutenant," Mark answered.

"Were there any new developments prior to this?"

The detectives' gazes fell to the ground. Lieutenant Michaels pulled back a little. "Look, I know you two don't handle cases like this, but keep at it."

Cassie surveyed the scene again, paying particular attention to the firefighters still around. That was when she realized someone was missing. Her brow furrowed. "Mark? Where's Melanie?"

Mark glanced about. She had accompanied the firefighters inside to put out the blaze, but once they removed the lieutenant's body, she had disappeared. After a bit, Mark spotted her about a hundred yards away, sitting on the curb. He pocketed his notebook and walked over to her. Eventually, he got close enough to see that her firefighter's mask was buried in her hair, and her head in her hands. The tank on her shoulders wobbled. He knew how she felt, but now was not the time and this was not the place. He squatted down next to her. "Melanie?"

"He's . . . dead! He's really dead!" she whispered to the curb.

"Melanie, it was an accident. He knew the risk of smoking in bed. I'm surprised that he did smoke, given his profession."

Melanie looked up at Mark. Mark could tell that what he had said had offered her little comfort. "He was my teacher!" she screeched. "He was the best at his job! I always went to him when I had a problem about a case! He took the heat from Heather when she went off on me! How am I going to help you now? I can't! Not without him!"

"You've already been a big help, Melanie. Don't you know that?"

She looked at him and hiccupped, blinking the tears out of her green eyes. "Really?"

"Really."

Mark smiled. She reached up to wipe her face. "You know, when I first met him, I teased him that he was going to die with a cigarette in his hand. I never thought that it would actually come true."

He took her trembling hands into his. "Melanie, I know how hard this is for you. I know that all you want to do is give up, but you can't. The lieutenant wouldn't have wanted that of any of us, but especially not from you."

They stared into each other's eyes, taking what little comfort they could manage for now. Finally, Melanie nodded. "Okay," she hiccupped.

Mark gave her a nod and pulled her to her feet. "C'mon. We have a job to do and Cassie and I need your help to do it."

Melanie enjoyed the feel of his hand in hers for a few moments, before wiping the last of the tears away from her face. She gave him a shaky nod, and then slid the tank off her back. Mark grabbed onto a free strap, and together, they walked back toward the others.

As crowds continued to congregate around the site, Julie walked up the street. She had been up at the farm when NIK informed her about the fire. She teleported back to her apartment, drove to the location, and parked a few blocks away to avoid detection. She made her way toward the crowds that had gathered across the street. She didn't see Heather anywhere, and she wondered where she was. She did spot Renee among the hovering media, in position to pick up any tidbits as to what was happening. Julie made sure to give her an extremely wide berth.

While walking behind the crowds, she observed Melanie, Mark, and Cassie, standing with Lieutenant Michaels. As she drew closer, the image of the screaming girl hit again. It was so strong, Julie actually felt the sting of the slap that accompanied it. She stared at Lieutenant Rutherford's former home. That made four places now where she had seen the image. Julie was now convinced that whoever this girl is, she was their arsonist. What was her name? Where was she now? Why was she doing it, and why was Julie detecting her here?

"A shame, isn't it?" she heard a female voice say.

Julie turned at the sound. She stood next to a tall, thin older woman, dressed in baby pink satin pajamas and robe. "Yes, it is," Julie replied. "Did you know him well?"

"For more than 20 years. I can tell you one thing: dying in a fire was not the way he wanted to depart this good earth." She turned to face Julie. "I've never seen you before. Do you live around here?"

"No. He was investigating a fire for me. Someone destroyed the historical house my company owns up on Harlan."

"Oh dear. I visited there a few times. I always enjoyed it. I'm so sorry for your loss."

"Thank you. I'm Julie Warren, by the way."

"Grace Waters." She motioned to the police and firefighters still milling in front of her neighbor's home. "I haven't been able to hear anything. Do they know what caused it?"

"I think so." Julie scanned Mark's thoughts quickly. "From what I've heard, they think that his bed caught fire when a lit cigarette fell on his mattress."

Mrs. Waters stared at her in disbelief. "No! That's not possible."

"What?"

"I'll believe a heart attack, or stroke, or even cancer, the way he smoked, but smoking in bed? Never."

"I don't understand."

"Lawrence never smoked in bed. He told me that he had seen too many people die that way, and he was determined he wasn't going to be one of them. Besides, he never slept in his bed. He always slept in his armchair, if he slept at all."

"Slept at all?"

"Yes. Lawrence suffered from insomnia."

*   *   *

The early peeks of sunrise were breaking in the eastern horizon when Mark parked his truck next to Julie's. He stared at it, then up to the dark windows that marked her home. A wave of guilt touched his conscience. Since yesterday morning, she had not made any inquiries into the investigation. He was glad for it. He had nothing to tell her, and loathed to see the look of disappointment in her eyes when he informed her of what happened to the lieutenant.

He showered, changed into a fresh pair of jeans, a T-shirt and a red plaid shirt, grabbed a quick bite to eat, and headed back downtown. To relieve some of the tension within him, he stopped at the range. He pretended the targets were the evidence posted on the wall in the conference room, and the bullets were darts that he aimed at it, trying to pinpoint exactly what piece would lead him to the correct conclusion. He blew perfect scores in all of his targets, but it didn't help him find an answer. On his way into the building, he called Tyler and asked him to check Lieutenant Rutherford's phone logs for the last few days to see if anything was there. With the lieutenant gone and Melanie going to pieces, it was all he had. As he entered the squad room, he spied Cassie in the conference room, staring at something with a look of profound disgust. He headed her direction and opened the door. "Cassie? What is it?"

"Our worst nightmare," she told him, picking up the plastic bag that sat on the table and handing it to him. "Apparently, one of the investigators found these in the lieutenant's study. He made out the name of one of our victims on it and assumed that they were part of our case."

Mark raised an eyebrow and wondered why they had even bothered to retrieve them. The bag reeked of stale water and smoke, and the papers were so water smeared and smoke-stained, it was a wonder they survived. The only things he could make out were Della Torre's name and a bunch of washed-out red felt-tip lines that went off the page. "These aren't the originals, are they?"

"No. Those are still here. He must've made copies. However, if he found something new, we'll never know."

Mark cursed under his breath. He tossed them into an empty chair, flung himself into a second one, and began to rub his forehead. Cassie took a position beside him. "You all right, partner?"

Mark stared at the display before him. After a few moments, he closed his eyes. He could still see them wheeling the lieutenant's body away from the scene, and Melanie's tear-streaked face while they did it. It intermingled with what he imagined his mother looked like when they retrieved her body. "I don't know, Cass," Mark breathed.

Cassie placed a reassuring hand on his weary shoulder. "We'll figure it out, Mark. It'll come to us sooner or later. It has to."

There was a knock and the door opened. The detectives turned. Heather stood before them. She glanced about the room and frowned. "He's not here either, huh?"

"Pardon?" Mark asked.

"Lieutenant Rutherford. I've been looking for him. He isn't upstairs, and neither is his trainee. I thought they might be hiding in here. He's overdue with those reports I asked for yesterday afternoon."

Cassie and Mark exchanged awkward glances. "I doubt that you'll get those reports, Heather," Mark assured her.

"Why? Did something happen to poor Lawrence?" Heather sauntered into the room, a supreme smile on her face. "Did he up and confess to committing these crimes and he's downstairs in holding? Do I need to get some hankies for the rookie?"

Cassie gave Heather her interrogator stare. "So you've haven't heard?"

"Heard? Heard what?"

Cassie looked at Mark. He turned toward Heather. He stood, squared himself to her, and crossed his arms. "Lieutenant Rutherford died last night," he said in a low voice. "His home apparently caught fire while he was sleeping."

Heather's hardened features softened instantly and her face began to pale. "What?"

Cassie crossed her arms as well. "Don't tell me that you didn't know."

"No. After I saw the Sullivans, I went to Yale to investigate another claim. I didn't get a chance to watch any television. On my drive back into town, I heard on the radio that there was a fire, but . . ." Heather looked to Cassie, and then to Mark in disbelief. "It was Lieutenant Rutherford who died?"

"Yes."

Heather stumbled toward a chair. Her arms shook as she gripped it and guided herself into a sitting position. She began to rub her hands together. They were silent for a moment. Then Heather spoke again: "The lieutenant's fire? Do you think it's connected to your case?"

"No," Mark replied. "The initial investigators didn't find any evidence of a break-in, or any type of accelerant, gas or otherwise. It looks like a home accident."

"A home accident?"

Mark stuffed his hands in his pockets. "They discovered him in bed. He must've been smoking in it, and he . . . fell asleep."

"Oh, that's just great. What about the case? Do you have any new leads?"

"No," Cassie replied.

"Well, where's Melanie?"

Mark and Cassie looked at each other. Last time they saw Melanie, she was walking toward her car, her fire gear still on. They hadn't seen or heard from her since they arrived back at the precinct. "We're not certain," Cassie admitted.

"Well, you better go find her. She'll have to take over."

"Heather, take it easy. She's just had a huge shock. We all have. Maybe we should take a day or two to regroup and . . ."

Heather stood. Her eyes were afire. "Any other time, I might agree, but I have people to answer to as well. Despite what's happened, she has a job to do, and she's going to do it. Do you have a problem with that?"

Mark and Cassie stared at each other. Finally, Mark turned to face Heather, a hardened look on his face. "No."

There was a knock at the door. Cassie walked over to it and answered it. Detective Ed Peabody stood on the other side. "You might want to read this," he informed her. "The call just came in."

"Thanks, Ed." Cassie took the paper and began to read. She let out a sigh. "Finally, a break."

"What kind of break?" Mark asked.

"They just got anonymous call on that hotline we set up. According to it, our caller was driving through Lieutenant Rutherford's neighborhood just before the fire broke out. She thinks that she saw a woman wearing some sort of navy blue uniform exit it."

"Did they leave a description?"

"They didn't catch much; just a woman of average height, wearing gold glasses and blonde-brown hair in a braid."

Cassie paused in her reading and looked at Mark. His face was somber, but she knew what he was probably thinking. A new face appeared at the doorway. He gave the frame a tentative knock, and then opened the door. "Detective Daniels?"

"Yes?"

The man handed Mark two sheets of paper. One contained a list of highlighted addresses. The other contained a preliminary report on the lieutenant's fire. Mark stole a quick glance at it. Then he paused to reread it. He looked up at the man who brought it to him. He leaned forward to whisper an explanation of what Mark read. When he was done, Mark stepped back to look at him. "You're sure?"

"Yes, sir."

Mark reread the information there. Finally, he let out a long sigh. "Thanks." He jerked his head to the door. "C'mon, Cassie, and you may want to come along, Heather."

Heather pointed to herself. "Me?"

"Yes."

Stunned that they would even want her there, Heather followed. They took the stairs up to the ninth floor and walked into the arson squad room. They spied Melanie seated at her desk. She seemed unaware of anyone or anything around her. Her face still had soot all over it, and her navy uniform and hair reeked of smoke. She held a pen in her hand, and a piece of paper in front of her. It looked like she was trying to fill out some sort of report, but she had written nothing down. Mark put a firm hand on her shoulder. "Melanie?"

She shuddered in her seat. She finally looked up. When she recognized who was there, she tried to smile. "Hi, Mark. I . . . just got in. I went to bed last night, hoping to convince myself that it was all some sort of bad dream." She looked over in the direction of Lieutenant Rutherford's empty desk. Someone had placed a firefighter's hat on it. A red rose in a vase sat in front of its brim. She sighed. "I guess it wasn't, was it?"

He looked at Cassie, who was totally lost as to what Mark might be doing. Then he turned back to look at the junior investigator. "Melanie, if you have a moment, I need to take a look at your car."

"My car?"

"Yes."

"Why?"

"It's nothing important. I just need to check something, that's all."

She looked at the women with him. Cassie's face was stoic; Heather's was neutral. She looked at Mark. She wasn't certain what was going on, but she didn't see any reason for why she should protest. She shrugged and stood. "Okay."

She made her way toward the back entrance. Mark made to follow her. He motioned Cassie to come closer. Confused, she approached him quickly. "What?" she whispered.

"Get two uniforms to meet us downstairs. Also, try to reach Julie. Have her come in and see whether she can identify Melanie's car as the one she saw leaving the scene of the Sullivan warehouse fire."

"Mark? What's going on?"

He handed her the paper listing the addresses and the preliminary report. He pointed to the results at the bottom. Cassie read the highlighted address and then the report. She looked up at Mark in disbelief. His face held a neutral posture, but she saw something different in his eyes. She paused in her walking and pulled out her cell phone. Mark jotted down Julie's cell phone number on the paper and joined Melanie on the elevator. "We'll meet you downstairs," he told the women, as the doors closed in front of them.

Cassie waited until she heard the elevator engage before hitting the "Down" button again. She pulled out her cell phone and dialed the front desk. She gave them Mark's instructions, and then cleared the line. Heather sidled up to Cassie, intrigued. "What's going on?" she whispered, even though there was no one else about.

Cassie pressed the paper to her chest so that Heather could not see, while she dialed Julie's cell phone number. "Later," she murmured.

Melanie led Mark to where she had parked her car, well away from the building. She drove a well used, late-model blue Ford Escort. Mark took in every ding and dent on its rusting blue exterior. Later, he hoped to check with Forensics to see if there were any matches to samples collected from the arson scenes. Melanie watched from a distance. She began to feel a little uneasy. The last time she had seen that look on Mark's face, they had been questioning suspects. Suddenly, she felt as if she had become one. "Mark? Is there something wrong?"

"Melanie, are you still receiving mail at your Seattle home?" Mark asked her without looking up.

There was a soft jangle of metal on metal. Melanie looked behind her. Cassie and Heather had arrived. Two uniformed officers had joined them. Uncertain as to what was going on, and unnerved by the fact they were there, she faced Mark again. "Y . . . yes. I have to go there on occasion. Only my important mail comes here. Why?"

"That's a good question," Heather interjected. "Why does it matter where her mail goes?"

Mark glanced up from his car inspection. He nodded to Cassie, who handed Heather the sheet of addresses she had been shielding. She took the list and began to scrutinize it carefully. Then she read the preliminary arson report. When she finished, Heather looked at Melanie, flabbergasted. "What!" Melanie screamed.

She snatched the list from Heather's hand. She saw her name and address highlighted on it. Then she realized the information it revealed. She shook her head. "No," she said in a firm voice. "I didn't order this!"

"There's more, Melanie."

"More?"

"The preliminary lab results also found a scant trace of the accelerant in the lieutenant's mattress. The fire chief informed me that the lieutenant was found in his bed." His eyes narrowed onto Melanie's face. "The intent was to make it look like he fell asleep while smoking, wasn't it Melanie?"

"Bed? No, that can't be right. Lawrence never . . ."

"Can I have your keys?"

"K . . . keys?"

"Keys."

Melanie hesitated, then fished in her uniform pocket and handed them to him. Her hands shook as she did so. "It's unlocked," she assured him. "I never do. There's nothing in it worth stealing."

Mark reached into his jeans pocket and pulled out a set of rubber gloves. He made to slip them on, and then moved toward Melanie's car. He noted that Cassie had taken a position aside of Melanie that would allow her to block her retreat, if necessary. Heather stood with the officers, the look on her face growing more confounded by the moment. He opened the driver side door, but he didn't smell any lavender perfume. However, Melanie hadn't been lying when she said she wasn't the neatest person in the world. Discarded fast food wrappers, empty soda cans, and crumpled paper littered most of its surface. He looked at the space behind the passenger seat. Sticking out amongst the trash was a gallon water jug. He turned to Melanie and pointed to it. "What's that?"

Melanie tried to smile, but inside, her stomach was a bundle of nerves. She didn't understand what was going on. "With this wacky weather, I've been having problems with my radiator overheating. I . . . have to keep a bottle of water handy. Why?"

Mark opened the back door and reached for it. It felt heavier that a water jug should, and it looked like there was about a quarter cup of liquid missing from it. Mark uncapped it and took a sniff. Then he stuck a gloved finger inside and pulled it out. The contents were slippery on his gloves. He turned to look at Melanie and his eyes narrowed. "*Romantic Interlude*, I believe. You should wear it more often, Mel."

Melanie caught wind of the scent coming off his fingers. In disbelief, she reached in a finger to touch the liquid. She rubbed it between her thumb and forefinger, staring at them in dismay. She turned to look at Mark. "I . . . don't know where that came from."

"Oh? I thought you made it?"

"Made . . . ?" Melanie stepped away from Mark and gave him a blank stare. "No. I . . . I don't like perfume! I didn't make that! I wouldn't know how to . . ."

"But you have the chemistry background to do it, and daily access to a lab with all the ingredients necessary for it? You also were the one who determined its chemical makeup." Mark placed the cap back on it and handed the jug to Cassie. "I'm certain that if we search your place here and in Seattle, we'll find more, won't we?"

Melanie stared into Mark's face. Hours ago, those sensual brown eyes were comforting and consoling. Now they seemed cold and distant. Her eyes filled with tears. "I . . . I didn't . . . I don't . . ."

"Melanie, where were you between the hours of 9:00 p.m. and 10:30 p.m. last night?"

Melanie's eyes darted to the others. "I was here until a little after nine, working."

"Did anyone see you?"

Her chin dropped to her chest. "No," she croaked. "I was here alone. I called the lieutenant before I left."

"From the office?"

"No, from my cell phone."

"Where did you go when you left here?"

"I was hungry, so I stopped at my favorite Mexican place. I went through the drive-thru. There was a line of cars. It took a while."

"Do you have a receipt?"

Melanie's lower lip trembled. "Why are you doing this?" she rasped. "Why are you treating me like this?"

"Melanie, we have an anonymous witness who says they saw a woman meeting your description leaving Lieutenant Rutherford's home roughly ten minutes before you claim you arrived. You told me at the scene that you went to see him last night. You were the first one at the scene. You made the 9-1-1 call." His gaze turned conciliatory. "If killing Lieutenant Rutherford was an attempt to cover up your actions these past few months, now would be the time to admit to it," he concluded in a soft voice.

"My . . . my actions?" She looked at Cassie, whose face looked as if were chiseled out of granite, and then Heather, who watched the scene unfolding before her with her mouth hanging open. Tears fell from Melanie's eyes and left trails on her soot-covered cheeks. "I didn't kill him!" she screamed. "I didn't try to kill anyone! I'm not the one!"

Mark made to recap the bottle of liquid and nodded to the uniformed men behind Cassie, who began to approach. "Melanie Keegan, you're under arrest for arson, and the murders of Anthony of Della Torre and Lawrence Rutherford," he murmured.

"Arrest? But I . . . I didn't do it! I'm not the one!"

The first officer to reach her jerked her left arm behind her. The click of the handcuffs in her ears did little to dispel the reality of what was happening. She collapsed to the ground, screaming Mark's name. The officer handcuffing her anticipated this. He bent down with her and dragged Melanie back to a half-standing position. The other retrieved the bottle of accelerant from Mark. "Make sure to get that to the lab and have it tested," he instructed him. "Have this car impounded and checked for additional evidence, and make sure Ms. Keegan is made aware of her rights."

The officer nodded and with his free hand, ensnared Melanie's other arm. Together, the officers escorted her back to the precinct. Melanie kicked and squirmed, and tried to drag her feet, but the officers' grip was firm. She stared at the trio as if they were some alien race taking her to meet her doom. Mark wrenched his gaze away. Cassie and Heather watched until they saw the officers and Melanie disappear into the building. It was a bit before any of them could move. Finally, Heather handed Cassie back the preliminary report on Lieutenant Rutherford's fire. She looked at Mark. "You're certain about the accelerant in the mattress?"

"Not completely, Mark admitted. "According to the report, the sample was just enough to be detected. There's no way of knowing if it actually caused the fire."

"So there may be no truth to what you just said about her killing her mentor."

Mark looked back toward the double doors that the officers took Melanie through. "I don't know."

Cassie let out a sigh of disgust. "I can't believe this. I thought I knew her. We hit it off so well." She stared at the sun now beating down on them. "I don't know about you two, but I need out of this heat."

Mark and Heather gave Cassie reluctant nods of agreement. The trio walked back indoors. They took the stairs rather than the elevator, but said nothing. Mark held the door open for them, and followed the women out to the main lobby. It was becoming crowded. He turned to Heather. "Well, it looks like you can pay out on those insurance claims, now that we found our arsonist."

Heather jerked back to reality. "What? Oh, yes. I . . . guess I should get on those, shouldn't I?" She clutched at herself as if she were cold, even though her shirt now stuck to her sweaty back. "I just . . . can't believe that it was her," she murmured.

"Funny. You practically accused her of it yesterday!" Cassie snapped.

Heather's gaze turned hard. "Not the same thing, Detective Edwards. I was looking for a solution just as much as you were. This wasn't the one I thought I'd find. I mean, why kill the lieutenant? Why . . ."

She broke off and stared into the distance. Finally, she shook her head. Her hair slipped out of its ponytail holder, and the tie fell to the floor. "Look, get me the paperwork as soon as possible. I'll forward it to my supervisors in Olympia. I'll also get them started on paying out on those other claims. If you need me for anything, you can call me."

She hesitated for a moment, turning back toward the elevator banks, hoping that she might see Melanie emerge from one of them, and believing for a moment that what she just witnessed was one big mistake. Then slowly, Heather turned to make her way out of the building. Her feet shuffled along the linoleum. Cassie waited until she saw her disappear through the door on the far right side. Then she let out a snort. "Good riddance, I say."

"Cassie," Mark warned her.

"Look, at least she's out of our hair. Now maybe we can wrap up this case in peace." Cassie's gaze fell to the floor. "Although I have to admit, this wasn't the answer I wasn't expecting, either."

"Nor me." Mark took one last glance at the reports in his hand. Then he crumpled them up. "Why didn't I see this? Why didn't any of us see it?"

"Mark, you're not responsible. Who knows why she did it, or why she did any of it?"

"Then let's go try and figure that out, okay?"

Cassie nodded. They turned to make their way to the elevator. They entered the car with a few other people. Cassie made her way to its corner, gripped the elevator railing, closed her eyes, and took a deep breath. Mark regarded her, and then turned to face forward. The elevator lurched and began its ascent. "By the way, did you reach Julie?" Mark asked.

"I got her voice mail. Is it possible she's left town again?"

"It's possible. Even so, I still want her to look at Melanie's car. Having some eyewitness testimony would help bolster our case."

"But Julie said she didn't see who it was who lured her there, remember?"

Mark gave her a light tap on the arm and Cassie opened her eyes. They were at their floor. They headed for the conference room, but as they reached the door, Cassie grabbed his arm. "Mark? You don't really think Melanie's our arsonist, do you?"

"She has the capability to make it, Cassie. She knew what we were looking for, and she was in a prime position to prevent us from finding out what we needed to know. Besides, you saw how she adored fire."

"But it was a professional admiration, not of a pyromaniac. Anyway, why kill Anthony, and why go after Julie? More important, what does it have to do with any of the other fires?"

"Maybe nothing. Maybe there's no connection to any of the other fires, but . . ."

Just then, Mark's cell phone rang. He fished it out from his holder. "Detective Mark Daniels."

"It's me."

"Hey, Ty, what's going on?"

"I pulled Lieutenant Rutherford's phone records like you requested. You were right. He did make a call last night."

"To who?"

"Michelangelo Della Torre."

"Della Torre? About what time was that?"

"Nine twenty three p.m. The call was about seven minutes long."

"Thanks, Ty."

Mark broke the connection and tapped the phone against his chin. Mentally, Mark placed these newest pieces of the puzzle alongside the other evidence. According to the incident report, the fire company got the call around ten thirty. Melanie claimed she left work shortly after nine. Factoring in drive time, it left just enough time for Melanie to get to the lieutenant's house, knock him out, place him in his bed, and set his house ablaze. Mark's eyes fell to the notes sitting in the chair. Then again, if it was Melanie, why didn't she take the extra set of case notes?

"Mark?"

Mark turned. Cassie frowned. His face had that look on it: the one that she and those who most cared about him could not describe, except as one of a man obsessed and willing to find an answer to his question at any cost. "You wanna clue your partner into what you're thinking?"

"That we're still not seeing everything." He picked up the bag full of paper and shoved it into Cassie's hands. "See if you can get someone to make heads or tails of this, okay? I'll be back."

He headed back toward the main entrance. Curious, Cassie dropped the bag in a chair and followed him. "Mark? Where are you going?"

"To talk to Della Torre."

"Why?"

"Tyler says that according to the phone records, Lieutenant Rutherford called him shortly before he died. I'd like to know what they talked about."

"Right. A lot of good that'll do."

Mark turned back to face her. "Look, maybe we do have our arsonist. Maybe Melanie killed Anthony and tried to kill Julie. I'd like to know why, and maybe Della Torre knows. By the way, have we tracked down Kate yet?"

"No."

"Then get on that, too. I want her found."

"You think it's her?"

"She wears a similiar perfume. She also has the chemistry background. She works in a lab that has access to many of the chemicals that make up the accelerant. She didn't like Della Torre any more than the rest of us, and she's made the most recent threats to him. On top of that, she knew that Lieutenant Rutherford was working the case, and he was the same investigator that worked hers."

"But what does she have to do with the other arsons, and with Julie for that matter?"

"I don't know. Maybe if we find that connection, we can nail her for good. Call me if you find anything. I'll be back within the hour."

Cassie nodded and headed for her desk, while Mark headed for the elevators. The doors opened just as he made to hit the button. He stepped into it and jabbed at the ground level button. Within minutes, he was in his truck, heading for the business district. He tapped his fingers against the steering wheel, the events of the last 24 hours running through his head. The feeling that Della Torre was still the arsonist's true target had dogged him the moment he truly began to involve himself with the case. Lieutenant Rutherford must've started to believe the same thing. Why would he have called him, unless Lieutenant Rutherford thought that Della Torre knew who the arsonist was, even if Della Torre didn't realize it? Mark needed to get an answer from him, and warn him that he was still in danger.

Fifteen minutes later, Mark swung his truck into a visitor's parking spot and marched into the building's main lobby. He took the elevator to Della Torre's office floor. He walked out of the elevator just as Della Torre and his bodyguard emerged from the restroom. "Mr. Della Torre!" Mark called.

Della Torre turned. He eyed Mark as he approached. He didn't look happy to see him. In fact, he looked like he dreaded it. He glanced behind Mark, but saw no one else. "Detective Daniels, where's your environment-loving partner? I thought she would be with you, ready to go another round with me."

"Sir, I need to talk to you."

"Not right now. I have a client waiting."

He made to leave, but Mark stepped in his path. "It's about finding your son's killer, sir," Mark said loud enough for everyone to hear. "Surely, you can take five minutes out of your life for that."

Della Torre met his gaze. Except for the eyes, he would swear he was facing Robert Daniels in court again. Robert was one of the few attorneys who had made Della Torre earn his $500 an hour fee. Had Mark joined him, they would have been a formidable team. The two men continued their staring contest for about another thirty seconds. Then Della Torre straightened his tie and walked toward the glass doors. Once through them, he turned to the woman sitting in the lobby. "I'll be with you in a moment, Mrs. Gonzalez," he assured her. Then Della Torre gestured to his office door. "Come in, Detective," he murmured.

Mark stepped aside to let Della Torre lead the way into his office. Della Torre pointed to a chair, but Mark did not sit. Della Torre slammed the door shut and then made his way around to his chair, stopping to gaze out the window. "What is it you want to know, Detective?" Della Torre asked, not bothering to hold back his anger.

"Mr. Della Torre, are you aware that Lieutenant Rutherford died last night?"

Della Torre turned to face him, his gray eyebrows furrowed. "I read that there was a fire last night. I didn't realize that it was the lieutenant that died. You're certain?"

"Yes. However, when we pulled his phone records, they showed that he made a call to you last night, roughly an hour before the fire broke out."

"He did? Well, I don't remember hearing the phone ring. I must've missed him."

"You chatted for nearly seven minutes, sir."

There was silence between them. They stared at each other for some time. Finally, Della Torre blinked. "All right, Detective. Yes, the lieutenant did contact me. Satisfied?"

"Was it about this case?"

"He might've made mention of it."

"Are you certain, sir? You admit that he called you last night. Less than an hour later, a fire breaks out in his home, and he's found dead in his bed. We found copies of the case notes at his place. He was working on it there. Lieutenant Rutherford must've seen or read something that made him believe the arsonist is somehow connected to you alone. I need to determine how and why." Mark took a step toward Della Torre. Only Della Torre's desk stood between the two men. "Mr. Della Torre, if you know something, now would be the time to tell me," Mark added.

"I don't know anything."

"You have to know something. Why did the lieutenant call you last night? What did he ask you?"

Della Torre crossed his arms. "It's nothing, Detective."

"It has to be something for Lieutenant Rutherford to call you so late at night. You may have given him a clue to the identity of who's behind these fires. There's a part of me that still thinks that you were the intended target, and that maybe you still are."

"Why? Because I represented a client that I shouldn't have? Because like you, I'm good at my job? Believe me, I've seen and lived through more than my fair share of death threats. I'm beyond carrying now."

He does *know something.* Mark pressed forward. "What did he ask you, sir?"

"It was a silly question, Detective Daniels. In retrospect, I shouldn't have answered it. I doubt it has anything to do with what's happening now. Now, if you don't mind, I have a client waiting."

Believing that his words had their usual effect, he turned his back to Mark to stare at the pictures of his family and friends on the credenza behind his desk. After a few moments, his chin sank into his chest. He shook his head. "It can't be," Mark heard him mutter. "It simply can't be."

"Can't be what, sir?"

Della Torre turned back toward Mark, somewhat surprised that he still stood there. He looked as if he didn't want to tell Mark what was on his mind. Finally, Della Torre sighed. "The lieutenant asked me if I went by any nicknames."

"Nicknames?"

"One in particular." Della Torre blushed. "He asked if anyone ever called me 'Mickey.'"

Mark looked up from his note taking. "Mickey? Who called you that?"

"I'm certain a lot of people have behind my back. However, only one person was allowed to say it to my face; a little girl. Her name's Maggie Sinclair."

Mark's eyes opened wide. "I know that name. Her parents died in a fire. You represented her when she became a ward of the state."

Della Torre gave Mark a curious stare. "You know about that?"

"Your former secretary told us, but why would she call you that?"

"When I first met her, she had a hard time speaking. Her language skills were woefully underdeveloped. She couldn't pronounce my name, so I told her to call me that instead. It was an easy correlation for her to make." Della Torre's expression lightened somewhat, and he chuckled. "My hair was much darker then, you have to remember. I guess it helped her to remind her of the mouse."

For a fleeting moment, Mark could see why. With those eyes of his, darker hair, and his build, a child could see him as someone for whom they could seek comfort. He jotted this information down. "This girl, Maggie Sinclair? When was the last time you spoke to her?"

"The day her adoptive parents moved her out of the state, but that was 25 years ago."

"And you haven't had any contact with her?"

"She sent me a letter once when she was in her teens. I received another one from her in February, I believe. I didn't respond. She was one client that I didn't want to see or hear from again, if I could help it."

"Why is that, sir?"

Della Torre gave Mark a hard stare. "It's personal, Detective."

"Sir, I need to know. I thought from the start that you were the possible target. Now I'm positive, and that this Maggie Sinclair is behind these series of arsons."

Della Torre's expression turned into shock. He quickly recovered his courtroom demeanor. "No, Detective, I don't think so. Even if I was the target, then I understand why."

"Why would she want revenge on you?"

"I hurt her when she was small . . . betrayed her, is the best way to put it, I guess."

Mark stopped writing. "Betrayed," he murmured. Julie whispered the same thing at the storage facility site yesterday. What did Julie know that he didn't? He made a few more notations and then looked up again. He paused. In Della Torre's profile, Mark saw the grieving father emerge, but he thought he also saw something else. He wasn't sure, but to him, it seemed like a look of guilt. Had he tried to do something to help Maggie Sinclair that went beyond his representation as her attorney? "Mr. Della Torre, I'll ask you again: are you sure that you didn't know any of the other victims, or represent them in any way?"

"Outside of buying my wife's perfume at Sullivan's cosmetics counter, I had nothing to do with any of them. Their names don't ring any bells, and as for that house on Harlan? My wife and I aren't antique buffs."

"Perfume," Mark muttered. According to the chemical analysis, the arsonist scented their accelerant with a discontinued brand of perfume. Julie identified the scent the other day. Sullivan's Department Store probably sold it at one point. Did Maggie have some connection to the store? He realized that he needed to gain access to Maggie Sinclair's court files, even if they were still sealed. "Sir, do you still have that letter Maggie sent you?"

"No. I had my head of security burn it. She was obviously a troubled woman. It was the last thing my family needed to see."

"Why didn't you turn them over to the police?"

"It was one a thousands of threats. If I took every one of them seriously, I wouldn't be able to get out of bed, let alone leave my home."

"That may be true, sir, but turning them in may have helped to keep your son alive."

"Wait a minute. You don't really think she's responsible for all of this?"

"She might be sir, and I think I know where she is, and who she's become."

Without waiting for a response, Mark turned and made his way out of Della Torre's building. He reviewed what Della Torre had said. Apparently, Maggie Sinclair was alive and well, and now walking about as Katie Cetera. When he first arrested Melanie, he had not considered that a female might be behind these fires. Now it made sense, at least in the case of Della Torre. If she had such a beef with him, why didn't she kill him while he was representing her? More important, where was she now? He pulled out his cell phone and dialed Tyler's direct line. He answered on the first ring: "Tech Room, Sergeant Martin."

"Tyler, it's me. I need some more research done."

"Not on your tenant again? I'm getting stymied with that, just to warn you."

"No, I need you to run down some perfume for me."

There was a pause. Mark realized what he had said. Already, he could see Tyler's thin face breaking into a broad smile. "So, you're going to wine and dine her now to get the information you want. It's a smarter way to go, if you get my meaning. Just to let you know, Jessie would . . ."

"Not for Julie, Ty!" Mark argued, feeling his cheeks burn red hot. "Our arsonist is using a particular brand of perfume to scent their accelerant. Check to see if a Maggie Sinclair was one of the purchasers."

"You have the name of the brand?"

"Call upstairs to Lieutenant Michaels, or talk to Cassie. Get back to me ASAP. Also, double check on Katie Cetera's background. Find out if she was ever known by the name of Maggie Sinclair, okay?"

"I'm on it."

Mark hung up the phone. He reached his truck and heard a scratching sound behind him. He glanced back over his shoulder, but saw nothing. Shrugging, he dug for his keys. He hit the unlock button on his car remote. Then something pricked him in the back of the arm. A few seconds later, he became incredibly dizzy. He crumpled to the ground. Just before his eyes closed, he caught a look at the legs and feet of the person who had drugged him. All he saw were black stiletto heels. The scent of lavender perfume filled his nostrils. There was only one woman he knew who wore that combination, and she was the real arsonist. "Kate," he whispered. His eyes closed and he slumped over unconscious.

Christie stood over him, a gleeful look on her face. She expected him to be her with his smart-ass partner. Instead, he came alone. She bent down and moved his hair out of his face. "Nighty night, Detective," she said to him in a childish tone. "I have one hell of a bonfire planned, and you're the guest of honor."

XIV

Ambassador? Do you require assistance?

Julie made her way toward downtown Mason City in the late morning traffic. She reviewed what had occurred within the last 24 hours. First, she was attacked. With Julie's help, the detectives discovered the source of the mysterious scent she detected at the house and at the warehouse fire, only to have Lieutenant Rutherford die hours later. She recalled Heather's comment regarding the case, and her near accusation that the lieutenant or Melanie was the real culprit. Mark's confidence in them didn't offset the doubt forming within Julie's mind, especially after NIK discovered numerous case files where the arson investigator or a firefighter was found to be the party responsible. The investigators were convinced that the arsonist was a man; Julie wasn't. What about Melanie? Julie knew little about her. Could she be the girl that Julie was seeing? Was she the one causing all of this destruction? If so, why?

Ambassador? Did you not hear me?

Julie snapped out of her trance. "Sorry, NIK. I'm just lost in thought."

Your physical and emotional responses continue to oscillate between the same two points. Is there something you wish to discuss?

"No. Yes. I'm sorry, NIK. I'm just angry with myself. You know those files of Mr. Della Torre's? I was certain that there was something there. Those files were from 25 years ago, and all about children. I feel stupid for risking Russell to exposure. Then there's that girl I've been seeing and feeling. I'm convinced she's our arsonist. Why can't I find what it is that connects her to them?"

I have helped you as much as I can, Ambassador. I have not found a pattern in anything that you have provided. However, I have traced the symbol that you transmitted to me.

"You have? What is it?"

It appears to date back to Earth Calendar Year 350 B.C.E. It is closely linked to a nomad tribe that once resided in the jungles of what is now called Central America. From my analysis, it is meant to resemble a heart.

"A heart? I still don't see how it fits."

As Ambassador Magsimon stated, when your mind and body are rested, you will be able to see it. I must remind you that you have not slept in 80 Earth days.

Julie pulled into a parking spot on the garage's fourth floor. She shut off the engine, and then sighed. NIK was right. Her humanoid form was physically tired. She wanted to rest, but her mind would not close itself down.

If her thoughts were not on the fire, then they were on Anichia, the emergence ceremony, or a whole host of other things that kept her awake and chatting with NIK for hours into the night. How she longed to be able to share her worries with someone who actually breathed instead of with processors and microchips thousands of light years away, or bobbing orbs of energy that could never begin to understand.

She alighted from her vehicle, grabbed her messenger bag, and headed for the walkway, watching for Renee Blackwell the entire way. When she reached the lobby, a new thought occurred to her. Except for that brief chat in the conference room yesterday, she never really talked to the arson investigators, especially about the odd accelerant. With Lieutenant Rutherford dead, she needed to talk to Melanie. "No, I need to *touch* Melanie," she corrected herself. "It's the only way I'm going to know if they are the same person. Then all I have to do is convince Mark and Cassie of that, without telling them how I found out."

She walked through the main doors and once again, blinded their machines to the true contents of her bag. Then the thoughts of every person in the building hit her simultaneously. She paused long enough to re-establish her barriers, then adjusted her grip on her bag and walked to the elevator. She studied the marquee, learned where the arson investigators were housed, and rode the elevator to the ninth floor. As she reached the entrance a man emerged, his nose buried in a file. "Excuse me, could you tell me if Melanie Keegan is here?" Julie asked.

"No. She's downstairs in holding."

"Holding?"

His gaze moved from his file to her. "Yes. She's been arrested."

"Arrested?"

"Detective Daniels arrested her a few hours ago. She's being charged with those arsons she's been investigating."

Julie took a step back from him. "Which way are the holding cells?"

The man pointed toward the elevators she just exited. "Basement level." He took a quick perusal of Julie and her attire. "Although I'll doubt that you'll be allowed to see her."

"Why?"

"If she's smart, she'll wait until her attorney arrives."

Julie bit her bottom lip, considering her options. Then she realized there was nothing to consider. "Thank you."

She headed back to the elevators. A fellow passenger told her where the cells were. She journeyed down the narrow, beige-painted cement hallway. She sensed the anger, despair, fear, and hopelessness within the walls. She took a step back to collect herself. Then she rounded a corner, and walked into a tiny room. Two wooden chairs were against the left wall. To the right, at a metal desk too small for anyone to sit or work on, was a female officer. She was writing something on her clipboard and did not seem to hear Julie's approach. Julie thought it best not to disturb her until she was done. She folded her hands in front of her, watching the woman's actions, saying nothing. After about a minute, the clerk looked up. She peered over her half-rimmed spectacles at her, her expression one of irritation. "Yes?"

"I'd like to speak with Melanie Keegan, please?"

"Are you her attorney?"

Julie reached into her bag and retrieved her wallet. She flashed her bar card at the clerk. The guard grunted and pointed a finger. "Bag, please."

Julie handed her the messenger bag. The clerk rifled through it. She played with the buttons on Julie's phone long enough to satisfy herself that the device was not a bomb. Then she reached inside and retrieved a hollow aluminum pipe at the bottom of the main compartment. She tossed it up in the air a few times. It weighed almost nothing, but it did not stop her from feeling uneasy about its presence. She gave Julie a sardonic grin. "A runner, I take it?"

"It belonged to a friend of mine. It used to be his good luck charm."

"Right." The guard raised an eyebrow at her, then stuck the pipe back and handed Julie back her bag. She jerked her head backwards. "This way."

She opened the huge metal door that sectioned off the holding cells from the cramped waiting area. It seemed even tighter back here. Melanie was in the second to last cell. The clerk stopped in front of it and Julie peered around her. Melanie sat there on the strip of padding, staring at the gray cement wall that marked the left side of her cell. Fresh tear trails were visible on her still soot-covered face, and her half-braided hair was a wreck. She smelled of smoke. Her hands absently toyed with the zipper to her soiled jumpsuit, pulling it up and down. Julie heard the teeth opening and closing. The clerk banged on the cell with her clipboard. The hallway filled with a ringing metallic sound. Julie cringed at it. Melanie jumped and turned in the direction of the sound. She saw Julie before she saw the clerk, and her eyes opened wide. The clerk jerked her head toward Julie. "Your attorney's here," she barked.

Melanie was stunned. Then she nearly laughed aloud. Julie gave her a quick shake of her head. *Don't laugh,* Melanie thought she heard her say. *I want to help you.* Melanie gave Julie a look of disdain, leaned back against the cold cement wall, and crossed her arms. Julie turned to the officer. "I'd like to speak with my client alone, please," she said in a quiet voice.

The officer gave Julie and then Melanie a hard stare. Melanie continued to look at Julie with a questioning eye. Julie gave her a slight nod. For some reason, Melanie felt comforted by the look of sincerity in Julie's eyes. Melanie turned to the clerk and gave her a nod of acknowledgement. The officer glared at Julie, who just smiled. Finally, she grunted and turned back to her desk. The women listened to her hard steps and clinking gun belt. Then the door banged shut behind her. Melanie waited a good ten seconds before turning to face Julie again. She raised an eyebrow. "You're my attorney?"

"Yes, for the next few minutes. I wanted to ensure that we could speak in private."

"So you're not an attorney."

"Actually, I am." Julie handed Melanie a business card. "I don't like to advertise the fact to others. It makes the negotiations I conduct that much more . . . complicated," Julie finished.

"I thought that's what attorneys do." Melanie shrugged. Whatever game Julie was playing, she would play along, so long as it meant she wouldn't be spending any more time than was necessary in this place. She laid the card down next to her on the metal bench and pulled her right leg up so that her knee touched her chest. She stared hard at Julie. "What do you want?"

Julie set her messenger bag down on the floor, but did not come any closer. "I'm here to help you if I can, and if you will let me."

"You? Help me?"

"Yes."

Melanie raised an eyebrow. "You realize that Detectives Edwards and Daniels are upstairs right now looking for more evidence so that they can charge me with trying to kill you, too?"

"No. Even if they are, they won't find it, because I know that you didn't try to kill me."

"You do?"

"Yes."

"Why?"

"Because I don't believe that you're the person behind these arsons, and if instinct serves me correctly, neither does Mark."

"Really? Well, excuse me if I don't believe the truth of that statement, especially since it was Detective

Daniels that placed the handcuffs on my wrists and ordered me dragged me down here."

Julie leaned back against the wall opposite of Melanie's cell. "I've talked to him about this case. His instincts are leading him down a different path, but he's not certain it's the right one, or of its destination."

"And what do your instincts say?"

"My instincts tell me that you're in there instead of the real person behind these crimes. I want to help him and you figure out who it is."

"And you expect me to believe that?"

"Not right away."

"Then why all the deception with the guard?"

"I needed to talk to you. I've been doing my own research on these cases. There're many similarities, but I've also discovered too many inconsistencies." Julie clasped her hands behind her back. She tilted her head to see into Melanie's face. "Also, I don't think that you would intentionally kill the man who was your biggest supporter. I also know he was a man who regarded you as being a daughter to him."

Melanie gave Julie a blank stare. How could someone who spent so little time with them know and understand how she and Lieutenant Rutherford felt about each other? She brought her other leg up and leaned forward to clutch them to her chest. Her posture took on the stature of someone who looked totally defeated. "I would never have done that to him, not in a million years," she whispered to her knees. "He cared about me. He really did. He wanted so much to teach me everything he knew, and I wanted to know everything he knew, you know? He was helping me to understand how much of a difference I could make, even if I couldn't work the pumps or carry the hoses. I wanted to be as good as him. I wanted to make him proud of me."

"From what I saw Melanie, he already was."

Melanie looked up. New tears filled her eyes. "No one thinks a girl can handle being an arson investigator, let alone a firefighter," she argued over the knot in her throat.

"If I may say so Melanie, I think you've proven that a woman of strength can do just about anything she sets out to do, provided that she's given an equal chance."

Melanie took in Julie's words of comfort. It was a full minute before she finally met Julie's gaze. She angrily wiped the tears away with the back of her hand. "So, what makes you so sure that I'm not the one?"

Julie lowered her head. That was the problem: she wasn't totally certain. The images of the girl would appear, but never stay long enough for Julie to pinpoint any details. All she registered was the anger, the pain, and the betrayal. "I don't know. I do have a few questions to ask you, if you don't mind."

Melanie stared about the gray-painted cement walls. "Why not? I'm not going anywhere for a while."

"Thank you. First, did you have any great tragedies in your life as a young child, say between the ages of five and eight?"

Melanie was taken aback by that question. "Well, my parents died when I was seven."

"How did they die?"

"In a car crash. It was a tough time, but I had lots of relatives to take care of me. Why's that important?"

Julie took a step backwards and began to pace in front of Melanie's cell. Melanie didn't understand the action. It was as if she was trying to reconcile something in her mind. "Julie? Are you all right?"

Julie gave her what Melanie interpreted to be a nod of acknowledgement. "You were a firefighter at one point, were you not?"

"I still am, in a way."

"But being an arson investigator wasn't your first ambition, was it?"

"No. I truly wanted to be a firefighter, but it's a tough, physical job. Yes, fire fascinates me, but not in the sense that I would become a pyromaniac."

Julie stopped pacing. "Fascinate?"

"Most pyromaniacs like to see things burn. It's . . ." Melanie thought to equate the thrill a pyromaniac feels to the sensations a man or woman experience during intercourse, but since she knew so little about Julie's background, she wasn't certain if Julie would take offense to the comparison. Instead, she put it into terms she thought Julie might better understand: "It's like being a chocoholic, and staring at a table where the world's best chocolate desserts are laid out before you. You'll get full after a while, but you'll keep on going back because of how good you feel from consuming it."

Julie beamed. "Yes, now I understand what Mark was trying to tell me the other night. The pyromaniac wants to see the fire consume whatever he's focused his anger on. He does it for the thrill, or for the power he feels when he sets one, and the power that he feels he lacks in his life."

"Correct. A lot of people in my field of work can develop that tendency, though in most it starts young; sometimes as young as four or five."

"And you still believe the arsonist to be a man?"

Melanie chuckled. "Why? You really think a woman's behind these fires?"

"I'm just trying to keep all of options open, that's all."

"Well, it's happened. If it's a woman, she's really gone off the deep end. There's no reason for burning what she's burning."

Unless they're personal to her, Julie thought, recalling the pain she felt every time the imagery came to her. If that were true, determining that relationship became more important than ever. "Melanie, how many female arson investigators are there in the state?"

"I don't know for certain. Why?"

"How did you wind up becoming an investigator? Why aren't you still putting out fires, instead of trying to determine what caused them?"

Melanie became intrigued. Julie had an actual curiosity about her! Melanie stood and walked over to the bars that separated them. As she grabbed them, Julie took note of their appearance. They were calloused and the nails bitten to the quick. However, the fingers were stubby, not long like the fingers she saw on the girl in her imagery. "I blew out my knee fighting a warehouse blaze in Seattle. Since I couldn't lug hoses for a time, they moved me into the investigation area. They figured with my knack for chemistry, and my somewhat curious nature, it would be a good fit. It was one of the few things they were right about, it seems."

Julie agreed. Melanie's dogged determination was the reason they had even found the accelerant at the last three arson scenes, and detected the perfume subtlety layered underneath it. It was probably also the key reason why Melanie sat in a jail cell instead of with the others in the conference room. "Melanie, does the perfume *Romantic Interlude* mean anything to you?"

"Other than it's the perfume mixed in with the accelerant our arsonist is using? No. However, I wish my sense of smell was as acute as yours. Maybe I could've sniffed the arsonist out."

Julie worked to keep her face neutral. She hoped that Melanie had learned something else that perhaps NIK had not discovered. NIK had already researched the perfume maker's manufacturer, their ingredient growers, their distributors, and all of its sales since it was discontinued from the market about a year ago, with no success. She gave Melanie a nod. "Thank you, Melanie. I'm going to go see what I can do to get you out of there. I'll be right back."

Julie picked up her bag. She had thrown the strap over her shoulder and was heading for the door, when Melanie called out to her: "Julie, wait!"

Julie faced her again. She thought Melanie had called her back because she didn't want to be in this place alone. Then she studied Melanie's face. It had a strange look on it. "Smell. That's it," she whispered.

"What's it, Melanie?"

"It's what I was trying to tell them upstairs. I can't stand most perfumes. If a perfume gets too potent, I have trouble breathing. In fact, when I first caught the scent at the warehouse, I thought I was going to have to go to the hospital. I hardly noticed it at Mr. Della Torre's storage place."

"Did you pick up the scent at my fire?"

"No, but then again, I was one of the last ones there. By then, your house was totally consumed, but at the warehouse, it was everywhere. I had to wear my firefighter's mask while we were outside. I knew that you got some on your clothes, so I thought it was you, but I never detected it from you after that night."

Melanie's voice trailed off. She looked as if she were in pain. "Melanie? What is it?"

Melanie gripped her hair and started pacing in a circle. "I thought . . . I'm certain that I caught the scent of this particular accelerant someplace else, but not here. It was in Seattle. It was the last fire I worked before I got hurt. A woman died in it. I think her name was Christie Augustine."

Julie suddenly realized what Melanie said. She too had picked up the scent somewhere else as well, but it wasn't at any of the sites. It was here, at this building, before she sniffed those perfumes for Mark. "Melanie, do you remember when that fire took place?"

"Gosh, it's been at least a year or two. I'm not sure."

Julie stared at her for a moment. Then she reached into her bag and pulled out her phone. She tapped on the screen a few times. Melanie watched Julie study what appeared on it. Julie looked up. There was a glimmer of something in her eyes that Melanie couldn't translate. Suddenly, Julie turned to leave. Frantic, Melanie reached through the bars and grabbed Julie's arm. Julie didn't expect the touch, and it startled her. Julie turned to look at her. There was no image of a screaming girl, no flashes of pain, no sense of betrayal. All she felt from Melanie was fear and uncertainty. "Wait! I thought you were going to help me!"

"I am, Melanie. I'm going to talk to the others." She smiled and patted Melanie's hand. "You'll be out of there soon. I promise."

Melanie bit her bottom lip. She didn't know or understand why she was placing her trust and her life in the hands of one of the would-be victims, or the arsonist herself. All she wanted was out of this place. She released her grip on Julie's arm. Julie gave her a reassuring smile. "I will get you out of there, Melanie. Trust me."

Melanie hesitated. Then she gave Julie a reluctant nod. "Okay."

Julie adjusted the bag on her shoulder and headed out of the cell area. She breezed past the guard who gave her a curious look as she departed, her mind focused on her next task. This one allowed her to tackle two issues at once. She took the elevator down one more level to the subbasement. She glanced at the sign before her, then turned right and headed to the end of the hall. She saw a series of doors on its left side. She followed the hall to the last one, a small, windowless room. She poked her head around the corner of the rack nearest her. A man sat in front of two high-resolution computer screens, concentrating on something. Julie knocked softly on the wall. He startled and whipped around in his chair. He made out the shape of her form against the blue-black darkness, but he didn't recognize her. A scowl came to his face. "Who are you?"

"I'm sorry to intrude. You're Tyler Martin, correct?"

"Who wants to know?"

"I'm Julie Warren? Mark's new tenant?"

Tyler wheeled his chair to the opposite wall and reached out to flick on the overhead light. Now that the light was better, he could tell why she intrigued Mark. He tried not to chuckle. *Hard to believe this kid controls more wealth than the top three billionaires in the world.* Tyler took a deep breath before standing up and holding out a hand. "It's nice to meet you."

"And you, Tyler. Mark's made mention of you a time or two. I understand that you and he are close."

"We're best friends, if that's what you mean."

"Yes. He trusts your judgment and you trust his."

He sat down at his desk again and adjusted his keyboard. He turned his chair around to face the monitor again, his back to Julie. "Civilians aren't allowed in here."

"I won't be long. I need a favor of you, that's all."

"A favor?"

Julie reached back and closed the door to his office. She turned off the overhead light, because she knew that was how he preferred to work. The research done on him, coupled with what Julie had gathered from shaking his hand, told her that this was the right course.

Outside of the blue-white glow from the monitor and the occasional blinking lights from the servers, the room was in compete darkness. "I was hoping that you could help me do a little research."

"What kind of research?"

"I'm trying to gather some information."

"Information?"

"In regards to these fires. I'm trying to help Mark, and I need your help to do it."

Computer keyboard keys clicked in their ears. "Why?"

"I heard that you're good."

"Who did you hear that from?"

"I have my sources."

"Well, whoever you talked to was exaggerating. I'm not that good. Now I think you need to go."

"That's not what I heard. Not only are you a brilliant researcher when it comes to computer-stored information, I understand that you're a gifted hacker; that you can dig up information discreetly and quickly. I need you to help me do the same thing." She took a step forward, which put her directly behind his chair. "Like the searches that you did on me," she added in a solemn tone. "The ones you haven't told Mark about?"

Julie saw his shoulders straighten and his jaw clench. His fingers stopped moving. "What searches?" he asked, trying to keep his tone conversational. "I don't even know you."

Julie leaned over his shoulder to stare at his monitor. Her mouth was only inches away from his right ear. "I know what you and Mark have been up to in relation to me," she said in a throaty tone, his breath tickling his earlobe. "Despite your skills, you should know that hacking is a criminal offense. If I were a vengeful person, I could have you thrown in jail for what you did, like they almost did when you were 16?"

Tyler glanced at her from the corner of his eyes. Beads of sweat formed on his head. His juvenile records were sealed once he completed his sentence, and no one outside of the police chief and the judge knew. "How do you know about that?" he asked, his voice shaking slightly.

"Let's just say I have methods for obtaining information that are far more reliable than yours," she assured him. She straightened, adjusted her bag, and crossed her arms. "Don't worry, Tyler. I won't say anything to anyone, but you have been warned."

Tyler turned to face her. The look in her eyes was one that meant business. "What kind of information do you need?"

"I'm looking for any suspicious fires set in Seattle over the last two years and the investigations conducted on them, both criminal and civil."

"Shouldn't you be checking with arson for that?"

"I would. Unfortunately, the best person to ask that question is dead."

"Oh."

Tyler turned back to his computer screen and tapped on a few more keys. After a few seconds, a list appeared. There were hundreds of newspaper clippings dealing with fires in the Seattle region. Several dealt with fires where there were fatalities. A few of them had photographs of the victims. As Julie read, she thought she recognized one of them, or at least she thought she did. Julie caught a glimpse of the dead woman's haunted green eyes and for an instant, saw the little girl on the porch again. She shuddered. Then she felt eyes on her. She looked to her right. Tyler was staring at her, his head propped up with his right hand, a "see all, know all" smile on his face. She gave him a confused look. "Is that all there is?"

"It's what's available to the public. Anything civil you'll have to go to the appropriate party, and unless you work for them or are one of the relatives, you won't get anything, and I won't get it for you." Tyler leaned back in his chair and crossed his arms. "So, any particular reason why you're interested in fires set in Seattle?"

"No, it's just something Miss Keegan mentioned."

"Ms. Keegan? As in Melanie Keegan, the arson investigator who's now under arrest?"

Julie didn't answer. That was enough for him. He reached out and with a keystroke, deleted the display. Tyler flicked on the overhead lamp again and stood up. He squared himself to her. "I think you better leave, Ms. Warren," he said, his tone guarded.

Julie straightened as well. "What I'm asking for is not out of line."

"Right, except that you're using police property and threats to get it."

"True, but . . ."

"Why the hell do you need it?"

"It's my belief that she's not the one responsible. I'm trying to help her."

Tyler crossed his arms. It was time to use what he knew about Julie Warren against her. "What are you, her attorney or something, because if you are . . ."

"It's research, nothing more."

They continued to stare at each other. She knew that her words didn't have the effect she desired. He still wore a look of distrust on his face. She nodded. "You're right, Tyler. Perhaps I have overstepped my bounds. However, I do appreciate what you've done."

She stepped away from him and made her way to the door. She only took two steps when Tyler called to her: "I plan to tell Mark that you were here."

"Yes, you could, but you won't."

"You wanna bet?"

He watched with delight as she paused in the doorway. The look on her face was one who was trying to find the best way to dissuade him from his planned course of action. She returned to his side. She gave him a humbled shrug and held out her hand. Tyler gave it a passing glance. "Bribes don't work on me."

"Tyler, I am trying to help Melanie, but I'm also trying to help Mark with his case. However, if you feel that I've overstepped my bounds, then please tell Mark I was here. I won't mind, nor will I hold it against you."

He exhaled and eyed her hand. Then he wiped his sweaty right hand on his jeans and grasped her extended hand. Once they connected, Julie traveled through his brain and deleted the brain impulses that had formed during his encounter with her. Within thirty seconds of her departure, Tyler wouldn't remember anything about this meeting. Meanwhile, NIK removed all traces of the search request from his computer. She signaled Julie of its completion. "Thank you, Tyler," she told him, a smile coming to her face. "I really do appreciate it."

"You're welcome, Ms. Warren."

"Oh, Ms. Warren's too formal. Please, call me Julie." Tyler shrugged. "Fine . . . Julie."

She chuckled and walked back to the doorway. She waited until he had resettled himself into his chair before turning and departing from the room. Before she was ten steps down the hallway, she knew her devilry had worked. She heard Tyler get up from his chair and approach his door. He seemed confused about something. After a bit, he returned to his chair and his work.

She rounded the corner and faced the elevator. Julie punched the button and looked up at the indicator. The sense of accomplishment she felt with Tyler was replaced with determination. Her face took on a hard look. "NIK?"

I crossed-checked the additional names you discovered. There was no connection to any of the other victims, and no correlation to you, the Foundation, Melanie Keegan, or Mr. Della Torre.

The doors opened and Julie made way for the police technicians on it to disembark. She entered the device and pressed the button for the seventh floor. "Yes there is, NIK, and the proof of it is upstairs. I need to get back into the conference room."

Ambassador, you have already transferred that information to my database. I could recall it for you, if you wish.

"No, NIK. I've missed something, I know I have, and something tells me that missing piece will put this whole mystery into clarity."

XV

The elevator doors opened up on the seventh floor and Julie disembarked. Blinding sunshine shown off the walls and the glass displays cases mounted on them. She gazed out past the cityscape toward the hazy, tree-filled horizon. Somewhere out there was a woman whose torturous past prompted her to kill two people, and perhaps more. Julie knew that Melanie wasn't that woman. Mark's arsonist was still out there. Julie needed to find her, or find a way to help Mark do it without exposing herself.

She turned from the window toward the precinct doors, pushed open the left door, and studied the surroundings. Then she looked toward the main conference room. Lieutenant Michaels and Cassie were inside, walking back and forth with papers in their hands. She deposited her messenger bag in Mark's chair, crossed the room, and knocked on the door. Lieutenant Michaels looked up from her reading. She waved Julie inside. Julie poked her head in the doorway. "Hello, ladies. How's it going?"

"Not well," Lieutenant Michaels mumbled. She paused long enough to look at her. "I take it you heard about Lieutenant Rutherford."

"Yes. I went to talk to Melanie about what happened, but someone there told me that she's been charged with his murder. Do you really think she's responsible?"

"That's what we're trying to determine."

"And not having Lieutenant Rutherford's experience is really hurting us right now," Cassie moaned, slamming the papers she clutched hard onto the table. It caused a breeze that ruffled the stacks of paper and blew some of them to the floor. Lieutenant Michaels glared at Cassie. Cassie caught her commander's gaze and contritely moved to straighten them.

"Where's Mark?"

"He went to see Della Torre to clear up something that Lieutenant Rutherford asked him."

Julie closed the door firmly behind her. She stepped around the near corner, and noticed a set of scorched and water-stained papers in a plastic bag. She frowned. "Where did you get those?" she asked the women, pointing at it.

"One of the junior investigators found copies of the case notes at Lieutenant Rutherford's place," Lieutenant Michaels said. "He was working on the file at home. According to his coworkers, it was routine."

"Was he looking at anything in particular?"

"From what we can tell, he had been focusing on the names of the owners. He must've thought there was some sort of connection, but even if he found one, they're too smoke and water stained to read."

Julie watched as the women busily shuffled papers about. She turned her attention to the board. They had added Lieutenant Rutherford's house to the list. Under his, they had added another name: Mickey. "Cassie?"

"Yes, Julie?"

"Where did that name come from?" Julie asked, pointing to the board.

"Mickey? It's one of the few words we were able to make out from those notes. We think it references Della Torre. That's what Mark went to check out."

"Mickey," Julie mumbled. She continued to stare at the board, working to stay out of their way, hoping that she missed something the first time she saw it. She focused in on the scant notes regarding Lieutenant Rutherford's fire. "Lieutenant Michaels?"

"Yes, Julie?"

"The fire at the lieutenant's home? Do we know what started it?"

"Melanie set fire to his mattress, we're thinking," Cassie replied.

Julie turned at the sound of that statement. "What did you say?"

"He was smoking in bed and he fell asleep. She used just enough accelerant to get the fire ablaze. He was so asleep that he didn't wake up. That's what the fire chief concluded."

Julie's thoughts continued to churn on this new development. Then she shook her head. "No, I don't think so."

Lieutenant Michaels paused in her actions. "Why?"

"I just came from talking to her. I don't believe she did it."

"Julie, an anonymous witness saw a woman meeting her description come out of the house shortly before the fire began. She was the first one at the scene. She made the 9-1-1 call," Cassie countered.

"But she didn't kill him," Julie disagreed.

"Melanie was feeling the heat and she acted. Even if don't believe that, you've met the man. You saw him! He might've been a really good arson investigator, but he was a chain smoker if I ever met one. Personally, I'm surprised that it didn't happened sooner."

"No, Cassie. I mean if Melanie killed him, she wouldn't have killed him in his bed."

Cassie folded her arms and began to tap her right foot against the floor. Granted, Mark may be smitten with Julie the way a professor was fascinated by an exceptional student, but she wasn't that great. If anything, she was becoming an insufferable know it all. "And, you know that how?"

"I stopped by the scene when you were there, and I talked to one of his neighbors. When I told her what was probably suspected, she told me that it was impossible."

"Impossible? Why would she say that?" Lieutenant Michaels asked.

"She told me that Lieutenant Rutherford was an insomniac," Julie replied.

Cassie unfolded her arms. She stared at Julie and then at his boss. Then she reached for a notebook situated in the middle of the table. She flipped through a few pages. She ran her fingers down until she hit a name halfway down the page. She and Mark interviewed the neighbors before they left the scene. Mark had an untidy scrawl, but he made the same notation. He had also put a question mark beside it. Cassie understood that shorthand note. He wanted to go back and clarify what the witness had said. "Grace Waters? Is that who you talked to?"

"Yes. She lived next to him. She told me that more than likely, he would have slept in his recliner, if he slept at all. She said she often saw him roaming the neighborhood at night, smoking and muttering about cases. Besides, Lieutenant Rutherford was more than Melanie's trainer. He was her mentor. They spent a lot of time together. Melanie would've known that. That's why I don't think she would have killed the lieutenant in his bed."

Cassie read Mark's notes again. She had dismissed what Mrs. Waters had said to Mark. Hearing Julie repeating it made her feel queasy. Lieutenant Michaels turned her attention to the board. "Judy Samuelson and Lloyd Branson," Lieutenant Michaels began to read, "Hubert Raich, Anthony Della Torre, Simon Birmingham III, Archie Sullivan, and possibly, Lawrence Rutherford. What do these people or the property they own have in common?"

There was a rap at the door and Detective Harry Carson stuck his head into the room. "Hey, boss? Tyler's on the phone. He's looking for something for Mark regarding these arsons."

"Thanks, Harry." Lieutenant Michaels turned to Julie. "Excuse me, Julie. Cassie, you had better come along. Let's check to see if Lieutenant Rutherford's insomnia is documented anywhere."

While Lieutenant Michaels and Cassie walked toward the lieutenant's office, Julie remained in the room. Her eyes moved back and forth across the board. Simultaneously, she recalled her notes and fought to find some sort of pattern. Then her eyes narrowed. She had already eliminated the Foundation's house from the list, and she felt safe about taking away Lieutenant Rutherford's fire. "It wasn't just the buildings the arsonist targeted, but the people. The arsonist and the victims have a relationship. I need to find it."

Julie looked to her left. Lieutenant Rutherford's plastic-covered notes were still on the chair. She looked out to see if the two women were approaching. Then she picked them up. Where the paper wasn't burned, the ink had ran or smeared. She placed a hand on top of the paper. With a thought, she sent a series of energy waves through the plastic that dried out the paper without melting or destroying anything else. Once they were dry, she began to study them. The ink was still smeared. However, Julie's immortal-enhanced eyesight could still read them. The top sheet was a list of all the properties and their owners. Lieutenant Rutherford had drawn a red line through her property. Like her, he had eliminated the Foundation's house from the list. Julie read further, her sight penetrating through the top page to the pages underneath. Two pages down, Lieutenant Rutherford had drawn arrows connecting all of the last names together to names and places outside of the case circle. He had started to draw another line, but it look like he had stopped midway. Julie followed its logical progression toward the lower left-hand corner. The name written there was Maggie Sinclair. "Maggie Sinclair," Julie whispered. "I've seen this name before, too."

She pushed her glasses up onto her forehead and looked closer. To her eyes, there was something else written on the page, but there was no ink. However, she felt the impression of words. Julie concluded that Lieutenant Rutherford had written something else on another piece of paper. She glanced to stare around the squad room and into Lieutenant Michael's office. She and Cassie were still there, deep in conversation. The rest of the staff was engaged in other activities. No one was paying attention to her. Julie returned her attention to the papers. She traced over the indentation with her index finger. With her powers, she penetrated the plastic and layers of papyrus to feel for the imprint his writing had left. It wasn't a trick she realized. Lieutenant Rutherford had rewritten two names: Michelangelo Della Torre and Maggie Sinclair. Next to Della Torre's name, Lieutenant Rutherford had written "Mickey." Next to Maggie's name, it looked like he had tried to write out something, but stopped after the first three letters: H, E, and A. Julie ran her fingers over it again to make sure that was what she felt. Disgusted, she sat the notes back down on the desk and studied the board again. *Hea? What kind of word is that?* Julie took one more look at the victims' names. Then the realization of what it could mean came to her. Was it possible? "NIK?"

Yes, Ambassador?

"Access the Washington State computer systems. Search their employee records for a Heather McCade, please. She should work for the state's insurance fraud division."

Accessing.

There was a moment of silence. Then NIK spoke: *Ambassador? There was one match for a Heather Elaine McCade. However, she worked for the state health care authority's mental health division. According to the records, she resigned from her position sixteen months ago.*

Even more confused, Julie retrieved the Illani scanner she kept in her bag. Then she searched for the business card Heather gave her that evening at the Foundation's house. The image of the little girl started there, when Julie tried to approach the house. Now in hindsight, maybe she didn't see the image because of her actions, but because Heather had approached her from behind. Her fingertips glided over its edge. The image returned almost at once. This time, the girl had Heather's expressionless face. She also had long, kinky brown hair, not the thin hair that Heather had, and green eyes, not brown. When the image faded, Julie stepped back for a minute, thinking hard. Why didn't she sense this from it before? Then again, were the girl and Heather truly the same person? She placed the business card on top of the scanner. "NIK, scan this card for traces of DNA or fingerprints. Run your results against every computer record you can access and against anything in the files Russell scanned."

Accessing.

The scanner glowed for a split second. Julie began to pace, staring at the board, then back at the file. "A condemned home, a vacant medical office building, a deserted department store warehouse, an attorney's storage facility, and an abandoned manufacturing plant: those targets I can somewhat understand. The Foundation's house is the oddity, the only residential property the arsonist burned. Why didn't the arsonist target the people's residences, or the people themselves?" Then she thought back to the image of the girl screaming when she had toured the damage of the Foundation's house. At two of the sites, they found that weird symbol. NIK concluded that it was an ancient version of a heart. "But not just any heart," Julie theorized. "It's a broken heart. She feels betrayed, angry, wronged. Could Heather be that girl? Was Della Torre the one who betrayed her? What about the others? What did they do to her?"

Ambassador, I have completed my search. I have concluded that the woman who gave you the business card is Maggie Sinclair.

"Heather is Maggie Sinclair? How's that possible?"

The fingerprint information for Heather McCade on file with the state does not match what is on the card. Additionally, I ran a comparison of the fingerprint and DNA information on the card against all records available. Two matches occurred: one for a Maggie Ann Sinclair, based on information gathered shortly after her parents died in Earth Calendar Year 1979, and one for a Christie Elizabeth Augustine, based on information gathered during her last physical five years ago. They are identical.

"Christie Augustine. Melanie mentioned that woman. She died in a Seattle fire, more than a year ago. NIK, how did you find Maggie's information?"

Maggie Sinclair's file survived the fire at the storage facility.

Julie turned to look at the board. "Go on."

According to that case file, Maggie Sinclair became a ward of the state after her parents' death. Michelangelo Della Torre was the attorney who represented her interests. I cross-referenced the Sinclairs. An Archibald Sullivan owned the department store where Maggie's mother worked. A Dr. Hubert Raich was Maggie's primary physician up until the age of seven. Lloyd Branson owned the manufacturing facility where Maggie's father worked until he was injured in a home-related accident.

"Good. Now most of the names made sense. Each building targeted was owned or ran by someone from Maggie's past; someone who had, at some point in time she felt had caused her some sort of harm or pain. What about the condemned house? Did her parents own it?"

No, Ambassador. According to their tax records, the Sinclairs may have rented it for a time until they moved into the home where they died. Judy Samuelson took ownership of the property after they vacated it. She held it until her death in Earth Calendar Year 1999.

Julie retrieved the photograph of the condemned house from the bulletin board. "When did they leave it?"

Approximately six weeks after her father was injured, according to the insurance records of his employer. He suffered burns in a fire they believed was deliberately set by a member of the family. They refused to pay his medical claim, and terminated his employment. According to court records, the property owner forced them to move.

"And that would explain why there were no matches when you ran that name check. Maggie's father never owned the condemned house; therefore it wouldn't have come up!"

Julie picked up the business card and then stared at the picture of the condemned home. Within it, Julie saw Heather as a child. She stood on the porch, her green eyes glaring back at her. Her brown hair was knotted and disheveled, her clothes ragtag and worn and at least a size to small for her. The bloody-nailed fingers that wrapped around the railing were long and thin, like Heather's were now. Julie saw deep red welts and bruises on her arms, and a yellow and purple bruise healing above her left eye. "NIK, outside of the fire, is there any evidence of childhood trauma in Maggie's past?"

There is a psychological profile in her file dated just after the fire took place. The examiner at the time indicated that she may have been physically and sexually abused, although there is nothing to indicate that in any of Dr. Raich's files. However, both Dr. Raich and the examiner noted her peculiar fascination with fire and anything associated with it. Counseling was strongly recommended.

"That explains the images that I've been seeing, but then why target our house? Simon and I didn't know her or her family. We had no reason to, unless she saw it." Julie stole another glance out the conference room window. Lieutenant Michaels and Cassie were approaching. "She had to have seen it at some point," Julie continued. "For some odd reason, it triggered a memory, perhaps something dealing with the abuse and the neglect. She dealt with it the only way she knew how: she burned the place to the ground. NIK, how did Maggie's parents die?"

Both parents were heavy smokers. According to the report, their bed caught on fire when a lit cigarette fell onto the mattress. Their deaths were ruled accidental.

"I doubt that. More than likely, Maggie set the fire herself. Already a firebug at age seven and no one caught it. Lieutenant Rutherford supposedly died while smoking in bed as well, but I don't believe that either. I think Maggie realized that he was coming closer to the truth, so she killed him and framed Melanie for it. What happened to the other owners?"

Lloyd Branson, Hubert Raich, and Archie Sullivan all died within the last five years in fires at their residences. The police are treating Dr. Raich's death as suspicious.

"Why?"

Dr. Raich and his wife died in a fire that started in his bedroom mattress. However, their medical histories showed they never smoked.

The doorknob clicked. "Thanks, NIK," she whispered, just as the door opened.

The women caught her voice as they walked inside. They looked around, then at Julie. They didn't notice a phone in her hand. "Who were you talking to?" Lieutenant Michaels asked curiously.

Julie smiled. "Myself. It's a habit of mine when I have a problem I can't solve."

"Well, we have one." Lieutenant Michaels closed the door and leaned against it, sighing. "I wish Mark was here. He'd probably have an answer for us in a snap."

"I think he did have the answer, Lieutenant," Julie said in a firm voice. "He just didn't realize it at the time."

Cassie and Lieutenant Michaels looked at her. "He did?" Lieutenant Michaels asked.

"I've been going over everything again, and I've reached a conclusion." Julie paused. "I think your arsonist is Heather McCade."

"Heather?" Cassie gave her a dubious look and snorted. "That's a new one."

"I'm serious, Cassie."

The two women looked at each other, then at Julie. "What makes you say that?" Lieutenant Michaels asked.

Julie picked up bag of notes, returning them to their original state before removing the scorched and waterlogged pages and spreading them on the table. She pointed to the circles Lieutenant Rutherford had drawn around the names and the notation for Maggie Sinclair. Then she pulled Mark's notebook toward her. "Mark had made a note regarding researching what happened to a Maggie Sinclair. When I saw the name,

I remembered looking at some of Della Torre's files that had survived the fire to see if there was any connection. One of the files that survived was for a girl named Maggie Sinclair."

Cassie looked at her. "Heather is Maggie Sinclair? The girl that his former secretary mentioned?"

Lieutenant Michaels shook her head. "I don't see the connection."

"According to the psychological case notes that were in it, there was evidence to suggest that Maggie may have been physically and sexually abused by her parents. Not only that, her parents died in a fire," Julie explained. "She was there and she witnessed it. She might have even started it, maybe in some desperate effort to stop the abuse. Somehow, in her traumatized mind, she found a way to justify their death. Fire became her way of coping with things. She knows its potential. Melanie told me that pyromaniacs see fire as a way of having power and control. It's possible that she views it as some way of exercising control over others. I believe she's taking revenge on those who caused her so much pain."

"But how did she become Heather McCade?" Cassie asked.

"Her name's actually Christie Augustine. My guess is that someone had it legally changed, hoping that it would distance herself from her past, and help her adjust. The other victims all had contact with Maggie or her parents when she was a child. Except for Della Torre, all of these people are dead. They all died in fires originating in their bedrooms. I think Lieutenant

Rutherford finally discovered the pattern, but she killed him before he could prove it."

"But how did she become Heather?"

"My same friend checked the employee roster at the state's insurance bureau. There's no woman that works there named Heather McCade. There never has been. However, a Heather McCade worked for the state mental health division. It's possible that Christie was one of her cases."

Lieutenant Michaels stared at the file, then up at the board. "That's a bit of a leap, don't you think?"

"My friend backtracked both of their living addresses. Heather lived and worked in Seattle up until about sixteen months ago, when she suddenly resigned her position. Christie did as well, up until there was a fire at her residence. She died in it."

Cassie turned to stare at Lieutenant Michaels. The expression on her boss' face told her she had just reached the same conclusion. "Christie torched her own place, but she didn't die. Heather did," she said aloud.

"We'll have to verify that, but it doesn't matter," Lieutenant Michaels told them. "We can reason out what happens next. Maggie or Christie waits a few months until the fervor dies down and then assumes Heather's identity."

Julie nodded. "When I spoke to Melanie, she told me she had only been an investigator for a little a year. She also told me that she thought she smelled the scent of that perfume once before, but in Seattle, not here. She told me that she worked that fire, and she remembered the scent. She didn't quite make the connection."

"But Maggie did, and her subterfuge gave her advantage over all of you," Lieutenant Michaels realized. "By masquerading as an insurance fraud investigator, she could keep up with the cases. Then she learned that Melanie trained in Seattle at one point. Once she realized that Melanie could recognize that scent, she would recall that fire, so Maggie framed her for Lieutenant Rutherford's death."

Cassie mulled over these conclusions. It seemed impossible, but there was some fragment of logic to it all. "But what's your role in this, and the Samuelson place? Why burn it down, and why come after you? You didn't even know her until a few days ago."

"The Samuelson house was the house Maggie was raised in for a time, and maybe the house she was abused in. I think my house was just an impulsive reaction. It may have triggered a memory that she couldn't cope with. As for me? I have no idea."

"You were a threat, just like Melanie and Lieutenant Rutherford," Lieutenant Michaels argued. "You did or said something that made her think that, and she acted. However, it still doesn't explain the nickname."

"It was in Lieutenant Rutherford's notes," Cassie said. "It's what he probably called Della Torre about. The only other person we know of who called him that is Kate, but she has an alibi for last night. We checked."

"And Heather?"

"She claimed she was in Yale."

"But what if she wasn't?" Lieutenant Michaels looked around the precinct, and then glanced at the nearby wall clock. It was already well past lunchtime.

She glanced over at Cassie. "Mark's been gone a while. Shouldn't he be back from talking to Della Torre by now?"

"Yeah. His office isn't that far from here, and he said he wouldn't be long."

"Did Heather know where he was going?"

"No. He decided to go there after she had left."

The conference room phone rang. Lieutenant Michaels answered it. Cassie and Julie watched as her face turned stern. "You're certain? All right. Thanks." The lieutenant hung up. "That was Dr. Foster. He's completing the autopsy on Lieutenant Rutherford. He said that someone struck him on the side of the head prior to the fire that killed him. Cassie, try to reach Mark, right now."

Cassie bolted out into the squad room. Julie turned to the lieutenant. She had a worried look on her face. "Lieutenant, what's wrong?"

"Mark called in to Tyler, asking us to do some checking on a Maggie Sinclair," she explained as they followed Cassie out of the room. "I think he's starting to put the pieces together, like you and the lieutenant did. Hopefully, he'll reach the same conclusions that you did."

"He's not answering his phone."

Cassie slammed the receiver back into its cradle and rifled through her desk drawer for Heather's business card. When she found it, she dialed all the numbers on them. "None of them work. They're all disconnected," she announced.

"Where's Della Torre's office?" Julie asked.

"It's only a few blocks from here, but if Mark's already been there, Lord knows where he could be."

"I'll call Della Torre," Lieutenant Michaels told them. "I'll also have Tyler do a search to see if there are any more properties here that our victims might've owned, and to check to see where she's really been living. In the meantime, you get going. We need to find her before she strikes again."

Cassie gave her superior a brisk nod and darted for the door. Julie walked toward Mark's desk. She reached out a hand to run alongside the edge. As she touched it, she suddenly sensed him. She could not tell where he was. She could tell that that he was in fear for his life. Julie hesitated for a moment. Then she grabbed her messenger bag from his chair and started to follow Cassie. "Wait, Julie!" Lieutenant Michaels called.

Cassie paused in the doorway, realizing that Julie was just a few steps behind her. Julie turned to face the lieutenant. A look of steel had crossed the lieutenant's face. "This is an ongoing investigation. You need to stay here. Let Cassie and my officers handle this."

"Lieutenant Michaels, I want to help," Julie argued. "Look, you know that I talk people out of doing foolish things for a living. If she's holding Mark hostage, maybe I can convince her to let him go, turn herself in, and take responsibility for what she's done." Julie sighed. "I hate to be facetious, but she's probably on a really short fuse. If you don't act quickly, Mark's going to die."

Lieutenant Michaels bit her lip. Then she gave Cassie a cold, hard stare. "You're in charge of her safety," she barked, pointing a finger at Cassie.

Cassie's jaw dropped. Lieutenant Michaels motioned for her to approach. Cassie glared at Julie, who gave her a pleading stare in return. She straightened her holster and walked toward the lieutenant. "Please tell me the heat's gotten to you, ma'am," Cassie whispered.

Lieutenant Michaels pulled her closer. "Detective, I understand your fear," she said in low voice, "but as she said, she is trained for this. It's going to take some time to locate the county's hostage negotiator, anyway. Let her try, but if it's doesn't work, get her to a safe place until the fire and rescue squads get there. Got me?"

Cassie gave her a reluctant nod. The lieutenant released her and gave Julie a nod. Julie saw the look in Lieutenant Michaels's eye and understood its meaning. Meanwhile, Cassie approached her. She gave Julie a reproachful gaze. "C'mon."

Cassie brushed past Julie and headed for the elevator. The touch told Julie who was in charge. Julie gave a nod of thanks to the lieutenant and bolted after Cassie. Lieutenant Michaels watched them leave. She let out a sigh. It was going to be bad enough if Mark died. She didn't want to hear what the Chief would say if he learned which civilian's life she put on the line to try and save him. She turned to Harry. "Get Tyler busy researching those records. We need to figure out where Heather took Mark, before we're too late."

XVI

When he first came to, Mark felt hot and sticky. He tried to move his limbs, but they would not budge. He sat on something hard. He blinked, trying to clear the grogginess from his head. Dust particles flew into his eyes and he shut them tight again. He shook his head, blinked hard, and opened his eyes again. The light was dim, and the air heavy with dust and stiff with humidity. He smelled fresh varnish and paint, and the subtle scent of lavender perfume. He heard joints pop in his neck as he glanced upward. A metal chandelier with a few naked light bulbs glowed high above him. He grimaced and tried to move his head take in more of his surroundings. He was in some large room with huge wooden beams. Stacks of boxes surrounded him, along with cans of unused paint and varnish. One wall was nothing but picture windows. The opposite had a set of sliding doors that led out to the deck and a lake vista. He continued to struggle against his bonds until he heard heavy footfalls thump against the hardwood. He strained to listen. They were coming closer. "Hello?" he called out. "Is someone there?"

The footfalls moved closer. Mark tried to determine which direction they were coming from. He struggled to turn himself so that he could see the doorways. "Kate? Is that you? Who's there?"

A figure moved into the doorway to his left. After a few moments, a strange sight appeared to Mark's eyes. He blinked a few times, hoping whatever had knocked him out was causing him to hallucinate. His captor now wore a pair of heavy boots, jeans and a thin T-shirt. She carried four jugs of a clear liquid in her gloved hands. Her thin hair hung limp around her face. Her glasses were gone, and without them, her pale green eyes were small, and had a haunted look about them. He did a double take. *Green? Her eyes were brown this morning.* "Heather?" he whispered.

She continued walking toward him. She said nothing. Mark studied her expression. It was one of malice and absolute hatred. "Heather?" Mark asked again, struggling against his bonds. "Heather, what's going on?"

She glanced up at him. She gave him the once-over, as if she was measuring him and comparing him to the mental notes she made. "You're awake, finally. I thought you might miss everything."

"Miss everything?"

"Don't you know? It's time for your reunion." Heather set the jugs down next to his chair, and squatted down behind him to tighten the ropes around Mark's hands. He could feel them digging into his wrists. "Your fiery reunion, I should clarify."

"Heather, what's going on? Untie me, right now!"

Heather stopped tugging at his bonds. She grabbed one of the abandoned jugs. She walked toward the fireplace behind him. "Just so you know, my name's not really Heather. My adoptive parents called me Christie. My real parents called me Maggie."

"Maggie?"

She moved to face him and stared him deep in the eye. "Maggie Sinclair?"

She took a step away and tugged at her hair. It came off in one fluid motion. Mark's eyes widened. It was an adult version of the female Catherine Tinnon had described. She did a pirouette for him. There was no hair spinning about behind her, for her real hair was gone. Her skull was nothing but patches of other skin grafted into its place. He also made out the faint outlines of the healed burns she suffered that fateful night. "Oh my God!"

Heather tossed the wig into his face and gave him a smirk. "Oh come now, Detective Daniels. You're so good at what you do, yet you can't accept the fact that women can be firebugs as well? After all, your stellar deductive skills got Melanie locked up for my handiwork."

Mark thought on her appearance now, and then remembered what Mrs. Tinnon said about Maggie and what had happened to her. Then he recalled his recent conversation with Della Torre. "Della Torre must've changed your name when you became a ward of the state," he said to himself.

"Yes. Mr. Della Torre, my attorney and so-called friend, changed it when my parents died. He thought it would help me heal." She shook her head, and a cold look came across her face. "But I could never heal," she said bitterly. "How could I, after what Mickey and the others did to me?"

Mark heard her feet shuffling, and he tried to look behind him. He watched her shadow while it moved across the floor. Its movements indicated that Heather was coating the room with whatever was in that jug. He picked up the lavender scent, and realized that it was the accelerant. When she was done, she tossed it aside, and retrieved a new one. Mark knew that he had to keep her mind away on what she wanted to do to him, and thinking rationally again. "Heather, why? Why did you do it?"

"Why not? After all, they all betrayed me. I told them what was happening to me. They all told me that they would do something, that they would help me. I thought they should know how much their betrayal hurt."

"But what did they do?"

"Nothing, Detective Daniels. Absolutely nothing."

She turned away from him. The filth and disgust began to rise faster than any time she could remember. She sniffed and wiped her nose. Then she regained her composure. She moved away from him about five feet. She tipped the full gallon of liquid. It began to pour out slowly, and stayed where it landed. She began to walk in a distinct pattern. "You should know that you were the most challenging one to deal with. Figuring out how to eliminate Lieutenant Rutherford and discredit Melanie was easy. However, I needed to find a way to eliminate you; the one other person who could put it all together. Then I overheard Melanie talking to Cassie about your mother's death. I went and pulled the records. That's when I decided that you should die just like the others did, with a little twist."

She paused in her pouring to retrieve a prescription bottle from of her pocket. She shook it back and forth. Mark heard no sound, which meant that it was empty. "Just so you know, the entire place has been laden with accelerant. I've also lit the candle. It has a ten-minute burn cycle." She glanced at her watch. "I say you have about three, maybe four minutes before this place catches fire and you burn to death. It's not a pleasant way to go, but at least, you'll know how your mother felt when she died at your hands."

She set the pill bottle down on the floor and met his gaze, a wicked smile on her face. He gave her a blank stare. He didn't understand. What did swallowing pills have to do with his mother's death? Heather looked amused by his confused expression. She clicked her tongue. "What a pity. Daddy didn't tell you the truth? Looks like I wasn't the only one betrayed by someone who claimed they loved them."

Mark was dumbfounded. He wanted to know more, but getting out alive was more important. He continued to struggle against his bonds. "What about your parents? What about your fire? You watched them die in it!"

"Oh, I did watch. I watched with total delight, at least before I got hurt. You see, I set the fire that killed them. As you can tell, I didn't get away completely unscathed." Maggie reached up to touch her head and frowned. "Even so, it was a fitting end. To them, I was lower than dirt. Daddy liked fucking his little girl, and Mommy beat me for it. They were going to burn in hell anyway, just like the preachers said. I thought they should experience it a little sooner than that."

She continued her walk in front of Mark's chair. He watched her movements, but it was a bit before he realized the pattern she was making. It was the strange symbol found at two of the sites, and he was right in front of it. When it went up, the light would probably blind him. *Keep her talking. Keep her distracted,* he kept thinking, *but what do I call her?* "Heather? Christie? Maggie? Please, listen to me!"

"Fire," Heather murmured in a dreamlike tone, "it's so wonderful, Mark. After all, you know all about it. Once started, it has a life of its own. It can rage on, gathering strength as it gathers its fuel. Nature uses it to clean out the old wood in forests, so that new trees can grow. I use it to cleanse away the hurt, the pain, and the sadness caused by those who clamed they cared for me, like my parents, the others, and him."

Mark thought about this. There was only one logical conclusion. The Look came to his face. "But you missed one," Mark argued, "and you're wrong. I care for you, too."

"Oh, right, Detective. I saw the look of contempt you gave me every time I walked into the room. You didn't give a damn about me. Admit it, Mark. You would've paid attention to me if you'd know who I really was, wouldn't you? It's why you spend that time trying to find out all you could about me, wasn't it?"

The case notes ran through his head, and then all the actions he took to gain more information to supplement them. He recalled the night at the library when he went searching for information on Maggie's fire. More things began to make sense. "The newspaper microfiche that went missing at the library," he said aloud. "I tried to study up on your fire. I wanted to get some understanding of how you coped with your loss, but you stole them so that no one would make the connection. It's also why you dogged the lieutenant and why you humiliated Melanie, to make me suspicious of them, but you slipped up."

He saw Heather pause. He must've hit a nerve. Then he realized what probably happened. "Taking those microfiche was your first mistake. Then there was yesterday, when Julie came to identify the perfume? You came in with papers. Somehow, you got some of your notes mixed in with ours. Lieutenant Rutherford must've found them. You realized that if the lieutenant recognized your handwriting, he would reason out the truth, so you killed him, and framed Melanie for it."

A sadistic smile came to her face. "You are such a clever detective, Mark."

"Not clever enough. I remember your statement regarding people close to the fire investigations. Insurance people get damn close themselves. That should've tipped me."

Heather tossed aside the empty bottle without responding. She went to get the final one, and headed toward the last set of boxes. She sensed Mark's cold stare following her about, and delighted in the fact there was nothing that he could do to prevent his death. "The other day, Lieutenant Rutherford reminded us that all the property owners were dead, except one," Mark continued. "You killed them all and destroyed everything they had built, all to get back at them because they didn't act to help you."

"Oh, they could've stopped it. Dr. Raich knew what my parents were doing. He saw the signs, but he didn't want to see me taken away from what he called 'a loving home.' He just didn't want to be labeled as a snitch. He told me so before I killed him. The others knew too. I know they did. That's why Mr. Branson fired my father. It just gave my father more opportunity to have his way with me, and Mr. Sullivan? He just worked my mother to the ground. Mom took her anger toward Mr. Sullivan and my dad out on me. They all confessed to me before they died, and pleaded with me to spare their lives. Well they didn't spare mine."

"But Della Torre found out after the fact, Heather. He couldn't have prevented it from happening."

"Oh, don't give me that bullshit! He knew exactly what he was doing when he tossed me aside like an old rag. What doe he do now? He defends those who don't deserve it; people like Walter, and Kate, and those greedy corporate types who polluted Puget Sound. I was his last case, the last child case he ever took. Did he tell you that?"

"No, he didn't, but I can understand why . . . Christie."

"Don't call me that!"

She threw the bottle across the room. It collided with the glass door and spilt all over it. She stomped over to Mark, grabbing him by his chin with her right hand, forcing him to look up at her. Some of the accelerant was on her glove, and now it was on his face. "Don't ever call me that!" she shrieked, her green eyes alive with fire. "Christie doesn't exist!"

Mark met her icy gaze. "Yes, she does," he muttered. "I think deep down inside, she does exist. She's the little girl that Della Torre sought to help all those years ago, the child he wanted to give her a better life; a life that her parents didn't give her, and should have."

"No. Christie was just a name. Mickey thought it was cute. He wanted to name his daughter that, if he ever had one. He has a girl, too, but he never named her that. I wonder why."

Her fingers dug deeper into his cheeks. Mark fought not to flinch in her iron grip. "Maybe because when he thought of that name, he thought of the hurt little girl he tried to protect from further harm. I think the name reminded him of a case that hit too close to home. I think it reminded him of the little girl he somehow betrayed."

Heather's face took on a look of mock astonishment. "I never thought I see the day. Could it be? You actually give a fuck about the most asinine lawyer in town. He's the man who made my life what it is today."

"No, he didn't. You did that yourself. He didn't teach you how to kill. He tried to save you."

"Right, just like he used to call me his pet, his love. He claimed he cared for me, and then he turned around and dumped me. I didn't manage to kill him, but I took away something that he cared about."

"No. I think Della Torre saw something else. I think the little girl he came to care for is still there, just underneath the surface. I talked to him about her. He still cares for you. I think that if she truly thought about what she was about to do to me, she would stop it."

Heather's face broke out in a devilish smile. "You don't know Christie. You never did. It's always been Maggie. Christie never existed, except in Della Torre's mind, and on paper."

She yanked her hand away from him and checked her watch. Mark realized he was on his last chance. "Heather, let me go. Let's get out of here. Let me get you help!"

"It's too late for that, just like it's too late for you. Now, if you don't mind, I have one more person I need to see. I think he'll die in his office. It'll be fitting. I so want to see his face when he sees me again." Heather gave him a cold smile. "Say hello to your mother for me."

She spun about to leave, but turned too quickly. She collided with the stack of boxes behind her. They began to sway, and then fall forward. A few of them popped open. They were filled with heavy law books. They tumbled out of their cartons and fell on top of her. She screamed and fell backwards toward him. She raised her arms to block them from hitting her, rather than bracing herself for the fall. One of the books struck her right temple. She crumpled to the ground. Mark heard her head hit the floor hard. She bounced a bit. She let out a soft moan, and then her body went limp. She was out cold. Mark watched in horror. "Oh, shit! Heather? Heather!"

He tried to hop his chair toward her. It teetered, and he braced his feet. He righted himself, and tried to remain calm. If he wasn't careful, he was going to land in the accelerant and if that happens, there may be no saving him. He stared up at the roof above him. His conscious finally became aware of the sweat that rolled down the nape of his neck and back, and soaked the folds of his shirt tucked under his arms. How far away was the street? He couldn't see it from where he sat. Were there any other houses about? What about the workers? If there were any about, would they hear him?

Off in the distance, he heard a sudden "whoosh." He froze. Seconds later, he heard something begin the crackle and burn. Burning wood and melting plastic began to replace the smell of new paint, cardboard, and carpet. It was a haunting mix of sensations indicating that a small fire was growing into a raging inferno. He stared at the prone Heather, and realized that the fire he should've died in was finally going to consume him 30 years after the fact. "Help!" he screamed at the top of his lungs. "Someone help me!"

*   *   *

Julie followed Cassie as she raced down the short outside steps to her black Taurus. Cassie threw her siren up in the window and gunned the engine to life. Julie barely had time to close the door, before she sped away in a squeal of rubber. As they reached Main Street, Cassie's phone rang. She grabbed it. "Mark, is that you?"

"It's Ed, Cassie. Lieutenant Michaels just spoke to Della Torre. He told her that Mark left his office more than an hour ago."

"Did he tell Della Torre where he was going?"

"He thought Mark was heading back here."

"Thanks, Ed." Cassie hung up the phone and looked back at Julie. "We just missed him at Della Torre's," she said.

"Where could he be then?"

"I don't know."

Cassie leaned on her horn. Cars slowly pulled over to make way for her. As they barreled down the road, Cassie's phone rang again. She answered it: "Edwards."

"It's Lieutenant Michaels. Tyler's found a possible hit."

Cassie listened as the lieutenant gave her the address and directions from her current location. "Got it." She hung up, and then tried dialing Mark's cell phone number again. Julie gripped the door handle, staring at the blur of buildings whizzing by them. Her stomach started to churn. Cassie's driving was having an effect similar to what she experienced when Julie traveled by ship or intergalactic portal. She hated traveling through either means. Meanwhile, Cassie had one hand on the steering wheel, and the other pressing the "Send" button on her cell phone every ten seconds, trying to get a hold of Mark. When he still didn't answer, she threw the phone in the back seat of the car. She ran her free hand through her hair. Her face took on a look of despair. "I hope we're not too late," Cassie muttered.

No, Julie thought. Even through the chaos her stomach felt, she still sensed Mark. Although she couldn't exactly where he was, she knew that he was still alive. "Where are we headed?" she asked aloud.

"Towards Grass Dunes Lake. Della Torre is building his new house there. Tyler found it when he did that property search. When Lieutenant Michaels called to verify it, he said he was supposed to move into it two weeks ago."

"What stopped him?"

"Construction delays? Anthony's death? Who knows?"

Cassie made a hard right and Julie grasped the door handle tighter. The houses began to grow larger and more spread out. She heard the tires squeal as they fought to grip the pavement. Cars and pedestrians moved out their way. Julie bit her tongue to stop the meal she ate two days ago from making a return visit. She closed her eyes against the images around them. "Could you not drive so fast?"

Cassie couldn't help but smile. She had noticed the slight gray pallor to Julie's dark face. "Hey, you're the one who wanted to come."

"Yes, but I'd like to get there in one piece, please."

Della Torre's new home was in a new residential complex that abutted Grass Dunes Lake, a manmade reservoir that was a result of the hydroelectric dam constructed more than 65 years ago. The street itself was short, and dead-ended about a thousand yards from the lakeshore. There were no other homes about. Cassie parked at the barrier. She gestured to the right. "There it is," she informed Julie.

Julie stared at the newly built, four-level structure. Its design allowed each room to take in the lakeshore view. Toward the left side of the house was a two-story wooden deck on stilts that jutted out into the lake. From the bottom level, a boat dock extended out another 50 feet. Julie studied the bay windows on the second floor. They faced out toward the lake. At first, Julie didn't sense anyone within. Then she spotted the vehicle parked by the garage, its back end facing it. "Cassie, that looks like the car I saw at the warehouse the other night."

Cassie climbed out of the car and reached for her discarded cell phone to dial 9-1-1. "This is Detective Cassandra Edwards, Serious Crimes," she said when the connection was made. "Have fire and rescue crews sent to 3021 Vinson, immediately!"

She stuffed her phone into her jacket pocket and retrieved her gun. Julie climbed out of the car and grabbed her messenger bag, a frown on her face. "You're dealing with an emotionally unstable person," Julie warned her.

"All the more reason to be cautious." She put a restraining hand on Julie's shoulders, remembering Lieutenant Michaels parting words. She gestured to the car. "Look, maybe you should wait here."

"I'm the one who talks to people for a living, remember? She might listen to me."

"She also tried to kill you, remember? What makes you think that she's going to listen to you now?"

"Nothing, but I'm not going to stand aside and watch you shoot her, either."

"I don't intend to shoot her, not if I don't have to." Cassie pointed to her car and handed Julie the keys. "Lock yourself inside, or even better: drive it out of here and get to a safe spot. Let me handle this."

"Cassie . . ."

Cassie raised a finger. "Look, you shouldn't be here in the first place, and I don't know why the lieutenant allowed it. However, she's not here now, so you'll do as I tell you. Got it?"

Julie bit her bottom lip to keep from responding. Cassie gave her a curt nod and turned back to head into the building. "Cassie!" Julie called.

Cassie turned back to her. She had a look on her face that told Julie that there was no arguing with her. She gripped Cassie's keys tight in her hand. "Just . . . be careful," she whispered.

Cassie nodded. Cocking her weapon, she ran up the embankment toward the back of the house. Julie sighed and stared at the outside of the building. She reached out with her thoughts. In her mind, she saw Mark. He was tied up in the center of some huge room, struggling to escape. Heather lay on the floor in front of him, partially covered by heavy books and boxes. She seemed to be unconscious. Her appearance also wasn't what Julie was used to seeing. The top of her head was covered with scars of burnt skin, and her hair was completely gone. Cassie had made it inside unnoticed and was weaving her way through the kitchen. She was only a room or two away from him, but she soon would be trapped as well. In the dining room table, the candle had burned through to the accelerant. Flames began to shoot up. In seconds, that room and the floor above it were ablaze. Soon after, the house would be too. Julie needed to do something. She set down her bag near the right front tire of Cassie's car and began to walk up the embankment toward the front door.

Stop, Halbrina.

Julie stopped walking. She knew who spoke to her. She clenched her hands. "I need to get in there," she argued in a low tone.

You know our laws.

"No! I can't just let them die, not if there's some way that I can prevent it!"

You cannot help them, Halbrina.

There was an explosion toward the back of the house. Then the windows nearest her began to shatter. Glass shards flew through the air. Julie immediately shielded herself. The back of the house was now engulfed. Sheets of flames jutted out from the blown-out window frames. Julie stared at the structure. None of them would survive this blaze, not without Julie intervening in some way. "NIK, how soon until the fire department gets here?"

Approximately five point three seven minutes.

Julie shook her head. "It'll be too late. They would all be dead before then, if not from the smoke, then from flames and the intense heat Heather's custom accelerant generated." She stared at the structure again. Using her powers to hold the fire back would do the trick, if it wasn't for the fact that she couldn't. Too many questions would lead them to her, and her chance to live here would be gone before it ever really got started. She had to find a physical way to do this, and yet fool their minds into what they were seeing. How could she when she was incapable of changing her form? Cassie's car keys jabbed her palm. She looked down at them, and an idea came to her.

She glanced about, and then refocused her thoughts. In an instant, her ability to will herself from one spot to another transported her from the front yard of Della Torre's home to the center of Mark's living room. Once she was settled, she glanced about. She had a way to enter Cassie's mind. Now, she needed a way to enter Mark's. Despite their close contact, her link to him was not strong enough to enter Mark's thoughts without touching him. With her humanoid exhaustion, she didn't want to chance doing it without something physical of his in her hands. She turned in a circle. "Find something, Halbrina!"

She paused and turned in the opposite direction. Her gaze rested on the bookcase in the corner, and its assortment of photographs. She walked over to it and picked up the one of Mark and his mother. The effect was instantaneous. She felt herself within Mark's mind. He had just kicked a bottle or something. The memories of his fire flashed through at that moment. His mother's face floated in his thoughts. Julie gripped the frame tight and smiled. She knew how to get them out.

Meanwhile, Cassie had made it into the structure undetected. The interior decorator in her could only take in its layout for a moment. The scent of perfume greeted her nostrils. It was also incredibly hot. She looked down at her favorite white denim jacket she was wearing. "Whatever possessed me to put this on?" she asked herself.

She glanced about the kitchen. Everything was brand new, and covered with a slick liquid that smelled like lavender. "Accelerant," she mumbled. "I'm in the right place. Mark? Mark, are you here?"

Off in the distance, she smelled cardboard burning. She looked to her right and saw the flames in the dining room. They were rushing toward her. She quickened her pace, weaving in and out of the boxes stacked in the hallway. She knew she should pause to check every room, but she knew she didn't have time. "Mark? Mark! Where are you?"

Mark smelled the cardboard burning too. He heard the crackling and popping sound the paper made as it caught fire. The heat began to build, and the humidity levels increased. He started to gasp for air. Then he sat up straighter, concentrating on the sound of the voice he heard crying out for him. He wasn't certain if he had heard right. "Cassie? Cassie!" he yelled.

A few seconds later, Cassie's gun, and then her head appeared in the doorway. She stared down at the still form of Heather. She didn't look anything like she had these past few days. She glanced over at Mark's sweat-filled face. "Mark, what . . ."

There was a small boom, and then a sizzling sound. Cassie turned. She dove toward Mark, making it into his inner circle just as the flames began to reach the accelerant around them. There was a roar, as the flames shot around the room. Before they knew it, they were surrounded by fire. Cassie stared at him. He could see the flames glowing against her skin and reflected in her eyes. "Are you all right?"

"I will be once we get out of here!"

She stowed her gun in her holster and squatted down in front of him, patting down his pockets. She looked flustered. She had seen it more than once. He had to have it on him. "Your knife!"

"Right pocket!"

He twisted himself and turned his hips as upward as he could so that she could reach inside it. She managed to wriggle his Swiss Army knife out of his pocket. She sawed through the ropes that bound his hands and feet, and he stood. The glass doors that led to the deck outside exploded. Mark instinctively pulled Cassie toward him. They ducked down in time to miss the shards flying in all directions. He heard wood and more boxes snapping and popping. The roof was now on fire and so was the fireplace. The boxes stacked near them began to ignite. The heat became stifling. Before they knew it, they were both sweating.

He released Cassie and staying low to the ground, crawled toward Heather. As he did so, his left hand struck the pill bottle that Heather dropped. It skirted across the floor and ricocheted off something. The sound reverberated in his ears. He wiped his face and made to touch Heather's still form. Instead, he saw his mother lying there, unconscious. "No," he muttered. "I'm not going to focus on that."

He checked Heather's pulse. It was still there, but appeared to be getting weaker. Cassie forced her gaze from the growing firewall to him. "How is she?" she asked, her voice muffled by the jacket sleeve she had placed over her mouth and nose.

"I don't know!"

He stripped off his plaid shirt to cover Heather's face and torso, and then moved the non-burning boxes and books off her. They helped to provide a temporary barrier to the firewall. He struggled to pick her up. He grunted with the effort. He felt a knot grow in his stomach, as he stared at the flames. "We need to get out of here, Cass!"

"My thought exactly! Any ideas how?"

They frantically turned in all directions, but all they saw were flames. The terror of his fire began to fill his heart with dread. He wasn't going to make it. He knew it. Then somewhere within the roar of the fire, he thought he heard a voice calling his name. He cocked his head. He heard it again. It was a woman's voice; a voice he hadn't heard in more than 30 years.

Mark! Come this way!

He paused, concentrating on the direction it seemed to be coming. Then he turned and looked toward the dining room entrance. He thought he saw a figure illuminated in the flames. He squinted. A woman of Cassie's height stood within them, but he could see the fire behind her. She wore a simple white dress. Her brunette hair flowed around her face, as if the heat and wind from the inferno blew it and the bottom of her dress about. A smile came across her face. Mark forgot about the fire for a moment. What was he seeing? An elaborate illusion? A ghost? He blinked his eyes hard. Then he focused in on her face. A familiar pair of brown eyes stared back at him. They were his eyes. His jaw went slack. "Mom?" he whispered.

Cassie looked in the same direction. She held her hand up to shield her eyes from the glare of the flames, and saw the heat waves rising around them. Otherwise, she saw nothing. She looked up at Mark. Mark had that distant look in his eyes again, the look he had had when they had been at Della Torre's storage facility. He looked as if he had stepped into another world. "Not now, Mark. Don't lose it now!" Cassie begged.

Run, Mark! Run!

"Run? Run where?" he asked the empty air.

Cassie put an unsteady hand on his shoulder. "Mark? Who are you talking to?"

Mark stared as his mother nodded her head to their left. A cool breeze whistled past him and he turned that direction. There, hidden by the smoke and flames was another picture window that overlooked the water. Just before it, Mark thought he saw a path between a set of boxes that the fire had not reached. Perhaps with timing and a little luck, he and Cassie could get to the deck without injury. He watched as the fire moved closer to the path and to them, trying to judge how long they had. He turned to Cassie. "There!" he screamed, jerking his head in the direction of the narrow path.

Cassie looked at where he pointed, then at the inferno rapidly heading toward the boxes. She looked at Mark. "Are you joking? We're not going to make it through there!"

"Yes, we are!"

He looked straight at his destination. His mom had moved, and now stood in the center of it. She smiled softly and nodded at him. *Run, Mark Anthony! Run now!*

At first, he was uncertain. Then the Look came to his face. He took a deep breath, adjusted Heather's weight in his arms, and started walking toward the shadow that looked like his mother. "C'mon, Cassie," he instructed her.

"Mark, where are we . . ."

"C'mon!"

Cassie shook her head. Saying a silent prayer, she grabbed onto him, avoiding Heather's swinging arm. As they moved closer to the flames, she buried her face into his side, peeking out from underneath his arms. Her fingernails dug into his lower back. The heat grew around them. The boxes had started to catch fire. She smelled her hair beginning to burn. "Mark, we're not going to make it!"

"Yes we are!" he shouted back. Tears stung his eyes, and the searing heat of the smoke and the flames stifled his breathing. He concentrated on the weight of in his arms and the feel of Cassie's body pressed against his. He struggled to move forward, his thoughts focused on the goal he sought to complete all those years ago. *Yes, we are. We're going to make it this time, Mom. I won't fail you this time. I'm going to get you out.*

He twisted his body to get by the boxes without Heather's dangling arms or legs touching them, or without having Cassie collide into them. Halfway through, Heather's weight, coupled with the overwhelming heat and the building smoke, began to drag him down. He stumbled and Heather's legs knocked over a flaming box. It barely missed Cassie. Its contents spilled over the floor and caught fire immediately. The smoke began to grow dense. He coughed. The memories of his own fire still filled his head, but this time, Mom was there. He couldn't see her, but he felt her love surrounding him, protecting and guiding him through the fiery maze. Her soft hands held onto his, assuring him that he was on the right path, and the scent of cinnamon seemed to touch his nostrils, overpowering the smell of the burning cardboard and his singed hair. Then her touch began to fade away. He narrowed his eyes, trying to stare through the thickening smoke, concentrating on the now-crushing weight in his arms, and Cassie's fingers digging into his side. He struggled to breathe. "Mom! Don't leave me!" he whispered.

As he spoke the words, he saw some kind of light shining ahead of him. With a last surge of energy, he pushed himself forward. He collided with the door. It burst open. He took an uncertain step and overbalanced. He took two more and crashed through what remained of the frame into the burning wooden railing. It gave way. He tumbled into the water with Heather. Cassie fell in right behind him. A few seconds later, they came back up. They stared at each other in bewilderment, then up at the flaming structure. Then they realized that

Heather had not surfaced with them. They dove back under the water. A few moments later, they re-emerged. The sudden dip into the cold water seemed to have awakened her. "No," she moaned. "Let me go!"

The sounds of sirens threatened to deafen them. The ground rumbled as the fire trucks pulled up to the house. Voices barked orders and they thought they heard the sound of a crane engaging. Mark and Cassie struggled to reach the shore, dragging Heather with them. "Help!" Mark called out, fighting to keep him and Heather afloat. He heard Cassie splashing beside him. He frantically scanned the grassy shore. "Help! Down here!"

"Mark? Cassie!"

They looked up at the top of the hillside nearest the barrier. Lieutenant Michaels had arrived on the scene. Her eyes were wide with fright and relief. They saw her turn and stare behind her, then back at their bobbing heads. "What . . . how . . ."

"Never mind!" Mark screamed. "Throw us a line, and get an ambulance over here, quick!"

She disappeared. Seconds later, an ambulance took up the space where she once stood. Doors slammed shut and they heard Lieutenant Michaels shouting instructions. They heard more footsteps. Seconds later, some firefighters and uniformed officers came over the hillside, carrying a portable gurney. Lieutenant Michaels reappeared. Moments later, Julie joined her. She looked as shocked at Lieutenant Michaels. "Mark!"

"Julie!" Mark exclaimed. "What are you doing here?"

"Cassie brought me. I'm sorry I disobeyed you, Cassie."

Cassie spat out water from her mouth. She glared up at the people staring at them. "Is someone going to help us out of here?" she barked.

Towing Heather, they swam toward shore, where two of the firefighters had scrambled down the embankment. They handed Heather to them, and then Cassie and Mark climbed out. As Mark reached the top of the embankment, he saw them load her onto the portable gurney, and the attending paramedics rushed her toward the waiting ambulance. "She's taken some kind of medication, a lot of it, I think," Mark called to them, fighting for breath. "I don't know what kind."

"We'll get on it," a third paramedic assured him, wrapping a blanket around Mark's wet, trembling body. "In the meantime, you need to come with us."

A second ambulance parked in the spot the first one abandoned, and the paramedics and firefighters ushered Cassie and Mark inside. They sat down. He caught a look at her appearance now and frowned. Cassie's favorite jacket was black with soot and had burn holes along its arms and on its back. Then he caught sight of Cassie's soaking wet hair, the ends of it now singed. He reached out to touch it. Cassie slapped his hand away. "No getting fresh, Detective," she warned him.

"What? I can't show even a little concern for my partner?"

"If you had, you wouldn't have performed that little stunt you just did, even if it did save my life." Her face softened and she looked at him. "What the hell did you see, anyway?"

As the ambulance door closed, Mark looked back at the inferno. Even if he told Cassie what he thought he had saw, she would not believe him. Had he imagined seeing and feeling Mom inside there? He looked at Julie, who stood next to Lieutenant Michaels. Julie's face still carried a look of disbelief. Once again, the feeling that someone sent Julie to watch over him returned. Last time he felt it, he thought Jessie had sent her. This time, he was certain it had been Mom.

The ambulance jerked and took off, and he watched Julie and the inferno she stood beside shrink in the distance. Lieutenant Michaels pulled Julie out of the way as a group of firefighters raced toward them, dragging hoses. When they were a safe distance from the scene, she put a comforting hand on Julie's shoulder. The look that was on Julie's face was probably still on her own. "Are you all right?" Lieutenant Michaels asked.

"I can't believe he and Cassie survived that," she whispered, gesturing to the orange fireball.

"Hey, I'm still having a hard time believing you survived that warehouse fire." Lieutenant Michaels stared up at what now remained of Della Torre's new home. "How did they make it out of there? Did you see them exit?"

"No."

"Well, at least they're all right. I'll assume that you'll be heading to the hospital to make sure of that?"

Julie was shocked. "Why would I want to do that, ma'am?"

"Oh, I don't know. I haven't known you long, Julie, but you seem to be fond of Detective Daniels, and I know that he's developed something of a soft spot for you."

"He has?"

"Yes. I don't know why, but for some reason, you intrigue him."

"There's nothing between us, Lieutenant. He's just my landlord."

Lieutenant Michaels gave her a knowing stare. "Well, after you've gone to see him at the hospital, come back to the station. There's a few things we need to get cleared up."

The lieutenant smiled, and then walked away. Julie turned back toward the inferno. A group of firefighters ran past the remains of the front doorway. Julie paused. For a moment, Julie thought she saw something within it. She stared harder. A woman slightly shorter than her and dressed in a white gown stared back. She had long, flowing brown hair and eyes just like Mark's. She was smiling at her. Julie looked at her empty hands. She had made sure to tuck Mark's photograph in her bag before Lieutenant Michaels and the fire trucks arrived. She would take it back to his place once she was free to leave here, so how was she seeing Mark's mother? She looked up at the sky, then toward the woman again. She was gone. Julie took an uncertain step toward the building. As she did so, she thought she heard a woman's voice say: *Thank you.*

Julie glanced about again. There was no one near her. Did she see what she thought she saw? It didn't matter. She glanced back up at the sky, took in a deep breath, and smiled. *No, Mrs. Daniels. Thank you.*

XVII

Suspect Arrested in Mason City Arson Spree

By Renee E. Blackwell
City Crime Reporter

Mason City Police yesterday arrested a suspect in the fires that have plagued the city for the past several months, killed two people, and destroyed several buildings, including a well-known historical site.

Detectives Mark Daniels and Cassie Edwards arrested former Mason City resident Maggie Sinclair after rescuing her from a fire that she allegedly started in a home on Vinson Street. Mason

County District Attorney Natalie Bishop announced yesterday afternoon that the suspect would be indicted on seven counts of arson, as well as the murders of Lawrence Rutherford, a 20-year arson investigation veteran, and Anthony Della Torre, the son of noted defense attorney Michelangelo Della Torre.

The alleged suspect remains under heavy guard at Mason City General Hospital. She is listed in serious but stable condition, recovering from a suspected drug overdose and smoke inhalation.

Sources close to the investigation report that law enforcement officials in Arizona, Florida, and Colorado are also inquiring into Ms. Sinclair, now known as Christie Augustine. Ms. Sinclair has become the prime suspect in the deaths of Dr. Hubert Raich, Branson Manufacturing owner Lloyd Branson, and department store owner Archie Sullivan, all who once owned and operated businesses in Mason City. Each man died as a result of fires set to their homes as they slept . . . .

Attorney Robert Sebastian Daniels sat in his corner office in Seattle. He perused the article in front of him with interest. He smiled, as he saw his son's name mentioned in it. Mark's name was mentioned often in the local papers. Della Torre had called to talk to him earlier that evening, to tell him how impressed he was with Mark and his detective skills. Robert had never liked his son's vocational choice, but Mark seemed to have inherited his instincts for figuring out problems, and he enjoyed his work. Perhaps he should stop pressing him to quit and work with his dad, instead.

As he continued to read, he heard a knock on his door. He wasn't expecting any visitors this late in the day. He quickly folded the paper up and tossed it in the recycling bin under his desk. He put his hand on the security buzzer, although it must be someone he knew. Otherwise, the security desk wouldn't have let them in. "Come!" he barked.

The door opened and Mark's tall frame filled it. He stood there awkwardly, staring at the man within the dim-lit room. "Hi, Dad."

Robert took his hand away from the buzzer. His brow furrowed. "Mark? What brings you here at this time of night?"

Mark shrugged, stepping inside his dad's office. He noticed that his dad looked like he was ready to go to court, even though it was well after 8:00 p.m. He hadn't even loosened the knot in his tie. *In control of everything until the very end.* Mark shoved back that stubborn lock of hair. "No particular reason. I just . . . wanted to know if you realized what anniversary it was this week."

Robert stood. He sensed that there was something more to his son's question. He leaned his head to the side. "I did. Is that all?"

"I . . . wanted to ask you something. I wanted to talk to you about Mom, and about the night she died."

Robert stepped away from his desk and toward Mark. "Son, we've talked about this. Every year we talk about this. Why do you still insist on beating yourself up over her death?"

Mark swallowed hard. He remembered what Heather said. She had researched the fire. She was going to re-enact it, she had said. "As you might know, I've been investigating some fires back in Mason City. It brought up some memories, and it got me thinking. I just want to understand what happened, Dad, and I also want to understand why it happened."

Robert sighed and crossed his arms. He dropped his gaze and pinched the bridge of his nose. "What is it that you want to talk about?"

"I think you should know, Dad, that before I came here, I went and pulled the records about the fire."

Robert stopped pinching his nose. Slowly, he raised his head to look him. Mark thought he saw something come across his father's face, like a shadow. Mark wondered if it similar to the one Julie saw in his face when he had a problem he was trying to solve. "I see."

Mark watched while his father walked over to a corner of the room, where a tray of glass decanters shimmered in the light. He stared at his son's reflection in the mirror. "Tell me something, Mark. Why would you want to do that?"

"Because I wanted to know the truth about what happened that day, once and for all."

"Did you find it?"

"I think so."

Robert reached for the decanter nearest to him and poured himself a glass of Scotch. He methodically placed the glass stopper back into it. "Oh? I'm curious as to what you found."

"Well, I read the arson investigator's report, as well as the newspaper articles, and . . ."

Mark paused. Robert nodded his head toward Mark's direction. "And?"

"I found the autopsy report on Mom. I found out why I couldn't wake her up."

Mark thought he saw his father's shoulders stiffen ever so slightly. He pulled out his notebook and opened to a page. He really didn't need to. He had memorized the report. "According to the medical examiner, she died of asphyxiation brought on by smoke inhalation. However, even if the fire hadn't happened, she probably still would've died."

"Is that so?" Robert picked up his glass, staring at its contents. "Are you a medical doctor now?"

Mark's eyes remained fixed on his notes. "Mom's final toxicology report showed about 200 milligrams of Carazin in her system. The medical examiner concluded that Mom had taken some sleeping pills; an overdose of sleeping pills. She was already dying when I started the fire, he concluded. They wouldn't have been able to revive her, even the fire never took place."

Mark looked up from his reading, watching his father. "He also noted that the arson investigator found the half-melted pill bottle in the debris. It was the one she dropped when she was heading back to the bedroom," he continued. "I knocked it down the stairs when I went to look for her." Mark paused. "He also found part of her note to you, still taped to the bedroom mirror frame."

Robert carried his glass back toward his desk. Mark noticed that his father's hand trembled. For the first time that Mark could remember, his father seemed weak. Mark stepped forward. The hand that held his notebook dropped to his side. The pages flapped in the breeze. "Why, Dad? Why didn't you tell me this? Why did you lie about how she died?"

His father set his untouched glass down on his desk. He ran his fingers along its rim. He couldn't bring himself to meet his son's gaze. "I never lied to you son," Robert replied, a touch of shakiness to his voice. "I just . . . didn't tell you the entire truth."

He abandoned the drink and turned to face the Seattle night skyline. He pressed his left hand to the glass, as if seeking out some force that would help him say what was on his mind. "She suffered from severe depression," Robert began. "You were too young to realize it, and I was too busy working to truly deal with it. They had prescribed her other medications, but it didn't seem to be working. Her new doctor prescribed her the Carazin to help her sleep, but it wasn't sleep that she needed. I think it was understanding, comforting . . . love that she needed. It was the love that I felt for her the moment I saw her, but didn't have the time of day to give her; the love that I couldn't find the time to give her because I was so hell bent on becoming a partner, of making a better life for her, and for you."

Mark realized that his knees were knocking. He slid into a chair in front of his father's desk. He stared at his reflection in his father's pristine desk surface. "Why, Dad? Why was she depressed? What caused it?"

"She suffered from it for most of her life. She felt neglected as a child, not beaten or anything like that; just misunderstood, I guess, not loved the way she wanted to be and needed to be. She had troubled relationships in the past before she met me. She married me thinking that I would bring the happiness she longed for. You did a little, Mark. I saw it in her face every time that she looked at you, held you." Mr. Daniels' gaze fell to the floor. "But I didn't, and as much as she tried, she couldn't break the cycle of depression. Nothing could. Not the doctors, not her friends, her family, not you, and in the end, not even me."

Mark thought back to that late spring afternoon, everything his mother did before she went upstairs. She took him shopping and bought him the wind-up pop gun he had been bugging her about for weeks. She made him his favorite cookies and let him eat them in the living room. She never did that before. Then he remembered something else. He stared off into the darkness. "She kissed me," Mark whispered. "I always thought it odd that she would leave me alone downstairs. She never left me alone, but it wasn't a good night kiss. It was . . . it was a goodbye kiss."

The senior Daniels hung his head. "When they told me about what they had found, I couldn't bring myself to tell you," he murmured. "I didn't want you to think that your mother had given up on herself, on her life."

"Given up on herself? Dad, for 30 years, I thought *I* killed her. Every time you looked at me, all I saw was the blame in your eyes. Did you even know? Did you care? I can't even begin to tell you how guilty you made me feel!"

His father let out a heartless chuckle. He closed his eyes and shook his head. "Guilt? Son, you don't know guilt, not until you lived with mine."

Robert turned to look at him. Mark was surprised to see tears in his green eyes. "Your mother's eyes? You have them, you know?" his father whispered. "Every time I look at you? *Every* time I look into your eyes, all I see is her staring back at me, reminding me of what happened . . . of what I didn't do, and what I did to you. It got to the point that the only way I could escape the guilt was to come here, bury myself in my work, but I couldn't really escape it. Eventually, I had to come home to you. Sooner or later, I would have to look into your face, into her eyes . . . your eyes again, and be reminded of the fact that I wasn't there for her."

Mr. Daniels' gaze fell to his desk. "I never intended to make you feel as if you caused her death," he murmured. "I know you didn't do it Mark. I know it, because I did it. I killed her with neglect, with my lack of commitment to her, and to you. I killed her because I wanted to provide a good home, to make sure that you and she were cared for, and had all you needed. I didn't realize that all she really wanted was to be held and caressed, and for me to tell her that I loved her, and that I would do anything to help her overcome this mountain that seemed to be crushing her. In the end though, the mountain won."

Mark stared at his father. For the first time in 30 years, the guilt he felt fully lifted from his shoulders. He felt lighter, yet a part of him felt so much heavier. His gaze fell to his father's immaculate desk surface. He began to crush the notebook in his hand, trying to come to grips with everything he learned and heard. Then he realized something else: Julie had been right about his father. Again, he found himself wondering how she knew.

"Mark?"

Mark forced himself to meet his father's tear-filled gaze. "Son, I know you probably hate me for not telling you everything, and you have every right to." Robert moved to take a step forward toward him, but found himself pulling back again. Why couldn't he reach out to even touch his only child? How long before his chances for reconciliation expired? "I did it because I didn't want to see you hurt any more than you were, except . . . ." He paused. "If you want to talk . . . need to talk . . ."

Mark found it hard to keep meeting his father's gaze. What he had heard shook him to his soul. He fought back a sob. "Maybe later," he murmured. "I'll call."

Mark turned from his dad, slipped his notebook back into his jacket, and left his father's office. Robert waited until he heard the elevator door close behind his son. Then he reached down to his bottom left desk drawer and opened it. Inside of it were two framed photographs. He pulled each one out. The first one was of Mark and Jessie on their wedding day. Jessie had sent it to him. Mark stood there in his tuxedo, his brown eyes so enchanted by the extraordinary woman in white gazing up at him. They looked so radiant, so full of life. He smiled and traced his son's face on it. After a few minutes, he set it aside and picked up the other one. It was one taken of Mark and his wife Rebecca when he was six, a few weeks before the fire. Mark had the same photo in his home. His mother held him in her arms. Her smile couldn't hide the pain in her eyes that now, Robert could plainly see. He held it up, leaning back into his chair. Then his will dissolved. He clutched the picture to his chest, brought his knees to his chest, and broke down into sobs.

*   *   *

Two days later, Mark pulled up to the site where old Malachi Wallace's house once stood. As he climbed out, he saw Julie and a man wearing a hard hat standing where the front door once was, mulling over blueprints. They turned when they heard his door slam. Julie's face lit up when she saw him. "Hi, Mark."

"Hey." He pointed toward where the house once stood. A backhoe dug out the remaining debris, and placed it inside of a dump truck. Mounds of dirt were off in another corner of the lot, and there were stacks of timber nearby. "So, I see you decided to rebuild."

She nodded to the contractor, who picked up the blueprints and walked over toward some of his crew.

She headed toward his truck, and then stared back at the empty space where the house once sat. "Yes. Simon and I thought it would be best."

"Simon?"

"My guardian? I had to call and tell him, of course. He wasn't happy, but not because of the fire. Apparently, he decided he would drop by unexpectedly, and planned to stay there. Now, he'll have to stay with me." Julie sighed. "I'm trying to talk him out of it."

"C'mon. He can't be that bad?"

"No. That picky."

She smiled broadly. Mark chuckled. She studied his face for a moment. They had not talked since the events of three days ago. "You mentioned that you were going to see your dad. You didn't say why. Did you go visit him?"

"Yeah. Heather had said something about my mom's death. I went to talk to him about it. You know, you were right about him still grieving, and blaming himself for it. How did you know?"

Julie shrugged. Like most everything that she knew about him, she could never tell him how she knew it. "I don't know, really. Based on what you told me, it seemed a logical conclusion."

She turned and leaned back against his truck. He positioned himself next to her. "I owe you a debt of gratitude. I talked with Cassie and the lieutenant after we transported Christie to the hospital. They tell me that you were the one who pulled everything together."

"Not really. It was a team effort. You, Cassie, Melanie, and Lieutenant Rutherford had already done all the legwork. If Christie hadn't been trying to keep you guys off the trail, you would have probably figured it out sooner. Also, if you hadn't become obsessed with finding out about Maggie Sinclair, I don't think I would've figured it out. By the way, how is Melanie?"

"Out of jail and heading back to Seattle. They're paying to send her back to school for her degree, and for continual training. They're also giving her a huge raise. I'm glad for her. She's going to be a damn good investigator, Julie, just like her mentor."

"Yes. I agree with that statement."

They stood in silence for a moment. Then Mark turned to her. "Can I ask you something else?"

"Yes."

"How did you figure out that Christie and Maggie were the same person? You see, I read Della Torre's file notes from the destroyed storage unit. There's no mention of a name change. The court's copies of her name change petition are still sealed. I also talked to Della Torre again. He said that her new guardians came up with the name, not him, and they asked him not to tell anyone. He didn't. Not even his old secretary knew."

Julie's face screwed up in thought. She reminded herself not be too forward with the information that NIK supplied her. "From a friend of mine, who happens to be a really good researcher. How is Christie, or Maggie, I should say?"

"Physically, she's still in the hospital, recovering from the burns she suffered. Mentally and emotionally, I don't know. It's going to take a lot of therapy to help her cope with what happened to her and what she did. Even so, I don't think she'll ever recover."

"What about the charges?"

"She'll have to serve some time, but probably in some sort of mental facility. Just so you know, Della Torre's representing her."

"You're kidding."

"Nope. He's going for an insanity defense, and knowing his reputation, he's going to get it. He feels responsible. It turns out that he tried to adopt her himself, but was turned down."

"Why?"

"He was still single at the time, working non-stop. You have to remember that Maggie was already a traumatized child. The state didn't think he could provide a stable enough home environment for her. That's why she felt he had betrayed her. No one knew about it except her. He had the paperwork done by another company, and in a pseudonym, so that no one would find out."

"Wow," Julie whispered, although she already knew that. NIK had informed her of such when she had finished the research on Maggie/Christie and Della Torre. "That was such a nice gesture, but if he had not showered with all that attention, would any of this had happened?" She pointed to the site. "Would the house still be standing? Would his son, the lieutenant, and the others still be alive?"

"Who knows?"

They stared off at the site for a moment. Julie sensed he wanted to ask her another one, but she put a hand on his chest, stopping him. "No more questions for me. I have a question for you."

"Shoot."

"Based on the photos that I saw later on, there's no way that you three should have survived that fire. I know, because I was there, and I still think it was impossible. How did you find your way out of there?"

Mark thought back on the events in the fire. He remembered staring into his mother's eyes again, and the feeling of hope and safety he felt she provided within the inferno. He stared out at the construction site. "Would you believe me, if I told you that my mom showed me the way out?"

Julie's jaw went slack. Then her expression turned cynical. Mark smiled at her response. "I didn't think so," he said. His gaze grew wistful, and he stared back at the site again. "You know, if I didn't know better, I thought I could've reached out and touched her, and for a moment there, I thought she reached out and touched me. She seemed so real, yet I know she wasn't. She's been gone for 30 years."

Julie gazed up to the sky. "Maybe in a way she was there, Mark. Even though they may not be here physically, those we care about are never truly gone. They're always watching and they're never far away. So long as we keep them in our hearts and remain willing to ask for their help when we need it, they'll be there."

Mark took in her words and thought about his mom and Jessie. Then he thought about Julie's deceased parents. He gave her a welcome smile. "Spoken like someone who knows a little something about that."

She thought on his statement a moment. Then she smiled. "Yes."

They watched the workers moving the earth and debris in silence. Out of the corner of his eye, Mark saw a handsome African-American male limousine driver approach them. He stopped a few feet away from them. He acted as if he didn't want to disturb her. "Excuse me, Miss Warren?"

"Yes, Thomas?"

"Ms. McIntire just telephoned. The Beijing office is being insistent. They need you to return there at your earliest convenience."

Julie sighed. She kicked at a pebble with her right foot. "Thanks, Thomas. Do me a favor, please? Call Jennifer to let her know that I'm on my way. Also call the airport, and have the plane readied."

Thomas nodded, then gazed at Mark and headed back toward the limousine, parked just down the street from the site. Mark looked at her. "Off again, huh?"

"I guess so." She stared up into the sky again. Simon was in distress. War had been declared, and the people of Beata and Quartan were taking up arms. Their limited knowledge of the worlds outside of their island meant they treated all strangers with suspicion. Thus, Simon could not leave on his own accord. She needed to help keep the fighting confined and to get Simon out of there. "I have a lot of work to do."

"You don't have to, you know? You're the CEO. Get someone else to go."

"No, Mark. This is something I need to handle personally."

"Julie, you don't have to try and save the world by yourself. Don't you believe in giving yourself a day off, or a vacation?"

Julie thought back to the promise that she made to the Illani so long ago. "No."

Mark stared back out at the rebuilding site. "So, can I ask when you'll be back?"

"I don't know. Hopefully, after this heat wave lifts."

"Well, I'll work on it for you."

Mark walked her over to the limousine. He held the door open for her and she climbed inside. Inside was cool and refreshing. He admired its luxurious interior, wondering when he would have the opportunity to ride in it. He thought he detected a cinnamon scent coming from within it. It reminded him of the cookies she had made for him. Another thought crossed his mind. He leaned on the top edge of the door. "By the way, I've been searching for a good oatmeal raisin cookie recipe to give to Jessie's mom. Where did you get yours?"

"From your mom."

"My mom?"

Thomas glanced at her from his rearview mirror. He shot her a thought. Julie fought to recover: "Well, at least I think it was your mom. I found it while rummaging through some old cooking magazines. Someone had submitted one." She pretended to think. "Rebecca? That was your mother's first name, correct?"

Mark nodded slowly.

"Well, then it's probably hers. I'll tell you what? When I get back, I'll dig it up for you. I'll see you later."

"Yeah. See you."

He closed the door and watched as her limousine pulled away from the curb and headed toward the end of the street. He thought back to what she had just told him. Unlike everything else, her story did not have an ounce of truth to it. He knew that his mother had never written down the recipe, and her cookbooks had burned in the fire. He stared at the empty hole where the house once stood. Then he turned back to her departing car. The Look came to his face. Once again, she had left him with more questions. Now, he was more determined to find the answers.

About The Author

Detectives and aliens are two of my favorite subjects in fiction, but rarely seen together in a modern-day format. It's taken some time to get my imaginary friend from my head to paper. I believe this combination of characters makes for intriguing and entertaining reading. This series focuses on the relationship between featuring Mark Daniels, a police detective seeking to reclaim his life after a series of tragedies, and Julie Warren, his mysterious new tenant. She's an immoral with the ability to kill with a thought, and an addiction to chocolate, coming to Earth in the hopes of reclaiming her humanity before the planet learns of her true nature.

A graduate of Penn State University and Thomas M. Cooley Law School, A.P. Lynn resides in Michigan.